YOU
broke
ME FIRST

C.R. JOHNSON

ISBN: 9798862217681

Edited by: Amanda Rash
Cover Design and formatting by: Melissa @To.All.The.Books.I.Love

Trigger Warning

Murder
Graphic violence
Physical violence
Consensual/non-consent
Age-gap
Mafia themes
Dark themes
Bondage
Torture/Mutilation
Humiliation
Grooming
Rape
Cheating
Sex toys
Anal
Degradation
Asphyxiation
Jealous/Possessive
Drug use

Playlist

Someone To You by The Banners
Dandelions by Ruth B.
This is Me from The Greatest Showman Soundtrack
My Girl by Dylan Scott
Issues by Julia Michaels
You Broke Me First by Tate McRae (Bedroom Sessions)
Perfectly Broken by The Banners
I Only Date Cowboys by Kylie Morgan
Gunpowder and Lead by Miranda Lambert
Wild as Her by Corey Kent
Take It Out On Me by Florida Georgia Line
Last Night by Morgan Wallen
Porch Swing Angel by Muscadine Bloodline
Fall into Me by Forest Black
Baby Outlaw by Elle King
Wildest Dreams by Taylor Swift
Feel Like This by Ingred Andress
Bitch by Meredith Brooks
Goddess by Xana
Dark Side by Bishop Briggs
Nightmare by Halsey
I Hope UR Miserable Until Your Dead by Nessa Barreett

Break You by Marion Raven
Bitter Sweet Symphony by The Verve
Love Makes You Blind by Kaylee Rose

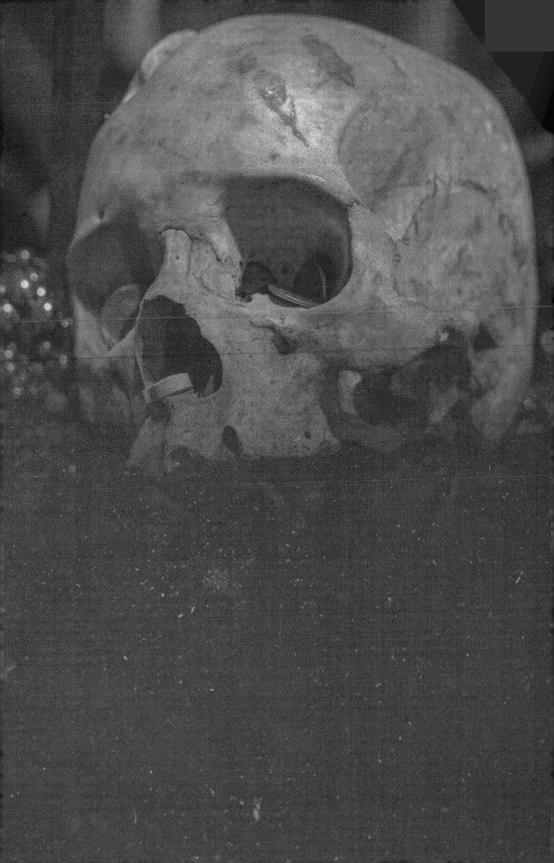

PROLOGUE
Sebastian/Bash

She is going to hate me, but I can't tell her the truth. I'm trying to be a better man, for her. Telling her would put a bigger mark on her head, because of me. If they find me here with her, they will know my weakness and hers. Something I swore would never happen; I fell in love with her. I know she is young and has her entire life ahead of her, but she has been like a drug since the moment I saw her in that cute little cheerleading uniform with royal blue ribbons in her sleek black ponytail, bouncing around laughing with her friends. She was breathtaking. She looked so much like Charlotte; I thought maybe her ghost had finally come back to haunt me. Sylvia didn't mention the fact that this girl could practically be Lottie's twin. Seems she didn't tell me everything she knew about her. She has to be a relative.

I knew I wanted her to be mine from the moment I realized she was real. It only made me want her even more when I saw her at the gym kicking the shit out of a decent-sized asshole. She is fucking perfect. I'm a twenty-seven-year-old man in love with a seventeen-year-old girl, who actually isn't even seventeen yet. In my defense, she doesn't look or act sixteen. She is so much different than Lottie was. My Savvy girl has a fire in her that burns fiercely, whereas Lottie only had a spark in comparison.

The last eight months have been so amazing with Savvy. She is smart, tough as nails, and has a mouth on her that would make a sailor blush, but she is so much more than that. She has a heart of gold and

1

always takes care of everyone else. I know I'm a selfish asshole who doesn't deserve her. I'm still the dickhead I have always been, but I want to be better for her. I can't do that here. I have to go home and face my family. Sylvia had me do this one off the books, so they think I'm just hiding from them.

I will love her from a distance for now, until I can get my family off my ass and get back to her. I love that I got to spend this last day worshipping her like the princess she is, and now I have to leave her until it's safe to take her with me. When she hears the rumors—and she will—they will kill her, and she may never forgive me. But I have to keep her safe and go home, even if she hates me for all of it. She will forgive me in time. I'll make sure of it.

She thinks I'm from Dallas. I have lied to her a lot—about my age, who I really am, where I'm from, even my name—in the hopes my past never comes back to haunt her. I take one last look at my sleeping beauty with her jet-black curls splayed around her head, a vast contrast to the white satin sheets. I gently kiss her forehead, breathing her in one last time. God, I hope I never forget that intoxicating scent. I wish I could see those bright blue eyes just one more time. I whisper, "I love you, my Savvy girl." Then I leave, because if I stay one more second, I will pick her up, throw her over my shoulder, and take her with me. Consequences be damned.

My heart is already aching as I pull my black Hummer out of the driveway of our place, our cabin, in the woods by the lake. I look out at the boat dock and remember our first picnic. Her bright blue eyes lit up my soul that day, letting me into her real world, not the façade she shows everyone else, and I knew then that I could never truly let her go. She always loved lying out there in her tiny bikinis with her hair in a messy bun on top of her head, reading her books while she soaked up the summer Oklahoma sun like it was her lifeline.

"I will come back for you," I vow aloud, hoping the words will somehow make it true, and I drive away. New Orleans is a good twelve hours from Ketchum, Oklahoma. I plug in my new phone and turn on Savvy's playlist. The Banners start singing "Somebody To

You", and I almost turn the SUV around. I keep going despite the pain I feel in my chest the farther I drive away from her. I grasp the necklace around my neck, holding the broken half of a heart, hoping it will help guide her to me.

Savannah/Savvy

I wake up with a white daisy and a pink Post-it note next to me with the words "I'm sorry, but I have to go. Forget about me and live your life."

Is this a joke?

I get up searching for Jake, going through the entire cabin, realizing he is gone, like gone, gone. His closet is empty, the furniture that came with the place is the only thing left other than the grey Tulane football T-shirt I am wearing of his with Bash on the back with the number thirteen. I take a deep breath, lifting the shirt and putting it to my nose. It smells like him, woods, musk, and ocean. I sit on the floor of the living room, grasping onto my shirt tighter and tighter as the sobs finally rack my chest and escape. Tears stream freely down my face as the images of last night flood my brain, recreating every moment in my head like a movie reel.

We came in late last night. I was pretty intoxicated as per usual with Jake. He always let me have my fun and last night was no different at Monkey Island, until we got back to his cabin. He did things to me you only read about in books. He made love to me, he was him, but slow and sensual. Last night wasn't about dominance. It was about us and how much he loved me. That's what he kept saying over and over all night. That doesn't happen very often, he is usually a dominant freak, in the best way possible. I smile through the tears at the thought.

I think about our first time together. I lost my virginity to him about eight months ago. I think about the day I realized that Jake wasn't just some guy trying to get in my pants, but that he genuinely cared about me. We had hung out a couple of times before that but

3

just at the gym. He invited me for dinner here at his cabin, it was our first date. He made us what he called voodoo chicken with rice and beans and a weird spicy sausage, and we ate out on the boat dock. He called it a picnic, which I realized quickly that his idea of a picnic is very different from mine. He got me to open up about things that I had never told a soul. I was too afraid of my mother to tell anyone. Until him.

I had started reading *Fifty Shades of Grey* by E.L. James at this point with some of the girls at school, so I was extremely curious. That night was the most magical night I could have ever asked for. He made love to me then too. I felt things with him that I had never really felt before, and then over the months, I fell in love with him. I love him. I sit up, still crying on the floor, at the realization that I really do love him.

Then I realize he isn't coming back.

I keep trying to call his cell, but his phone is disconnected. My heart is literally shattering into a million pieces, and I have no idea what to do. I have spent the last eight months ignoring my friends and being with Jake every spare moment I had. I couldn't get enough of him. No matter what we were doing, I was happy. Happiness has been foreign to me my entire life. Until him.

My light is gone, and there is darkness once again. I don't want to go back to being a shell of a person who is numb to the life around me with the fake smile that has everyone fooled. I'll leave as soon as I graduate and save up enough. I can't stay here in this tiny bible belt town with parents who couldn't give a shit less about me and a brother who never has time for me or anything else as long as he is shoving shit up his nose. Jake is the first person to show me what love really is. Was it all a lie?

CHAPTER 1
Savvy

I have to admit, I'm going to miss this little town. I put my phone on the charger after booking my hotel room for my first night in New Orleans and set it underneath the bar. No one really knows I'm leaving, besides the guys at work, and I doubt they really care to be honest, but I will miss my regulars at the yacht club who tip really well. I will miss the lake, our boat dock that I go to when I want to think or still feel some closeness to Jake, the dam when the gates open, rushing vast amounts of water down to the little blue swimming hole, and walking the freshwater creek looking for crawdads.

I won't miss being the town whore's daughter and the looks of pity from nearly everyone. I tried fitting in, moving out to my own place, and even dating. Problem is, when your mom is literally the tri-county whore, men expect you to be just like her. Not the case, exactly. I sleep with who I choose and will never apologize for it. I'm also not married. I know I do it to chase after the high I would get with Jake. I picture him a lot when I'm with other guys. It helps to get me off. Hey, dudes do it all the time, picturing whatever pinup in hustler they saw last or the tits bouncing from the movie they recently watched. I just picture the man who left me broken in the first place.

"Savannah, what time are you leaving tomorrow?" Aron asks from across the dark mahogany wood bar top as he fills little packets of sugar and fake sweetener at each perfectly set table.

"Seven a.m., why? I retort, knowing he wants to come over tonight, but won't come uninvited. He is a true gentleman, unfortunately. I'm just not in the mood to deal with any of my booty call drama. They are all nice guys, don't get me wrong, but most of them are clingy as fuck and I just can't deal with it when I'm going to be driving straight through tomorrow.

"Would you want to have a going away drink with me tonight?" he asks with a devilish grin on his face.

"No, thanks, I'm going straight to bed tonight after my shift. I'll catch ya next time I'm in town though," I reply with a sorry expression. He visibly slumps and looks like I just kicked his dog. See, pouting like a damn girl. Why would I want to fuck a sap? "Suck it up, buttercup. Darlene is my relief so you might still get lucky tonight. I know she likes you, so you should just give her a chance," I pick at Aron with a bounce to my step. I know Darlene has fawned over Aron for two years and he never gives her the time of day.

"You really think so?" Aron asks, almost dumbfounded.

"Open your eyes, bud, she has liked you for a while," I explain and watch his face morph from confusion to delight.

It's times like tonight I miss Jake. I know he will never come back, and even if he did, I was probably just a notch on his fucking belt anyway. I did love that belt though, it had a bite to it that others just don't, or was it the person using it? I'll probably never know. I found out he was fucking three other girls at the same time as me, and two of them went to my school. No matter how hard I try to forget Jake Bash, he always finds his way back into my head. He literally pops in there without warning, and it makes me wet every time. I hate him for that as much as I loved him for it when he would make me come over and over again. He didn't have the biggest dick, but at least he knew what to do with it. Only one guy has even come close to comparing, but it was only because he had the damn girth of a coke can and hit everything just right without even trying. Okay, maybe not a coke can, but you get the gist.

I finally end my shift and see that Aron is fast at work with

Darlene. I quickly say my goodbyes and head out the back to my black Jeep, laughing at how predictable that was. People almost never surprise me anymore with their bullshit, I wanna love you forever. They forget to say, I wanna love you forever until a fresh piece of ass comes my way. Men are fucking pigs, and in all honesty, getting my heart broken was maybe the best thing that could have ever happened. Too bad a submissive sex fiend was created in the process, but I like me so...

I count my tips and almost fist pump the air when I realize just how good I did. Four hundred bucks and some change. Not bad for a Thursday night. I start the Jeep, grabbing my brown leather-wrapped steering wheel and gripping it tight as "Dandelions" by Ruth B fills the empty space, making me freeze. I always think of Jake when this song comes on, remembering when I would sit by the boat dock after he first left, wishing on every single dandelion I could find that he would come back for me. I pull myself from my own thoughts, put my Jeep in drive, and sing at the top of my lungs, pushing him out of my mind with every tear I shed.

When I get to my little dilapidated trailer, I stop feeling sorry for myself and finish packing. Shoving everything into my Jeep, I realize not everything will fit, so I decide to leave behind the boxes marked yearbooks and mom's stuff. I don't need or want any more horrid memories making their way to New Orleans with me. It's not like I have much, some clothes, pictures, but mostly books. They are my one truth, that fiction is better than real life every time. I was able to get a fake ID with my birth certificate being forged with a new date stating I'm turning twenty-one in three days instead of twenty. It's from a friend who works at the Social Security office, so it's legit, and it didn't cost me much.

I will be able to work and do whatever I want in the city of magic and dreams. That's what Jake always called it. We talked about going because he had gone with some buddies and told me all about it. I guess that's why I picked New Orleans; I need to have a little magic and follow my dreams. It can't be worse than where I'm at. Plus, my favorite show is based in New Orleans, and I can't imagine going anywhere else. If I'm being honest, I hope we run into each other again, just so I can punch him in the face.

I eat a shrimp-flavored cup of ramen before I shower and go to bed. I left out the scrapbook I made of me and Jake. I look through the pages and pages of pictures, settling on one of us on the boat dock. I'm wearing a yellow spaghetti strap sundress, kissing Bash's cheek. He looks at the camera with his gorgeous, chiseled face set in a smile that shows off his perfectly straight, mega-white teeth. I look into his mesmerizing caramel eyes, imagining he really is here.

This is the picture I always look at when I'm horny and have to get myself off. Which is most of the time. I set the scrapbook up on the nightstand, not letting my eyes leave his. I slip my blue cotton boxer shorts down to my ankles and lie back on my bed. I close my eyes and think of Jake touching me as I move my hands to cup my breasts through my thin tank top, squeezing my nipples the way he used to. I imagine him hovering above me, looking into my eyes as I move my hands down to my already throbbing clit. I spread my wetness around, bucking my hips at the thought of his dick at my entrance. I shove two fingers in my slick pussy and moan his name. I picture him thrusting in and out of me as I rub my clit with my other hand. I can almost hear him gasp my name as I come. My pussy pulsates around my fingers as I picture running my nails down his back, scarring his beautiful dark skin. I always loved tugging on his dark curls to bring his lips to meet mine, when I wasn't tied up, at least. He disappears into a puff of smoke as I come down from my high. I let the tears fall, remembering him holding me after sex. He would always either hold me, caressing my back until I fell asleep, or he would carry me to the bathtub and bathe with me while holding me from behind. He treated me like I was the rarest diamond on earth. I would have given my soul to the devil to get him back before. Truth be told, I probably still would, even if it meant just one more night with him.

I wake up and look at the clock. It's only four a.m. I cried myself to sleep again.

I dress comfortably in black joggers, an Oklahoma State Cowboys T-shirt, and my black Nike tennis shoes. I throw my hair up in a messy bun and choose not to wear makeup today. My olive complexion in the depth of summer keeps me from having to wear much anyway. I look back at my reflection one last time in the rearview mirror. Bright blue eyes stare back at me like windows to the broken pieces that reside within my soul.

"You get to be Savvy again, not just plain old Savannah. It's time to start your new life, missy," I tell myself and crack up laughing at the fact I'm giving myself yet another pep talk. I look back at my old tin can of a home one last time. It wasn't much, but it was mine, and that was all I really needed. I turn on the playlist titled I'm not broken, I'm pissed. I made it just for the trip to get me going and keep me going. Music is just like listening to a book to me. Songs tell a story that, when done right, hits you just as hard as any book out there. "This Is Me" from *The Greatest Showman Soundtrack* starts blaring through the Jeep, giving me the push I need to put this thing in drive and say goodbye to my childhood and move on to bigger things.

I can't believe how long it has taken to get here. I had to stop four times to pee and get snacks. I'm amazed by all the scenery and perk up when I see the Superdome. My back has been killing me from being in the same position for too long, and the mounting headache that was forming is all feeling better now that I'm in my new city. I still can't believe I'm doing this. I can't believe I'm finally here.

"My Girl" by Dylan Scott flows through the Jeep, and I immediately have a slight panic attack, freak out crying, and hyperventilating to the point that I have to pull over. I, of course, have to listen to the rest of the song, blubbering out the words, and even dancing. It was a song Jake always sang to me.

Once I blow all the snot out of my nose and wipe away all the tears I shed for no apparent reason, I take a few deep breaths and hop out of the Jeep for some fresh air.

That is not fresh air, it is humid and rancid smelling. I crinkle my nose, trying to cover the awful smell with the back of my hand as I look up at the street sign and realize I had taken so many turns I didn't know where I was. The sign says Bourbon and Conti St. Well, that explains the smell. I was told that Bourbon St. always smells like ass until morning when the trucks come to clean the streets of vomit, shit, piss, and God only knows what else, leaving a lemon smell. I make a mental note to check that out tomorrow morning. It's six p.m. and I'm starving. I see a sign for food with an arrow pointing to another sign, Oceana Grill.

Sounds good.

I know I have enough money to last me a few weeks without a job, so I guess I should treat myself on my first night here.

"How many?" a young girl with sleek light brown hair asks without even looking up at me as I approach the hostess stand.

"One," I reply with a bright smile.

When the girl looks up at me with her chocolate doe eyes, she blinks a couple of times with a blush running up her cheeks before she smirks and replies, "Right this way." From the outside, this place did not look this fancy. It's dim with red lighting throughout, giving it a sexual ambiance. All the tables are set with fine deep red and white linens, small vases with pretty flowers, and candlelight. I also notice bubbling drinks mount every table. It's sleek, classy, and sensual with a hint of rustic vibes with natural wood beams lining the ceiling. Jazz plays softly over the chattering of the patrons enjoying not only their company but the food and drinks as I watch a man serve his lady a bite from his fork. She moans as she takes the bite slowly as we pass by. I almost feel bad watching, like I was intruding on an intimate moment. I realize quickly that I am underdressed for this place, and slightly regret coming in.

I follow the waitress upstairs and see that it's even fancier up here with beautiful chandeliers and another bar, somehow more elegant than the one downstairs, yet done in the same deep red and raw wood rustic theme.

Fuck, might as well make the most of it.

She sits me at a table in the back corner and I'm at least grateful for that. "This should be a fun experience for you. Are you new in town?" the doe-eyed girl asks in a thick southern accent much sweeter than mine.

"Is it that obvious I just made it to town, had a massive breakdown, and then strolled in here?" I ask, knowing I'm giving up too much information about myself but not caring either.

"Not *that* obvious, but yeah, pretty much." She laughs and nudges my arm. "I'm Chamomile, but everyone calls me Cami," she states with a sweet smile. Thank God she wasn't being a bitch bringing me up here. Maybe there are decent people still in the world.

"Thank you, Cami. I'm Savannah, but my friends call me Savvy," I reply with a soft smile.

"Nice to meet you. I'll send a waiter over with a drink menu. You look like you could use one." She walks away, giving me a bright smile.

I finally decide on the Redfish Oceana after the waiter basically says it is heaven on a plate. He brought me blackened gator bites with rémoulade sauce, his treat, because I needed to try it. I drink three swamp juices and devour every bite of everything the waiter brought out, practically moaning with each bite. I'm dying at this point, thankful for the joggers I'm wearing. My phone buzzes, pulling me out of my food induced coma.

Hunter: Where the fuck have you been?

13

I swallow the lump that forms in my throat and reply.

> Me: I moved, dickhead. Stay the fuck away from me!

> Hunter: You chasin' after some guy? You could help out here with the ranch! Why are you such a selfish whore?

That should have hurt or struck a nerve, but it doesn't. He is probably snorting that fucking white powder up his nose at this very moment. He can go to hell.

I sigh, putting my phone back in my purse and taking a long swig of my swamp juice, second guessing my decisions until a very handsome gentleman from the table over meets my eyes and gives me a nod and smile. I wipe my mouth with my napkin and smile back with a nod of my own.

"Hi, I'm Savannah, my friends call me Savvy," I say as I wave slightly.

"Mark Boudreaux," he replies in a deep, alluring voice, getting up from his table and joining me in my small booth. He grabs my hand, kissing it softly, never letting his eyes part from mine. He is big! At least six foot six. He is delish with intense green eyes, messy, dark brown hair, luscious lips, and a very defined jawline with the slightest bit of a five o'clock shadow showing.

I sink my teeth into my lower lip as he sits next to me and his warm, musky yet clean scent hits my nose. Fuck, now that is enticing. He smells and looks way too expensive for my tastes, yet I still want to mount him right here if I'm being honest.

"Tell me, cher', have you ever been tied up and fucked into submission for hours on end?" he asks nonchalantly as he raises my hand to his luscious lips again with a smirk that makes me clench my thighs. I honestly can't believe what just came out of his mouth.

I surprise him when I smirk, bat my eyelashes, and as seductively as I can muster while still allowing my accent to really drawl out of every word, reply, "You think you are worthy to be my Dom? I realize the way I'm dressed combined with my Southern belle charm has you thinking I would make the perfect sub for you to train and do with whatever you please." I move closer to him and whisper in his ear, "Handsome, I'm the Devil's worst nightmare." When I pull back with an evil smirk, he quirks his eyebrows in surprise, and I know he is shocked when his mouth is gaping open. I continue, "I am not as submissive as what you are used to I'm sure, and—"

He cuts me off as he grips my arm when my voice raises a few octaves. "I'm a sadist, so yes, I know I'm worthy, and I'm going to punish that dirty little fucking mouth of—"

"Can I get you two another drink?" the waiter asks, cutting him off. He lets my arm go at the stare down from the waiter. "No, thank you, just the bill," I reply.

"One more drink," Mark says obnoxiously, obviously annoyed. I have really let my mouth run with this Dom wannabe. I can tell he isn't the kind of guy who is used to hearing the word no.

"Just my check, thanks," I reply as I grab my drink and down it, grab my purse, and move to get up.

I have to admit, even though this is not a guy I want to get to know at all, he triggered the familiar throb between my legs that a dominant male seems to bring out without even trying.

Cami makes it to the booth just as I stand up and Mark moves to grab my arm again. "Ready to go?" she asks sweetly, bobbing her head. I look at her and get the all-knowing big eyes look all girls do by being obvious about something that they are trying to get you to not be obvious about.

"Yup, just need to pay the bill," I reply with a thank goodness smile as we walk away and go down the stairs. The waiter blocks Mark, and I have to remember to come back by here and thank him for that.

Cami pulls me outside before I can stop and pay my bill. "Cami, stop, I have to go back and pay." I protest against her still tugging.

C.R. Johnson

"Girl, your tab was paid right after you entered the building," she says, waving her hand in the air.

"By whom?" I ask, dumbfounded.

"I don't know. My boss told me, and I let Charlie know." Cami sighs as she explains. I get lightheaded and stumble, bracing myself on the car next to me. "Savvy, are you okay?" she asks, helping me to my Jeep.

Jake used to tell me all the time to not get into situations I can't get myself out of. I really miss that dickhead. He always put me in situations I didn't want to get out of. Sounded like Mark had the potential to do just that. Unfortunately, he was a bit scarier than Jake ever was. He made the hairs on the back of my neck stand on end when the Southern boy charm flipped to sadistic. He reminded me of my mother.

Cami decides to drive my Jeep to my hotel and help me check in since I'm stumbling and can barely form sentences. She helps me move the box in the front seat to the back, because I refuse to leave my Jeep.

We get to The Bourbon Orleans Hotel only to find out they gave my room away because check in was hours ago and I didn't respond to their calls. "I can just sleep in my Jeep tonight, no biggie," I slur as I try to lean the seat back and fail. I lay my head on the window, letting the cold air from the vent hit my face. Cami says something before I cannot keep my eyes open any longer, but I have no idea what it was.

CHAPTER 2
Savvy

I wake up to loud clanking and wince as I try to open my eyes. I grab my head, attempting to relieve the pounding. Holy shit, I haven't felt this bad from a hangover since last summer at Dripping Springs. That was a wild night, from what I remember.

"Well good morning, Savvy!" I hear a woman's voice and finally will my eyes to open.

"Cami, right?" I ask, embarrassed. "Where am I?" I question, mostly because this is not a hotel room. I'm lying on a very comfortable overstuffed black leather couch in a modest living room with eclectic trinkets and colorful décor throughout. I notice several fleurs-de-lis throughout the space and know I love the decorator.

"You never confirmed your reservation, so they gave away your room at the hotel, then you passed out in your Jeep, so I had Charlie help me get you here, in my house," she states with a big grin.

"Who's Charlie?" I ask, not knowing if I should know that name.

"Your waiter last night, and my boyfriend." She squeals and I swear I see hearts in her damn eyes. Poor girl is ruined already.

She bounces over to me and hands me a glass of water and a bottle of Excedrin. "You always make a habit of getting blackout drunk your first night in a new city?" She chuckles as she heads back into the other room.

I get up off the couch and realize I'm in my underwear. I look around and find my joggers and slip them on quickly. "Hey, Cami,

19

I'm really sorry for behaving that way, and I really appreciate you letting me crash here. I was on a roll of sorts, fighting my own demons last night, and I hope you won't hold it against me. You are literally the only person I know here, and I don't want you to think that badly of me. I only had three drinks the entire night, so I'm not sure what happened," I explain.

"Girl, if that's the worst you do, then you are my new bestie. Not usually a lightweight back home? Alcohol poured here is double what you are used to," she says cheerfully, putting a cup of coffee on the table for me. She points to the chair next to her at the pretty round oak table. I sit and take a sip. It's divine.

"I don't think I have ever had coffee this good." I moan in appreciation and keep sipping.

"It's a café au lait, you can get them just about anywhere in the city."

"Seriously? We do not have coffee like this back home," I reply, still moaning with every sip.

"Where is back home?" she asks curiously.

"Oklahoma," I reply, still enjoying my yummy cup of happiness.

"Here for vacation, or do you plan to stay?" she asks.

I give her a questioning look of surprise. "I plan on staying," I reply honestly.

"I figured with the way your Jeep was packed down. Have you found a place to live yet?" she asks with a smirk on her face.

"No, I plan on looking today. I had a reservation for the hotel for three days. I will see about another hotel room too," I say apologetically.

"Well, my roommate just moved out and I'm looking for one. Four hundred a month plus the water bill. I take care of the rest. If you want to skip the searching part," Cami says nonchalantly, like it's no big deal.

"Oh my God yes, that would be amazing. Are you sure you want to take in a straggler from small town Oklahoma to be your roommate?" I get excited, bouncing in my seat.

"I think you would be the perfect roommate. You actually seem like you have your shit together, other than the drunk thing last night, and I can tell you are a really good person. You have a nice orangey yellow aura around you. It's too pretty for you not to be a good person," she replies like she said something people say every day.

"My aura?" I question her.

"Yeah, I'm kind of a witch of sorts. It's in my blood anyway. I'm what you would call grandfathered in. I come from a long line of New Orleans witches," she responds as if she is making sense.

"Well, Jake always said that New Orleans was the most magical place on earth, so I guess I found the magic I needed to follow my dreams," I reply with a shrug of my shoulders.

"Who's Jake?" she questions, not knowing she is opening a can of worms I can't seem to close.

"He was my first love, only love really. I've dated other guys, or slept with them anyway, and no one else has ever compared. He is the man who broke me into a million tiny pieces and, honestly, the reason I chose New Orleans. He would talk about it incessantly, even though he said he only had one trip here, it really had an impact on him," I reply, spilling all my inner demons. I'm surprised at how easily I answer her honestly, without thinking about leaving the little details out. I swear it's like I've known her my whole life and can tell her anything.

"Jake sounds like he knows where to go, but the fact that he broke you has me stunned," she replies with her eyes wide as she sips her coffee.

"He was my first everything, and then he left without a trace, like a ghost. I couldn't even find anything on him when I googled him after he left. It's like he doesn't exist," I explain, sounding like a stalker.

"What's his name? I want to try and google him."

"Jake Bash. Good luck, you won't find anything."

"Bash?" she questions with her eyebrows raised.

"Yeah, he said his name was Jake Bash." I respond with a sigh at the sound of his name. "He liked to be called Bash at the gym, but I always called him Jake unless we were role playing, then I always called him Bash like he wanted," I explain with a chuckle, remembering how he would tie me up and make me call him Bash before he would let me come.

Cami looks deep in thought in another world when I fan my hand out in front of her face several times before she finally responds. "Sorry, so Bash, huh? And where did he say he was from?" she asks with a chuckle.

"Dallas, but I think he lied about that too if I'm being honest. Hell, for all I know he lives here as much as he talked about it. That was a different chapter of my life, and one I don't want to go back to. If I never see Jake Bash, or whatever his name is again, it will be too soon," I reply sarcastically, knowing I'm lying to myself.

"Well, NOLA has plenty of men who would die to shower you with attention. Just be careful, that guy from last night is a key player in this city. He is a big bank roller for investment property, and he likes his women for about as long as he takes to close a deal, so a no strings attached kinda guy," she explains, and I can tell she is being sincere.

"Explains the whole *"I'm a sadist"* thing he was trying to lure me in with." I laugh while making air quotes.

"Yeah, I'm glad you agreed to come with me instead. I knew a girl who got hot and heavy with him. She was in the hospital for months before she moved back to Georgia," she explains, putting her hand on my arm, making sure she has my attention. A chill runs down my spine at the thought of what could have happened to me had Cami not been there. I'm realizing quickly that New Orleans is nothing like Oklahoma.

"Who paid for my dinner last night? I don't remember ever paying the bill," I ask, realizing I already owe someone money after being in town one day.

"Charlie said he wasn't sure, but probably Mr. Boudreaux, the guy who almost took you home. I told you last night our boss just told me," she replies with a huff.

"I'll be sure to stay away from him," I retort.

I finish the last of my coffee and chat with Cami for a little bit before we decide to unload my Jeep. I finally take the time to really appreciate her house. It's quaint with modest furnishings and she called it a shotgun style. You basically have to go through every room of the house to get to the next. It's cozy and I love it. My room is painted dark gray with dark wood floors and a large window that lets in a ton of natural light. I have to go buy a bed, dresser, and curtains, but Cami said she knows some really good places where we could go shop. I figured I could just crash on the couch until I find something, but Cami was adamant about me having my own bed.

I guess I'm not going to have much luck finding a job on Sunday anyway, so we get cleaned up for the day and decide to go shopping. Cami showed me so much of the French Quarter, walking everywhere. My feet feel like they might fall off. She only jokingly made fun of me for a second when we made it in front of the cathedral, and I sat on the park bench where the finale of The Originals was filmed and cried for a second. Not just because it was an iconic spot, but at the fact that I made it. I did it on my own and I got out of small-town USA and am now sitting on the bench in the last scene with Klaus and Elijah. When I explained it to Cami, she just said I have an old soul and had every right to take a moment and appreciate what I have gone through to get here, and my love for a TV show. She sat with me on the bench and was just there with me, she didn't push for an explanation, just let me have my moment. God works in mysterious ways to bring light into your life when you need it most. If there is a God that is.

I found a bed and a dresser for under three hundred bucks at Keils Antiques on Royal St. It was the only one that was solid wood and I know I can make it beautiful again someday. They are even delivering it for free. We also stopped at a market, and she let me buy a few groceries. I love that there is music being played on every corner and people singing and dancing everywhere. I'm starting to understand why Jake loved this city so much.

"Hey Cami, is there a boxing gym or anything like that nearby?" I ask nervously.

"Yeah, NOLA boxing club is close by, why?" she asks, a little surprised.

"Well, I'm kind of a fighter. I kickboxed back home to get out all my aggression and it's how I work out. It's a great stress reliever. I don't really plan on boxing here, just working out. Gotta keep my face pretty for job interviews," I reply with a wink. Cami busts out laughing and changes our direction.

"Come on, I'll take you to the gym. It's on our way if we go this way," she replies with a grin. We come up to a big redbrick building with a sign in black and white that says Boxing Club. We enter the club and I'm immediately hit with the smell of sweat, blood, and leather. I close my eyes and take a deep breath, relishing in the familiar smell.

"Hey pretty ladies, I think you are in the wrong place," a chiseled, dark-complected man with curly black hair and the greenest eyes says with a mega-white smile.

"Actually, I was wondering if you train women here too, or just cocky jocks with little dicks trying to make up for it by making their muscles bulge a little bigger," I ask with sarcasm dripping from every word. He looks stunned at first and then chuckles at my brashness. I don't even crack a smile, knowing it will irritate the fucker more.

Just when he is about to reply, I hear my name being called out by a familiar voice. I look past the wannabe bodybuilder and I swear I see a ghost.

"Jake," I mouth his name. He is directly in front of me in an instant. I don't know what to say or do. I see him, but I can't believe it's him. He leans into me like he is about to hug me or kiss me, I'm not sure, but all of the sudden I see red when I realize he is real. Dropping my shopping bags, I punch him in the nose with as much force as I can muster, then grab his shoulders, forcing his body toward mine and knee him square in the balls. I watch him crumble to the floor before running out of the club.

Cami catches up to me in a second outside and I'm making a beeline in the wrong direction. She turns me around, hands me the bags I dropped, and we start walking again. I know I look like a maniac, huffing and puffing. When it turns to sobs, Cami stops me.

"Hey, we can stop and grab a drink if you want. I think you might need it, Rocky." She jokes and it actually makes me laugh.

"I'm sorry, Cami, I hope I didn't embarrass you. I don't know what came over me, I just saw red, and then went in for the kill. I guess I have a little pent-up anger toward Jake still." I apologize yet again for my poor behavior.

"Honey, his name is not Jake Bash, that was Sebastian Devereaux. AKA Bash. He just took over the biggest crime family in New Orleans a couple of years ago. He had left the city and his dad was looking for him for almost a year before he came back and took over. They have a very lucrative real estate development business that most say dabbles in the cocaine business and money laundering. They have never pinned anything on them, but it's common knowledge," she explains.

"Well fuck me, I had no idea," I reply dumbfounded as I play with my necklace. It's the only thing I kept that he gave me, other than the T-shirt I sleep in, and it's my nervous habit.

"Yeah, he isn't exactly the kind of guy you go around punching and kicking in the balls," she retorts with a little bit of fear in her voice.

"Yeah, well after what he did to me, he should be thanking me that that's all I did to him. Maybe he will see it as a warning to leave me the fuck alone," I reply with a slight chuckle. Even as I say the words, I'm regretting them, because all I want to do is run back to him and tell him how much I've missed him. I won't because I have more self-worth than that, but it doesn't keep me from wishing I could.

Cami took me to a place called Tropical Isle, right off the edge of Bourbon and Toulouse St. We drink hand grenade after hand grenade, comparing stories of our torrid pasts with men. I almost fall off the barstool when Jake, Bash, whatever his name is, sits down at the bar right next to me. My breath hitches at the sight of him as my thighs clench.

"You are not old enough to be drinking in here, baby girl." I feel his stubble graze my cheek as he whispers in my ear. Fuck, that voice, his intoxicating scent mixed with all the booze in my system makes heat go straight to my core and my clit to throb.

I smile mischievously. "You obviously don't remember how smart I am. I have an ID and birth certificate that could make you a liar again." I smirk as I take a slow methodical drink from my straw.

"Are you being bad, my Savvy girl?" he asks, and something in me snaps.

"I am. But not for you." My smile fades and I let him see just how much he broke me. I feel tears start to prick the corners of my eyes.

"Savvy, I didn't want to leave you, but you weren't eighteen yet, and I was trying to keep you safe," he tries to explain, cupping my cheek, making me look into those piercing caramel eyes." I still love you, and I haven't stopped thinking about you since I left," he replies, and he sounds so genuine.

"Do you have any idea what you did to me? The pure hell I went through after you left. I had nothing else to do with my time other than work and get fucked by every guy I could find trying to get some semblance of you back. I hate you," I reply, the alcohol giving me courage to say things I don't mean. I see the flash of hurt in his eyes and I almost feel bad for a second.

"So, Bash, since we will never be more than friends now, how about you explain why you left someone you say you loved so much." I lash out a little more, slurring the words, hoping to hit a nerve.

"You still love me, or you wouldn't keep fidgeting with the neck-lace I gave you." He pulls his necklace out as well, putting the two pieces close enough that the magnet catches, and once again, the two pieces of a heart are molded back together.

I pull away, quickly letting the pieces of the heart break apart once again and fall back to our chests. "You did that, just remember that." I let one tear escape that I was trying to hold in. He brushes the tear away with his thumb and I swat his hand away.

"That is the last tear I will ever shed for you, so enjoy it, asshole," I state with as much harshness as I can muster before standing up, grabbing my bags, and look at Cami to head out.

"Nothing like a woman scorned!" Cami belts out, shrugging her shoulders as we walk out the door.

It's once again dark out and we wasted the better part of the day drinking. I don't even know what time it is.

"I'm sorry, Cami, I know this is not how you wanted to spend your day." I apologize for what seems like the hundredth time to my new roommate who has bent over backwards trying to help me.

"Girl, I have had more fun in the last twenty-four hours than I have in a long time. Maybe I need a little firecracker in my life to make it more interesting." She laughs while texting. "We should have a ride here in about ten minutes." She giggles as she bounces down the street. I follow, stumbling slightly.

A black SUV rolls up and we both get in, thinking it's our Uber. Nope, just the asshole who broke my heart and is now making me relive it all over again.

"Fuck my life!" I yell as soon as I sit down and realize who is in the front seat of said Uber.

"Glad to know you still have your cute Southern accent and dirty mouth, baby," Bash replies to my two-year-old fit of stomping.

"I'm drunk and being dramatic at the moment so just shut up!" I yell at him with a huff as I cross my arms over my chest and pout.

"God, I have missed that mouth, Savvy. Don't make me punish you for letting it run out of line, baby," he replies with a lustful look.

"You wish I would let you punish me. Problem with that, I have to be willing, that was your first rule. You going to break your own rules, dickhead?" I question, my words obviously slurring now, and I giggle.

"Baby girl, don't test me right now. We will talk once you have sobered up." He basically orders, and I don't like it one bit.

"Maybe we could make some coffee and you two can talk while I keep Charlie company," Cami interrupts.

I bust out laughing, "At least one of us will get dick tonight. Hey driver, you got any plans after this?" I cackle, knowing it will piss Bash off.

"I wouldn't answer that if you want to live, Mike." Bash almost looks like he could kill the man driving the car.

"Mike? Nice name, is it your real name, or is he lying about your name too?" I ask the driver, laughing, knowing I'm getting under his skin.

"That's enough, Savannah," Bash bites out a little harsher than I've seen him before. He also has never used my full name. I shut up and finish the ride in silence knowing I won, kinda. I did stick my tongue out at him once and that made Cami burst with laughter. She keeps hitting his seat, taunting Bash which, in turn, I find hilarious. Bash, not so much.

When we finally make it to Cami's house, we both bolt out of the car and attempt to run up the stairs to her front door, determined not to let Bash in. Unfortunately, in our drunken stupor, we both fall on the steps and drop half the groceries on the way down. That is definitely going to leave a mark, I think to myself as I feel the warm ground beneath my body. I can't get up. I'm too exhausted, and I just don't want to. "I'm gonna sleep here tonight," I shout, giving up and rolling to my back, letting out a huff.

Charlie comes out when he hears the loud banging, helping Cami get up, and Bash comes over to me and picks me up like a sack of potatoes, throwing me over his shoulder. I kick and scream, and practically beg him to put me down. He flops me down on the couch and walks toward the door.

"That's right, go away, asshole." I screech as he whips around and stomps back toward me. I hunker down onto the couch, flinching. He stops abruptly, knowing my past and immediately softens. He cups my face, making me look at him. "I'm sorry, baby girl, I didn't mean to scare you. I would never hurt you; you know that," he explains with a melancholy tone.

He knows how I retract and what I grew up with. A tear slips down my face and I soften as well.

"How about some coffee, and then we can talk, yeah?" he asks with the sweetest voice, pushing my hair out of my face.

"Yeah." I finally relent in trying to hurt him. "Coffee sounds good, but the kind that Cami makes." I whine.

"I'm sure it's the same as it is all over New Orleans." He chuckles.

"That's what Cami said. How come you never made me coffee like that?" I ask, slightly aggravated that he kept something so amazing from me.

"Hold that thought while I go pick up the rest of the groceries you dropped." He goes out the front door.

My mind is racing, and I know I can't continue being mean to him, even though he deserves it. I still love him even though I hate him at the same time. He comes back in, and I'm slumped on the couch, lying down now. He looks delicious in his Nike shorts and tank top. I'm just realizing he never changed from the gym. My eyes keep getting heavier, and I know I'm never going to make it to drink a cup of coffee.

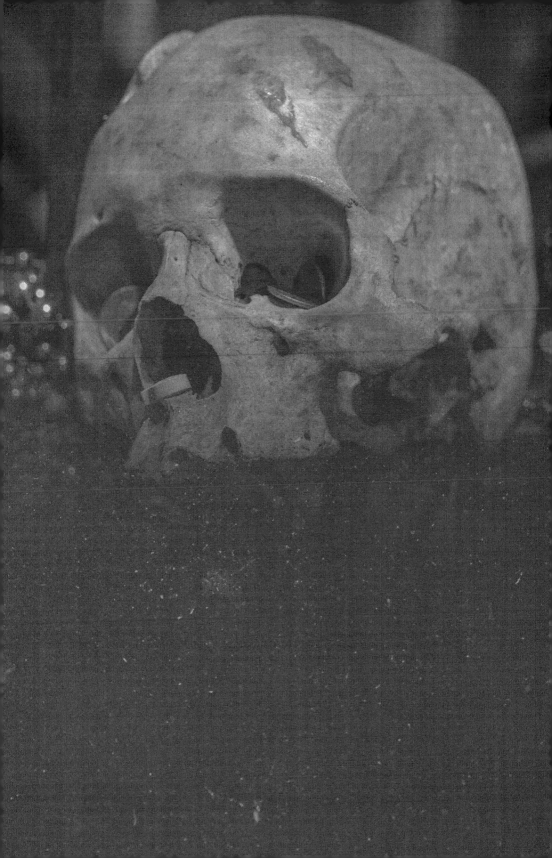

CHAPTER 3
Bash

She looks so beautiful sleeping. Her raven locks are in a messy bun with pieces poking out everywhere, and her beautiful olive skin looks perfect. She has turned into a beautiful little foul-mouthed vixen, and I can't wait to win her back. I can't believe she is here. I went back to get her several times, but every time I would find her looking happy living her life, and I didn't want to bring her into this life.

The last time I saw her, she was with a guy, making out in her Jeep. I had to leave so I didn't kill him. I'm a dangerous man who has more enemies than I can count, and Sylvia lying about who she was and wanting to find her. I was just trying to protect her, and now she hates me. I knew she would.

I told one of my little sluts that I had on the side there that we didn't have to keep our relationship a secret anymore. I knew she went to school with Savvy and hated her because she had me. The only time I allowed Mia around me was when Savvy couldn't get out from under her parents' thumbs. Mia was a freak who let me do anything to her body I wanted. She was a perfect little pet.

I make my way through the little shotgun house and realize there isn't a bed in the other bedroom. I got a huge view of Charlie's ass in the air and wish I hadn't while going through the small house. They only laughed when I apologized and closed the door abruptly. I take my phone out and have Mike pull the car back around. I whisk up my girl bridal style, she is passed smooth out. "Looks like you're going

31

home with me after all, my beautiful Savvy girl," I whisper to her as I make sure not to hit her head getting her in and out of the house or car.

"Take us home, Mike. I finally got my girl."

"Why exactly is this girl so important to you? You bang different chicks constantly. I mean, she is your type, but doesn't look much different than the rest," he questions with a surprised look.

"Make no mistake about it, Mike, she is very different. She is mine, and she will stay mine. I'm going to marry this girl. She came here after three years, not even knowing I was here. That's fate, my friend," I reply a little too excitedly.

"Oh, you found a chick when you were gone for like a year and your dad was ready to kill everyone. That's what had you so wrapped up that you couldn't come home and take over like you had promised," he replies more like a statement than a question.

"Yeah, she is. She was totally worth it too. I wear those scars proudly, knowing they belong to her," I explain with a wicked smile. I like pain, and it still baffles the men who watched me take all ten of my lashings from my father, the former boss, without making a sound, and without flinching. The hole that was left in my soul when I left her made me numb to pain. I beg for it because every once in a while I will feel something, and it reminds me how much I loved her.

I can feel the light that shines from her already healing a part of my soul. I feel again, only for her. She took me out of the darkest parts of myself and showed me the light that burns within her. I have missed its warmth, like morning glories, my heart has been opened once more by the sun that is Savannah Barrett. She is the only light I will ever need. I thought that I could live without her and just have my sluts on speed dial forever. It's not hard to get pussy in this city, women throw themselves at me, not because they want to know me, but because they can see I have money and they all want a piece of it.

Savvy loved me when she thought I had nothing. She comes from money, and all the small-town asshole ranchers and farmers bullshit that came with it. She didn't want any part of it. Her dad seemed decent enough, helping her barrel race, but her mother was a piece of work. She hit on me several times, begging me to fuck her in various places. That one I never touched, no matter how much she begged to suck my cock. Scarlett is something else, but nothing like her daughter.

Savvy always had bruises she couldn't explain, even from boxing. She finally confided in me that she went at least three rounds a week with her mom, but never hit her back. That was our first night together. I made sure that she knew what it was to feel loved. I knew it was her first time and how special it was for her to give herself to me in that way. She deserved to be made love to her first time, not some wham bam thank ya ma'am with some pimple-faced idiot teenager. Savvy deserved to be worshiped and cherished, like the beautiful sunflower she was.

Once we make it to the compound and into the parking garage, I gently lift Savvy out from the back of the SUV and carry her to the elevator, which is stifling with her signature perfume filling up the small space quickly. She literally smells like sunshine and the beach with hints of tropical flowers. Her scent is amazing. I feel my dick getting hard just having her this close to me. We finally make it upstairs and I take her straight to bed. I undress her and put one of my T-shirts on her, she always loved that. She snuggles into the pillow and comforter when I cover her up. "Jake," she sobs lightly as a tear goes down her nose onto the pillow. My heart breaks knowing that I caused her more sadness than she had already known.

I get into bed, trying to snuggle her and comfort her in her sleep, but once my arms snake around her waist, she turns to face me and kisses me like she used to, when she loved me. She lays her head back down, still asleep, and whispers, "I missed you." I knew she still loved me. She can fake hating me all she wants, but she will admit that she still loves me at some point.

I text Mike to pick up some clothes for Savvy and have them delivered to the penthouse. I remember her sizes and tell him to keep it classy with a whole new wardrobe. If I know my Savvy girl, she kept her style of sweats, band T-shirts, Levi's jeans and cut off shorts. Other than her black hair, she is basically Daisy Duke. I started sending her daisies as soon as we started dating. She was sixteen and I was twenty-six, trying to woo a girl. I had never wooed anyone. She also thought I was twenty-one. She made it so easy though and would always chastise me if I bought her something that she thought was too expensive. Money is the last thing Savvy cares about.

She almost died when I gave her the necklace she still wears. They were way more expensive being white gold. I lied and said they weren't that much, and to me they weren't, but to her, it was like a kid at Christmas getting a present for the first time. Each heart is engraved with 'The other half of my soul'. I had the magnets added inside to make sure they were unique. I had them engraved with a fleur-de-lis on each as well. Maybe I was hoping the magnet would be strong enough to pull her here one day, and the fleur-de-lis to help her know which way to go.

Maybe.

When she agreed to submit to me for the first time, she went above and beyond what I could have ever expected of her, and she loved it. She was a quick learner, as she was with most things, and while she allowed me to dominate her in the bedroom, she knew from the start that she had me wrapped around her little pinky. I would have done anything she asked of me, and things she would never ask because she is too good at heart.

I would kill for her whether she asked me to or not. The only reason her cunt of a mother is still alive is because, although she is worthy of a slow death, she was still her mother, and I don't think Savvy would appreciate me killing her mom. So, I let her live, for now.

Savvy got me going on Vampire Diaries, always telling me that I was a hotter, younger, beefier version of Damon with better hair than Stefan. She always made me laugh with how she described things. She could tell a story like no other. I know she didn't go to college. Maybe she will want to. I'll give her the world if she will let me.

I wake up to the sound of glass smashing on the floor. I jump out of bed, ready to shoot someone with my pistol drawn when the light comes on. A stunned Savvy is standing with her hands up in the middle of the room.

"Why the fuck are you holding me at gunpoint, Jake, Bash, Sebastian, whatever your stupid name is?" Savvy yells, picking up a pillow and throwing it at me.

"Why would you throw a pillow at someone pointing a gun at you, I taught you better than that," I tease, loving the rise I get out of her.

"Because I know you would never shoot me. You would never intentionally hurt me unless I gave you permission to. Same game, just a more grown-up player. Or was that it, because I was a virgin, was that why you toyed with me, and those other girls?" She is nearly sobbing now, and all signs of anger have left her.

"I swear I never fucked around with any of those other girls, I only started those rumors hoping you would get over me faster." I lie. It's much easier than telling her the truth, which would literally make her hate me more.

"You started those rumors about Mia and Abby? They didn't deny it!" She screeches and throws another pillow at me.

"I never did anything with any other girl once we were together." I lie to her again with both my hands up. I place my gun on the bedside table, letting out a deep breath.

"Why am I here?" She looks down with her shoulders slumped.

"Because you came back to me."

She looks up at me with a confused look on her face. "I didn't come here for you. I came here to start a new life and hopefully forget you. You always talked about NOLA like it was your favorite place on earth. Was everything a lie?" She finally asks the question that I'm sure she has asked herself a million times. If I answer honestly, she might leave, and I can't let that happen.

"Define everything?" I reply with my voice low and obviously broken.

She looks me dead in the eyes. "You never loved me." Her voice breaks at the end as tears fall down her gorgeous face.

"Savvy, I have loved you since the moment I laid eyes on you and that is the honest truth. Yes, I lied about almost everything else, but that is true." I know I'm laying it on thick, but she is broken, and not the way I prefer her to be broken. I want my Savvy girl back. The one who would gladly bow down to me on her knees and beg me to punish her.

"How would I ever trust you again?" She's obviously contemplating the question in her own head.

"Time. Give me time to win your heart back. Stay here with me and let's start our lives together," I plead, practically begging. I don't beg anyone, but for her, I will grovel till the day I die to have her back in my arms. Silence fills the room, and I can't take it. "Please say something, anything."

"No," she replies in an almost whisper.

"What?" I ask, obviously stunned, and a little hurt if I'm being honest. I knew this wouldn't be easy, but I thought she would fall right back in love with me.

"I don't want this." She finally speaks aloud, waving her hands around, looking at the vast space.

"You don't want this, or you don't want me?" I didn't expect this at all. She has definitely grown up.

Tears fall down her face as she looks back up at me. "I don't know. I came here thinking I was finally going to get a fresh start where no one knows me or my family. I wanted to experience the magic you always told me about. I hoped that eventually I would find my way and meet someone who would make me finally forget you. I'm going to go back to school and make something of myself, if for nothing else, for me. I owe this to myself." She is putting her walls back up and I know it's going to take me a long time to break them back down.

"I want you to have everything your heart has ever desired. I want you to be happy. Make no mistake though, no one will ever make you forget about me. I am the other half of your soul, and you will come back to me, willingly," I reply honestly. I know I'm right; it's written all over her face. I haven't missed the way her body reacts to mine. That is one thing that will never change, and she can't deny it.

Her eyes widen at my confession, and for a moment I see the lust in her eyes once again that she used to give me so willingly. Now I see her holding herself back again, only this time it's not from the fear of the unknown, but the fear of the known and how good I can make her feel.

"Jake, you want me? Fine, I will be your sub one last time. Then, we'll see. That's all I can give you right now. You get me for tonight and then maybe I'll let you take me on a date. I refuse to make you any promises. First, please tell me the truth about yourself so I don't feel like I'm fucking a stranger," she says pointedly with the slightest hint of a smirk at the end.

My Savvy little vixen never disappoints in telling it how it is. I start moving toward her like a lion stalking its prey, she doesn't back away "Savvy, of course I want you. We don't have to do anything tonight, as much as I would love to worship every inch of you, I wouldn't ask you to do that." I say the words and mean them, even though my dick is painfully telling me otherwise.

"Who said I was doing it for you?" She almost laughs as an evil smile creeps up her cheeks, one I've never seen before, but I know was created because of me. "I fuck who, when, and where I choose. I never fuck anyone just because. Except this one time about a year ago at Rocklahoma, but that's beside the point. I'm just saying, if I did this it would be for me, not you." She chastises me as if I'm the child here. Fuck, I like this side of my girl. She doesn't care what I want and is only thinking of herself for once. I'm proud. Stunned, but proud. I'll always give her what she craves.

"Are you going to tell me who you really are so we can enjoy one last night together or what?" she persists.

"Damn, you have gotten bossy over the years. I like it. My name is Sebastian Jackson Devereaux. I will be thirty on November first. I recently took over the biggest crime family in New Orleans. And my favorite color is blue. Anything else?" I ask, noting the surprised look on her face.

"You're almost thirty?" Is all she belts out with her hand over her mouth. I expected the crime family comment to be what shocked her.

"Yes, please don't dwell on our age difference. I did it for months before I finally gave in to my need for you," I tell her, knowing it is and isn't a big deal.

"I'm just surprised that you lied about your age, I wouldn't have cared either way. Explains how you were so good in bed," she replies with a duh expression, then laughs at my expense. Not saying I don't deserve it, but I can't stand the thought of another man touching her, and for her to be so coy about it, shoving it in my face. She is playing with fire.

"I don't want you as my submissive tonight, Savvy, I just want you," I admit honestly, because if I were to dominate her tonight, I might accidentally hurt her thinking of who all has had a taste of what's mine. I still might if she keeps running her mouth.

"Like the last night we were together before you left me?" she questions harshly. "You knew you were leaving me and wanted to actually love me before you left. That night still burns in my mind every time I close my eyes. How different and passionate you were, taking your time to show all of me just how much you loved me, just to rip that love away as if it meant nothing to you. I meant nothing to you. I'm done. Take me home please." She jerks the rug right out from underneath me, quickly dismissing me with her words.

"Savvy, it's three in the morning, let's just go back to sleep and talk more when you wake up, maybe over breakfast," I ask, hoping she won't push me away. I go to touch her arm, but she jerks it away, giving me a don't fuck with me glare. Her fists ball up, and I can see the redness go up her neck to her cheeks. She is seething, and I can't figure out why. I thought we were getting past all of this.

Next thing I know, she is pouncing on me. She wraps her arms around my neck, pulling me down and crashing my lips to hers. She jumps up the second my hands grab her ass and wraps her legs around my waist. Our teeth clank and our tongues dance together, remembering the feel of each other. I lay her on the bed gently, as if she were a delicate flower, never separating our bodies. I know she wants it rough, but I won't give in to that just yet. I snake my hand up her shirt and caress her breast before pinching her nipple, making her gasp and break our kiss. I pull her upright and swiftly remove her shirt and let her fall back on the bed again.

I take a moment and indulge in the sight of her again. She is a rare beauty that I will never get tired of staring at. Her black hair is splayed out on the white silk sheets with her arms above her head, ready for me to hold her down or tie her up. Her barely there black thong leaves nothing to the imagination. Her dark olive skin fading to her light pink nipples. I yank my boxers down and come back up, burying my face in her sweet little cunt. I move the tiny string aside and delve my tongue from her ass to her little nub popping out to see me. I give it a very nice greeting, making sure she is writhing with her hands on my head, pulling me in. I let out a low growl and she jerks her arms back up above her head just as I bite down on her clit. I'm gentle, but I will make it hurt and then soothe it all away, and she knows it. She remembers and she is testing me to see if I'm still me.

I pull back and sit up on my knees. She watches me and doesn't move a muscle. I may have said that I wouldn't dominate her tonight, but she is making it very difficult to stay true to my words. Fucking perfect little cock tease. I rip the little piece of fabric that was covering her pretty, bare pussy off her quickly. She yelps in response. I give my cock a few strokes before smacking her clit with the tip. Her hips buck in response.

"Eager, my little princess?" I ask before smacking her clit again with my dick. I slide it up and down her center, popping just the tip in, making her squirm and buck her hips, wanting more. "Say my name, baby, please?" I ask rather than command.

"Ja..." she almost whispers through her moans.

"Eh eh eh." I pull back from her entrance and smack her clit again. Her eyes pop open "What's my name again?" I see the glint in her eyes and the small smirk she was trying to hold back.

"Sebastian Jackson Devereaux." Her words are more than sultry, and the way she looks in my eyes, like she is looking into my soul, has me ready to explode already.

"My good Savvy girl." I give her praise as I sink into her slowly, enjoying every inch of her tight pussy clamping around me. "Fuck baby, still so tight." I grunt as I move forward, grasping her wrists in one hand and wrapping my other arm around her, grabbing her ass, pulling her hips into mine, making me go deeper. She moans out the sexiest sound I have ever heard as I move my hips, getting into a smooth rhythm. I kiss up her neck to her mouth, stifling her moans. I let her wrists go, but she leaves her arms above her head.

I pull back from her, slightly going deeper. Her head snaps back. "Oh God, Jake, please fuck me," she yells out, making me stop abruptly. She realizes her mistake quickly with a huff.

"Look at me, Savvy," I command. Her gorgeous lashes part for me to look into her mesmerizing blue eyes. I move my hips slowly, letting her still feel me. She holds my gaze without missing a beat. A soft moan leaves her lips.

"Bash," she says softly.

"What, baby girl, I can't hear you?" I ask, pumping my hips a little faster.

"Bash, please?" She yells out loud enough for most of the penthouse to hear.

That's all it takes. I pull out of her and flip her over. "Hands above your head, baby, grab those sheets and don't let go." I order her as I smack her ass, a little harder than I intended, but she doesn't seem to mind.

"Harder" she yells. I smack her ass again, harder this time, as I sink into her. She yells out, "yes, yes, more, please don't stop!"

"Rub your clit, baby," I order. She does as she is told. "Good girl, you want more?" I ask as I grab a fistful of her hair, wrapping it around my hand. I yank her head back, exposing her neck and earning me a yelp, and whisper in her ear, "We are going to try something new, baby. Do you remember our safe word?" I keep pumping in and out of her slowly, torturing her. I know she likes it fast and hard just like me. I used to anyway, until her.

"Pineapple." She almost sobs.

"Good girl, baby, now relax and enjoy the ride," I whisper in her ear and kiss her tear-streaked face before letting go of her hair.

I grab both hips, lifting her ass higher, exposing her tight little rosette. I spit on it just before pressing my thumb against it, applying pressure.

"Oh God, oh God." Her words are muffled by the sheets her face is now smashed into and holding onto for dear life. I pump into her harder as I slowly slide my thumb all the way in her ass to my knuckle.

"Rub your clit, baby, I want to see you come," I order in a raspy voice mixed with grunts. I'm so close, but I refuse to come before she does.

I pump in and out of her, harder and faster until I feel her walls tighten around my cock and my thumb. I finally let the dam burst, pumping in and out until I have nothing left to give. She is still moaning and shaking, coming down from her orgasm. I practically fall on top of her, finally pulling out and wrapping her in my arms, pulling her close.

"You're still my sweet Savvy girl," I whisper in her ear and kiss her shoulder.

CHAPTER 4
Savvy

I lay in his arms again for the first time in over three years, thinking about what was, what could be, and what I truly want. I know he expects this to go more his way, but I wanted what I wanted from him, and after breakfast, I will leave. I will go and start my new life. I'm not just going to give in to what he wants. I came here for me, I need to remember that when he looks at me, touches me, or is anywhere in my vicinity. I refuse to bow down to a man just because he makes my body sing like a fucking canary on a beach with a glorious sunrise.

I try to unwrap him from my body to go to the bathroom, but he refuses to let go.

"Baby, please just stay with me." He whines like a little kid.

"You don't have to get up, but I do. I need to pee, take a shower, and go find a job. Breakfast would be great too," I reply, nudging him again to let me go. He finally relents, loosening his grip on me. I jump out of the bed and make a beeline for the bathroom, but I forgot about the broken lamp and step on a big piece of glass. I scream out, cursing and jumping around when Bash sweeps me up, takes me into the bathroom, sets me on the counter, and starts assessing my wound.

I notice he has left his hair longer than before, his black curls hanging down around his eyes. He is still just as handsome as the day I met him. His tanned skin and chiseled jaw make him look more intense, but when I look into his caramel eyes, I see the sweet, care-free guy I fell in love with at the lake.

"Okay, Savvy, I'm gonna pull it out on three, baby. One, two..." He rips the glass out and I scream like a little girl.

"What happened to three? That shit fucking hurt," I wail at him.

Bash applies pressure with a big piece of gauze. I notice the cabinet below my legs is open, and he keeps pulling more medical supplies out. "It's bleeding pretty good, and the cut is deep. I can stitch it up, or I can call in our doc, baby, which do you want?" He looks at me, still holding my foot and applying pressure with a look of almost mortification at the fact I'm bleeding. Pain starts to register again, and I let a tear fall. Shit. I have to quit crying in front of him.

"Call the doc, you are not stitching up my foot," I practically yell at him, my eyes wide.

He gets up off the floor, grabs my hand and puts it on my foot, telling me to keep applying pressure, then walks back into the bedroom. I hear him bark out orders, sounding like a lunatic. I dare to look at my foot, removing the gauze. Nope, bad idea, blood pours out the second I release the pressure. I feel lightheaded and watch the ceiling come into view and a disgruntled Bash curse before every-thing goes black.

I wake back up to voices all around me, mainly Bash yelling at everyone to fix my foot, keep me comfortable, and to bring in break-fast before I wake up.

"Too late Mr. Grumpy Pants," I slur. "My tongue feels funny." I try to say but it comes out sounding strange.

"Are you allergic to any medications?" the gray-haired man in a suit and tie asks.

I think for a minute and try to put my hand on my face but can't because I have an IV pulling my arm. "Morphine, Norco, doxycy-cline, and sulfa drugs." I spew the list out per usual but have trouble pronouncing everything.

"Get her some Benadryl too." The older man asks softly, "Are you in any pain dear?"

"No, I feel great, like I'm floating on a cloud," I tell him almost excitedly.

"She is good, everyone out, I'll get her some Benadryl and change out the Morphine to Demerol. I got this, doc." Bash shoos everyone out of the room, coming back over to the bed and unhooking the drug pumping into my blood.

"Buzz kill," I joke with him. He laughs as he walks back into the bathroom, coming back with two little pink pills, Benadryl. "I hate Benadryl, it makes me loopy, and I don't want to sleep," I whine.

"Take your medicine like my good girl, Savvy," he orders.

"Fine, but only because I don't want my throat to close up." I give in, popping the pills in my mouth when he hands me a glass of water. I yawn and snuggle into the bed, watching Bash hook more drugs up to my IV.

"These won't make you as goofy, baby," he says sweetly, while inwardly laughing at me. "How about a movie?" he asks.

"Yes, I love movies," I squeal and bounce on the bed, clapping my hands. I quit when he finally busts out laughing at my childlike behavior. "Okay, no more drugs for me, I need my wits about me if I'm going to get a job." I whine some more.

"You have six stitches in your foot, you are not looking for a job walking around the city. You will reopen your wound and it will definitely get infected. I don't think you realize how deep your wound is." He chastises me like a child. Compared to him, I guess I am.

"I have to find a job! I saved up enough to get me here and live for a few weeks, but that's it. I already have to pay Cami rent since I did find a place to live. I even bought furniture yesterday, thinking I would get a job quickly. This isn't happening. Morphine makes me nuts, I don't like the crazy side effects," I explain to him, but I become a blubbering mess instead.

"Calm down and breathe, Savvy, it will all be okay. You can move in here with me and you won't have to get a job or work if you don't want to. Let me take care of you." Bash tries to calm me, stroking my hair, but he just makes the crying worse.

"No! Are you crazy? I just told you that I don't even know what to do with you and that I can't just be with you after everything, and you want me to move in and what, be one of your concubines? I don't think so, fuckboy!" I yell at him, obviously dumbfounded by his audacity to think that this will all just be fixed because he fucked me into submission once in the last three years. Fuck you.

I guess I'm in the stage of rage with morphine. I broke my hand in a boxing match when I was sixteen and had to have surgery. The docs realized very quickly that morphine wasn't my friend. I would go from laughing hysterically to crying while laughing to going completely nuts and throwing things, including my IV pole. Needless to say, they made it an allergy. The shakes are settling in now from it working its way out of my system. I'm not cold but to look at me shivering you would think I was a popsicle. Or a crack head. I can see the wheels turning in his head, trying to figure out how to keep me here, but I'm not backing down.

"Baby, you are high on meds, you're still angry with me, and you're not thinking straight. How about some breakfast? They should be bringing it in soon," Bash says softly, obviously getting the memo I want to hit something.

"You and I both know I burn through meds like this quickly. I'm starting to feel much more clear-headed." I seethe at him with my arms crossed over my chest.

"Oh right, the metabolism thing. You have hyperthyroidism. I did forget about that. I didn't forget about the morphine; I remember how nuts you went. I also remember you not having any pain at all after surgery for several hours. I honestly figured it would just knock you out for a little while, but that only lasted thirty minutes," he retorts with a scrunched-up face as if he was apologetic.

A knock on the door with a sing-song voice saying room service breaks the staring contest we are having. Bash opens the door and ushers in two blonde Barbie-looking women who I think are twins, but on these meds, I wouldn't swear to it, pushing in two carts.

"Savvy, these are my assistants Sky and Annie, they will be

helping you when I'm not around." Bash introduces me to Tweedle Dee and Tweedle Dumb. I'm sure he has fucked them both and that thought pisses me off.

"You want me to let your fuck toys help me when you're not here? I don't think so." I know I sound horrid, but I don't care.

I'm looking at these women, who now look mortified, and I just can't believe he would have the audacity. They are both stylishly dressed in business-looking outfits, they both have sleek, long blonde hair, one with bangs, one without. They are slender yet curvy in all the right places. Average height and conservative makeup.

"Savannah Grace Barrett..."

I cut Bash off before he can mutter another word. "I'm so sorry, Sky, and Annie, was it. I'm heavily medicated and saying things before I realize I'm saying them. You both seem like really nice women, but I won't be needing your help." I try to keep my voice calm, and not cry anymore. Crying is a weakness, my mother always used to tell me, after she would kick my ass. I suck it up and try to leave the bad memories behind, stuffing them down into the back of my brain.

"Savvy, please let me take care of you. I will take you back to Cami's and I'll take care of you there. I will only bring the girls in when Cami or I am unavailable to be there with you. They are twins by the way, I saw you studying them. I have never laid a hand on either of them. They are family and I would appreciate you treating them as such. I would also appreciate you giving me a little more credit. I haven't fucked a blonde since I met you." He sounds a bit angry.

"Again, sorry, girls," I say as apologetically as I can, looking over to both of them, then turn back to Bash. "I need you to realize I'm not the same teenage girl you made fall in love with a lie. I'm all grown up, and I need to do things on my own. I get that you have money and power, but that's not mine and it's not me. I had money growing up, and it didn't make my family happy, it was the evil that bound it together. I don't want to live like that. If I earn it on my own, it will

47

mean more to me than someone giving it freely. We both know that nothing in this world is free. I need you to let me go and be whoever I turn out to be. I'm not saying goodbye, I'm saying I'll see ya around. I may come back to you when I'm ready, I may not. You have to let me make that choice." I feel the tears fall at my own words, feeling the pain of an old wound being ripped open again. I'm weak.

I realize that Bash is staring at me, grasping his chest over his heart and clasping his necklace that matches mine, feeling the same anguish I have felt for the last three years. On one hand, I hope it fucking hurts, on the other hand, I want to wrap myself around him and never let go. Be strong, I tell myself.

"Baby, please don't shut me out." He lets a tear escape, weakness. I realize in that moment that is exactly what we are, each other's weakness. We are like the magnets placed in the broken hearts; a force greater than ourselves pulling us together. I am his and he is mine.

"I love you, but I am in love with someone who doesn't exist anymore. Jake, and you can't be that man anymore. I don't know you." I finally explain in a way that he understands. He has a look of understanding mixed with hope.

"Well, I think I introduced myself fairly well last night." I feel the blush go up my cheeks when the twins start giggling. Shit, I forgot they were there. "Thank you for bringing in breakfast, ladies, I'll call you back if we need anything else." Bash nicely asks them to leave, and they do, both with tears in their eyes.

"I hope to see you again soon, Savvy," one of them says as they close the door.

"Yes, Sebastian Jackson Devereaux. Where the hell did you come up with the name Jake anyway?

He laughs lightly. "Jake is my dog. It was the name I used on my fake ID when I left here and met you."

"Wait, you have a dog? Where is he? I love dogs," I belt out, bouncing. I wince when my foot moves the wrong way and I finally feel the pain of the gash.

"He died last year. His urn is above the mantle in the living room." His eyes turn sad again, but only for a moment.

"I'm sorry, I would be heartbroken too. I cried pretty hard when Fudge Bear died." I reach out for his hand, but he gets up quickly, going over to the wheeled-in tables of food. He lifts the lids on several, deciding on two and bringing them over to me in the bed.

"I have to admit, a girl could get used to this." I waggle my eyebrows at him and laugh an actual genuine laugh. I haven't heard that laugh myself in a long time.

"I would gladly serve you breakfast in bed every morning for the rest of our lives if you would let me." He says it almost condescendingly, but I let it slide and try to put him in a better mood.

"Maybe I should get a dog. Or we could find one and keep it here if Cami isn't a dog person. It could be like a fresh start for us as friends, ya know, like how we started out before."

First, he looks at me like I'm nuts, then he smiles wide. "Okay, I'll take it. It's a start, but not until your foot is better." His voice is back to chipper as he opens the tray in front of me and orders me to eat.

I'm surprised when I see that he got my favorite eggs benedict, hashbrowns, and he sets a cup of coffee on the bedside table next to me.

"I think this is the coffee you were raving about. I added sugar for you like you used to like," he says in a smooth yet almost sad voice. His eyes light up when I let out a soft moan when I take my first sip. "This is even better than Cami's, what is this?" I ask, genuinely needing to know.

"Café Du Monde, it's a very lucrative coffee and beignet shop by the French Market. It's been around since the 1860's and has expanded into a franchise throughout New Orleans. It's coffee with chicory." He explains almost like a tour guide.

"What's a beignet?" I ask, not really knowing what it could be. He laughs at my response.

"It's a pastry, love, with powdered sugar sprinkled on top. They

49

are amazing. I will get some brought in for you," he says sweetly, and I didn't miss him calling me love.

"Sebastian, one, please don't use words you don't understand. Two, you don't get to use the words of my favorite character on The Originals to try and woo me. I will give you an A plus for effort though," I taunt him, knowing that I would hit a nerve. He only called me love after he binged the show with me one weekend at the cabin.

"I knew you would come here at some point, and we would meet again, if for no other reason than that damn show and how much I loved the way it made you love New Orleans. I knew it would lead you back to me. Can't you see that we are supposed to be together. You came here hoping that one day I would come back here too. Admit it, Savvy, we are star crossed lovers just like Elena and Stefan in The Vampire Diaries." He uses the shows against me but obviously never finished them after he left me.

"The thing is, Stefan and Elena don't end up together. Not even in the books. No matter how hard the universe tries putting them together, she fell in love with Damon. Remember? That was in season four! You need to brush up on your TVD, mister." I poke fun at him while also making a valid point.

"They seriously don't end up together? I just figured she would go back to the ripper eventually and see that she only wanted to fuck Damon. What about Bonnie and the rest of them?" he asks, obviously stunned by my revelation. He did get pretty into the shows with me. I made him start from the beginning and watch them all in sequence. We only made it to season five and then started The Originals.

"How about you take me back to Cami's, and we can binge the shows again until I can walk or get you to give me some crutches. My bed and stuff I bought yesterday is supposed to be delivered today at noon," I ask sweetly before shoving another bite of eggs benedict in my mouth.

"If that's what you want," Bash concedes.

I look around the room, appreciating its beauty for the first time as I eat my breakfast. The walls are a deep shade of cream with an almost rust colored stucco, dark wood trim with intricately carved crown molding. The floors are a light natural wood, stained to show every grain in its natural shade. The furniture in the room is elegant yet masculine and screams antique with a four-poster bed with matching nightstands, armoire, and huge dresser all hand crafted with beautiful fleurs-de-lis carved into each piece. The navy comforter and white satin sheets on the bed pop as the only colors that really stand out in the room. I look over to the nightstand where a perfect dark blue glass lamp with a white fleur-de-lis painted on the front sits. I look to the other nightstand, knowing what I need to replace.

"I'm really sorry about your lamp. Where can I get you another one?" I ask, feeling bad about breaking something so beautiful.

"They are one of a kind, I will have to call my friend and see if he can make me another one. It's not a big deal," he responds nonchalantly, waving it off as he pops a piece of bacon in his mouth. He looks just like he used to, except for a few new scars on his back and a few new tattoos, but is he the same person I fell in love with?

CHAPTER 5
Bash

I finally got Savvy all set up in her room at her new place with Cami. I really wish she would just stay with me, considering I have staff that can help take care of her, but no, she wouldn't have it. I considered tying her to my bed and retraining her, but that's not my Savvy and I need to remember that.

I can tell that Cami and Charlie are good people and I love them for taking care of my girl like they did on Savvy's first night in the city. Cami told me about Mark Boudreaux hitting on her and getting her drunk that night. I remember his text the other night to let me know a beautiful, rare, dark-haired beauty showed up in town. I will make sure to have a chat with him about fucking with what's mine. I know he couldn't have known who she was, but if he had hurt her, I would have killed him. I know he drugged her. He always does. It's his MO, that's why they always leave willingly, or so it seems on the cameras. The little sluts look like they are hanging all over us when we leave half the time. The image of my Savvy in that position, with him of all people, sends anger coursing through me.

Calm down, he didn't touch her. The voice in my head reminds me.

I'm just glad someone was there to keep her from going anywhere with him. I'm a psycho, and that is bad enough, but he is sadistic in ways I would never dream of. That's why he is my top man. I know he works for others as well, but I always get first dibs. Perks of being the king.

"Keep the change," I tell the delivery driver, handing him a hundred. The teenager's eyes light up and I know I just made his day. I carry the pizza boxes into the kitchen and holler dinner toward the back of the house. Cami and Charlie come out looking like they are heading out for the night.

"I got dinner, guys, where are you going?" I ask, curious.

"It's Cami's birthday, so I'm taking her to dinner tonight, sorry, man," Charlie says as he winks at Cami.

"Shit, what is today?" I ask, knowing I probably have already fucked up. I knew it was getting close to Savvy's birthday, but the last couple of days have been a bit of a blur.

"Sunday," Cami says with a giggle, looking at me like I'm nuts.

"No, the date?" I ask, pulling out my phone.

"August 5th," Charlie replies, brows furrowed.

"Happy birthday to you, Cami, and our Savvy girl in the other room," I reply, running my hand through my hair, trying to figure out how to fix the fact that I haven't told her happy birthday yet and it's seven p.m.

"What? It's her birthday, and not one single person has even acknowledged her today. I didn't tell her it was mine because I didn't want her to feel bad. She probably did the same," Cami whisper shouts, obviously upset.

"My world has been turned upside down since she punched me in the nose yesterday, I'm lucky I remember my own name." I try to defend myself.

"You have so many names, I'm surprised you remember which one you're using at the moment," Cami jabs with a come at me bitch look. She really does care about Savvy.

"Hey, baby, let's not be rude, we only have one side of history here. Give Bash a chance, he obviously cares for Savvy. I can see it, and so can you if you are being honest with yourself. Look past what he did to her and ask for his reasoning. You'll see what I do," Charlie says in an almost riddled tone.

Cami looks at me and her face softens until her eyes are almost glassed over and she finally blinks. She smiles at me and says, "You actually have a blue aura that lightens to almost pure white. I have never seen someone go from the black fading to the red I saw before at the gym to such a pure color. She changes you."

I'm sure my mouth is open, gawking at Cami, not knowing how to respond to her. Then it hits me. "Fuck, you're a witch?" I ask, not really believing I'm saying it.

"Kind of, I've never really used my gift other than to help others and know who to stay away from. You were one I would have stayed away from before, but not when you're with her. She makes you better," Cami says, like it's no big deal.

"Okay, well, I don't know what to say to that except you're right. She does make me better. I have never been a good man, but she is the other half of my soul, and I'm in complete darkness without her. She is my light." I pour my heart out, not knowing why, because I don't tell anyone anything.

"That makes sense. Savvy's aura is bright yellow with splashes of orange. Her aura changes with her moods and when she drinks. She is like a sunrise with a hurricane coming in close behind her. When you said her name at the gym, she went from yellow to pink to red, and then the red almost looked like flames surrounding her when she kicked your ass." Cami throws out the information like it's a warning.

"Well, what are we going to do about her birthday?" Charlie asks, bringing us all back to the problem.

"I'll call one of my assistants to pick you both up a cake and have them pick up a few gifts and her favorite alcohol to make drinks. What else should I do?" I ask, only because I have never thrown a birthday party.

"One, she is on pain meds, alcohol probably isn't the best idea, and two, we will go to the store and get a cake mix and help you bake us a cake. She can't party, she is in bed for Christ's sake. Think, you got pizza already, she is waiting for you to watch her show, right?" Cami chastises me.

"Yeah, obviously. I don't have a gift, and it's too late to go get anything that's worthy of her," I reply, shaking my head.

"She will actually appreciate you making her a cake and remembering at all over something materialistic. She isn't the wine and dine kinda girl. When we were shopping, she wanted used furniture that she could refinish someday and make it what she wanted. It just had to be solid wood; she wouldn't buy anything that wasn't." Cami explains things that I already know but quickly forgot, just wanting to impress her. Savvy does not get impressed with lavish things. I know that. Why is it that the one girl I want isn't begging at my feet like the rest.

"I just need to spend time with her and make sure she knows how much I still care about her. I get it. Thank you," I reply as I get my wallet and open it to pull money out for them when they both stop me.

"We will pick up everything you will need for tonight. It can kind of be our gift to Savvy," Charlie says with a kind smile.

"Okay, but when Savvy is better, I'm taking us all out for a fun night, deal?" I ask, hoping they will say yes. I really like Savvy's new friends. They are a bit odd, but they are the kind of people she needs in her life. I want her to be happy, but I want her happy with me, and I don't see it going any other way.

"Are you coming back, or did you ghost me again?" Savvy shouts from her bedroom with laughter following. "No, seriously, did you fucking leave?" she shouts, sounding very angry when I don't answer her.

"Yes, love, I'm still here. I'll never leave you again unless you try to make me, and you have fun with that one, baby girl." I laugh at her. Cami and Charlie try to hold in their laughter when Savvy starts giggling again. I bolt out the door, grabbing two pizza boxes and head back to the bedroom.

Savvy looks adorable in my T-shirt and dark green boxer shorts.

"Mmmm, pizza. I was beginning to wonder if y'all had normal food here. Don't get me wrong, I have loved everything I've tried so far, but sometimes you just need pizza." Savvy smiles, taking a big bite out of a slice of pepperoni and moaning with her first bite.

I've missed the cute little noises she makes. "There is every kind of food imaginable here, you just tell me what you are wanting, and I'll get it for you," I explain as I take a bite of my own pizza.

"I may have to take you up on that, but if I keep eating everything I want, you may have to roll me out of this house," she jokes with a cute little chuckle.

I laugh out loud at the thought of Savvy being round like a ball. I smile at the thought of her having a rounded belly carrying my child.

"What are you smiling so big at me for?" she asks with a mouthful of pizza, and I bust out into laughter again.

"I was just picturing your belly all swollen with my child." I choose to be honest.

Savvy chokes on her pizza, grasping at her chest at my words. She takes a big drink of sweet tea before she starts yelling, "Have you lost your mind? I will not be swollen with anyone's baby any time soon, so get that thought out of your head. We are not even together."

I put my hand up to stop her because I don't want to hear it. "Savvy, I know you are not sure about us, but I will make you fall in love with me again, maybe not today, and maybe not even next week, but you will fall in love with me again. I will do everything in my power to make sure you feel what I have always felt for you." I reply honestly because that's all I've got going for me and that's what she needs from me at this moment.

"It's going to be difficult, yes, but you never lost me. I never stopped loving Jake. I also hate him, that is what you need to work on. You are Jake but you are also not Jake. You're going to have to let me fall in love with this version of you, Bash. I already know I love some piece of you, it's letting go of that piece, knowing he doesn't exist, that's the hard part." She shatters me yet gives me hope at the same time. I will give her time to fall in love with me, but she is mine whether she realizes it or not.

We watch an episode of The Vampire Diaries before Cami and Charlie make it back. I ask Savvy if she wants anything from the kitchen and push play on the next show so she will be kept busy while I bake her cake. I hurry to the kitchen and join in on the baking.

"I got candles, party hats, and party blowers. I hope she likes cherry chip cake with cream cheese frosting," Cami says as she gets the eggs out of the fridge to help me start mixing all the ingredients the box calls for.

"She loves anything cherry flavored, but she doesn't like cherries." I chuckle. "She also likes bananas but hates anything banana flavored. Something about medicine as a kid. She is a bit of a picky eater," I explain further, unable to contain my smile.

Cami and Charlie give each other a strange look at my revelation about Savvy.

"I haven't noticed her being picky at all, she just eats whatever," Charlie replies with a dumbfounded look. "She is too nice to say when she doesn't like something."

"She won't hurt anyone's feelings, but she has a list a mile long of foods she doesn't actually like." I realize I know her better than anyone. I never had interest in the things that the girls I fucked liked or didn't like, until her. I wanted to know everything about her, nothing was too small or minute when it came to her. At first, I'll admit it was a fascination with how similar she looked to Lottie. Then she became my everything, and now that I have her back, I refuse to let her go. I don't know that I could survive without her, especially knowing she is so close. That was one thing that kept me from her, the fact that she was so far away, yet I knew I could find her anytime I wanted to. I was banking on her eventually coming here. I'm just surprised it took her this long.

I finish baking the cake. Cami and Charlie finally went to dinner as planned when they realized I wouldn't burn the house down. I have been alone a long time; I can cook better than most. I set the timer on my phone and head back to the bedroom with Savvy.

She has tears falling down her face watching the show. I hurry over to the bed and snuggle up to her and watch the episode.

"Oh my god, Bonnie dies? What the hell, you didn't tell me she dies." I chastise her. I know she gets emotionally invested in her shows and feels all the emotions, and I always let her.

"This is just one of the times Bonnie dies. She dies a few times throughout the show, but she died early on too, in like season two I think." She sobs, tears still streaming down her cheeks.

"How can she come back just to die again?" I ask, knowing she will stop crying, laugh, and brutally explain in detail how.

"It's the Vampire Diaries, anyone who they really want to come back can, it's the beauty of fiction." She laughs at me, giving me a duh look.

"Fiction is always better than reality." I mouth the words, letting out only a whisper, remembering just how she used to say them to me when I would make fun of her for not wanting to get out of one of her books.

"You remembered," she says sweetly, leaning over and giving me the smallest peck on the lips.

"See, still me, baby girl," I reply, cupping her cheek.

"I know, it's just going to take time. I see you and still can't believe you are here with me. It's not just time with what happened, it's also time to get used to the fact that you are really here, and I still don't know exactly how to feel about it. It's like my mind and my heart are at war with each other." She tries to explain, and I get it.

"I will give you all the time you need, we have the rest of our lives," I tell her without ever breaking our stare down. I lean in to kiss her when the timer I set on my phone goes off. She jumps back startled.

"Who is that?" she asks with her brows furrowed, obviously as let down as I am that we were interrupted.

"Dessert, baby," I reply as I get up and turn quickly to kiss her before leaving the room. I leave her with a smile that way. I head to the kitchen and can smell the aroma of cake as I turn the corner. I take the cake out of the oven, flip it onto the cake pedestal and dust the crumbs into the trash, then place it on the counter to cool. I set another timer for fifteen minutes and go back with my girl.

"Where is dessert?" She pouts, puffing out her bottom lip.

"It's cooling, wouldn't want you to burn that sassy tongue of yours," I tease with a soft smile. She just laughs and hits play on the remote with an eye roll. Before, I would have spanked her for that, but now I think it's the cutest thing in the world, and I just laugh.

"Damn, Bash, Jake was much stricter than you." She is teasing me, and really drawing out her words, making her cute Southern accent even sexier than usual. My dick hardens instantly at her words as she looks at me with those beautiful eyes, and I know in this moment that she is right. I'm not Jake, or Bash, or anyone else when I'm with her, I'm just me, Sebastian. I don't want to play games or punish her. I just want her.

"Yeah, you make me a big softy. I can't help it, I just want to love you," I reply, catching her off guard. I see the tears well up in her eyes, and I break. I pull her to me, careful not to hurt her foot. She straddles me on the bed, and I just hold her like that, hugging her, smelling her neck, and I cry. I haven't shed a tear since the day I left her, and I never thought the dam could burst open.

"I'm so sorry for what I did to you." I sob, holding her tight. She has her arms wrapped around me tight while continuously rubbing my back. "I have been lost without you for so long, I never thought I would have the sunshine that is you back with me." I continue to cry, and she cries with me.

"I missed you for so long. I wished on every dandelion I ever saw at our cabin. I went there a lot to just feel you again in some way. Now I have you back and it's like a dream I don't want to wake up from." She opens up and lets me in finally.

Our moment is botched once again by the stupid alarm. I kiss her neck while placing her back on her pillows that are propped up. "I'll be back in a few with dessert," I tell her as I wipe tears from her cheeks, then practically run to the kitchen.

Holy shit, I didn't expect that. She is probably thinking what the hell kind of a fucking bitch have I turned into. I pull myself together, not used to feeling this much emotion. I ice her less-than-perfect cake and write in bright red icing Happy Birthday my Savvy Girl with a heart on the end. Then down lower on the cake I write in yellow, Cami too! I put twenty multi-colored candles scattered all over the cake. She can say twenty-one all she wants, but I know the truth and I want this to be authentic. I never got to celebrate her birthday with her, even though I buy a cake for her every year, blow out a single yellow candle, and eat it alone, wishing for her.

Cami and Charlie burst through the front door laughing and smiling. "You guys are back early!" I whisper shout.

"Yeah, dinner was a bust, and we wanted to get back here and celebrate with you guys," Cami replies, bouncing into the kitchen while clinging to Charlie's arm.

I light all the candles and we all three take the cake back to Savvy's room and start singing Happy Birthday. Her face is priceless. She sits up straight with her eyes as big as saucers, welling up with tears. When we get to the part of names, we all say Savvy and Cami and her eyes get bigger as she puts both hands up, covering her mouth.

"Cami, you didn't tell me it was your birthday." She laugh-shouts through sobs.

"Well, ditto, sister." Cami laughs at her.

"Both of you blow out the candles," Charlie demands, chuckling at both the girls. They both close their eyes and blow out all the candles, bouncing and giggling.

"Happy birthday, my Savvy girl. Did you make a wish?" I ask, knowing she would never miss the opportunity to make a wish on anything.

"Of course, I did, silly," she chastises me.

"Was it about me?" I ask with a cheesy grin.

"I'll never tell. It won't come true if I do, ya know." She waves her hand at me, and we all laugh.

"I'll go cut the cake and bring in the party favors," Charlie states as he takes the cake from me and leaves the room.

"I'll help," Cami says as she rushes out the door after him.

"Were you surprised, baby girl?" I ask as I snuggle up to her in the bed.

"I can't believe you remembered and baked a cake. Thank you, Bash. I don't remember the last time I celebrated my birthday with anyone I cared about, or at all if I'm being honest. I usually take the day off and spend it at our cabin on the dock with a bottle of liquor and my books. No one has moved into the cabin since you left. Sometimes I would go in and stay the night in the winter; no one ever changed the locks. I just loved being there. It was hard to stay away from a place that made me so happy. I'm sorry, I shouldn't be bringing it up. I just want you to know I really appreciate you remembering," she says with her head down. I can tell she is trying not to cry, she always hated crying.

I put my finger under her chin, forcing her to look at me. "Baby girl, we still own the cabin. I couldn't sell it because I wanted you to have a place to go when it got rough, or to just get away. The cabin is in both of our names. I assumed you would stay there; I kept all the bills paid to make sure you wouldn't have to worry when you left your parents. I have stayed there twice since I left, hoping you would come to me. I saw you the last time with a guy in the parking lot of the yacht club and forced myself to believe you were happy and decided to leave you alone. It broke my heart that the cabin remained empty. As for your birthday, next year and every year after that will just get better and better. I love you, Savvy. I want every day to be special for you," I explain, hoping to mend her heart a little more.

"We own the cabin? I could have stayed there the whole time? You came back for me? I don't understand, Bash. Why didn't you say anything? I could have been with you for how long?" Her voice goes from soft and confused to full-on pissed in less than a second just as

Charlie and Cami come running in with party poppers, twisting them, throwing confetti and bright colored string all over the room.

Cami looks to Savvy, then to me. "What did you do now?" she asks me pointedly. "Wait, before you answer, will pot help with the situation, or make it worse?" she asks us, shifting her eyes back and forth between us.

"Pot?" I ask, furrowing my brows.

"Yes!" Savvy shouts with a cheesy grin on her face.

"Good, cause this is my present to us!" Cami giggles, handing Savvy a joint and lighting the one in her mouth before handing Savvy the lighter. Charlie hands me one and proceeds to light his own, then hands me his lighter.

"Jesus, where did y'all get this? Is it a Sativa, an Indica, what strain is it?" I ask, knowing they know none of the above.

"I got them from a witchy friend, who may or may not have laced it with a spell for the night. He promised that Savvy would be able to relax and still have a good time with her injury," Cami states matter of fact as she gives me a pointed look. Savvy has already lit hers and started coughing on the first drag. She is at least smiling again.

"What the hell, might as well enjoy the night," I reply, lighting my own joint and taking a long drag from it. It's smooth and hits my throat, giving it a tingly feeling.

"What kind of spell did he put on it?" Savvy asks, taking in another long drag and holding it in.

"He just said that it would open our minds to all the possibilities and will help us with anything we have been struggling with," Charlie replies, blowing out a huge cloud of smoke.

"I'm glad I didn't know about the cabin. I was able to survive on my own with zero handouts, and I made it to the city of magic and dreams by myself. Sure, I had help knowing where I wanted to go because of all the little hints and my favorite show, but I made it here because of me. I haven't given myself the credit I think I deserve. I don't want to go to college, I want to start my own business," Savvy says, more to herself than anyone else.

"Oh my Goddess, girl, are you serious? You have overcome a lot of things already at twenty, you should be proud of yourself. Not everyone goes to college and gets a business degree before starting a business, you don't have to." Cami coughs, blowing another cloud of smoke. The room is filling quickly.

"Baby, you don't want to go to college?" I ask, thinking maybe she talked about it with Cami, which really bothers me. I want her to talk about these things with me.

"What crawled up your ass and died?" Savvy starts laughing hysterically.

"I don't know what's so funny, but it hurts that you haven't talked to me about this," I reply, taking another hit.

"You have only been back in my life for a couple of days, you haven't even earned what you've been given," Savvy states matter of fact, swaying her head with her brows furrowed. Great, I pissed her off again.

"I thought about walking away from my family business three years ago. Before I met Savvy, I was an asshole. I still am, but I hide it better than I used to. I knew I couldn't walk away, they would ultimately find me, and probably kill us both, or worse. I left Jake behind, knowing that I only got those ten months as a vacation, and that was it. I had to come back home and face my dad. I can't ever be Jake again. I'm Sebastian, and I'm a bad guy who does bad things."

Everyone's eyes are on me and looking shocked at what I just said.

"Would your family actually kill you for trying to walk away from your family business? I mean, is it like in the movies, where there is only one way out and that's in a shallow grave," Savvy asks, intrigued by the danger.

"I mean, my guys wouldn't, but others in my line of business might, if the price on my head was worth it, but my family would put the hit out. I keep all of it like it is now, where my brother just controls the cocaine and I handle everything else. I still get my hands dirty every now and then, but I let him handle it most of the time. He prefers crushing bones to crunching numbers." I try to explain without showing how bad of a guy I really am. I think Savvy would ultimately never speak to me again if she knew the whole truth.

"I want to marry you, Cami." Charlie jumps up from his seat on the bed and rushes over to where Cami sits. He kneels down on his left knee, pulling out a little red velvet box, opening it with both shaky hands up to Cami, saying, "Chamomile Elizabeth LeFey, I love you with all of my heart and soul, would you do me the honor of marrying me and making me the happiest man on earth?"

"Oh my Goddess, yes!" Cami shouts as she jumps down on the floor with Charlie, wrapping her arms around his neck as she kisses him with tears streaming down her face.

I look back to my angel and realize she has tears running down her face with no trace of happiness.

CHAPTER 6
Savvy

It's been two weeks since Charlie proposed to Cami. I don't know why, but it set emotions off in me that I can't explain. I'm happy for them, don't get me wrong, maybe I'm just jealous. I realize I want what they have. Love. A love so crippling that the loss of it shatters you into a million pieces. A love that no matter how hard you try to deny that it is there, in your soul you know it's real. A love that consumes you, body and soul, and burns so deep that you never crave warmth ever again because it's there to hold you and keep you safe from all your demons.

I have a love that is all of those things, yet he walked away from it three years ago without giving me a choice. I have a choice now, and I'm not taking that choice lightly. I kicked Bash out that night and have refused to talk to him since. Vases upon vases of flowers cover our entire house and porch at this point. Bash brings more every day, begging for me to talk to him, to explain what he did wrong. I know I'm probably not being fair right now, but I really need to evaluate what the fuck I want and quit worrying if he is the one or not. If he is, then it will eventually work out. Right.

I get up after staring at the ceiling for God knows how long, wallowing in my own self-pity, and head to the kitchen to make some coffee. My foot is healed, stitches came out a few days ago. Still smarts sometimes but all in all healed enough for me to go put in applications today. I've stayed in this house for the last two weeks, one to heal, and two to keep from having to talk to Bash. I know I'm being ridiculous, but damn it, I'm still pissed.

"Morning, Savvy," Cami sings sweetly as she hands me a cup of coffee.

"Morning, thanks," I reply as I plop down at the kitchen table.

"Okay, your aura is way off, honey. Bash loves you, and the longer you push him away, the more miserable you are making yourself. Go check at the front door, the answers are all there," she says cryptically, trying to lift me out of the chair by my arm and shoo me to the door.

I open the door to see none other than the perfection that is Bash standing there with another bouquet of lilies.

"Good morning, beautiful. Please don't shut me out anymore," he says as he drops to his knees. "Please give me a chance to be the man you need me to be. You can go to school, not go to school, open your own business, or not. You can dictate your life however you want, but please just admit that you are as wrecked as I have been these last two weeks. Baby, please let me back in, we can take it slow, or whatever pace you want, but please don't torture me anymore." His voice is shaky, and I have never seen a more beautiful sight than the man on his knees at my feet.

"Pick me up at seven and plan something fun. Show me who you really are, Bash," I reply, taking the flowers and closing the door in his face. Harsh, yes, but he deserves it.

I take the vase to the kitchen, set it by the window, and sit back at the table with a very happy with herself Cami.

"See, told ya." She nudges my arm.

"You suck, but I love you anyway," I reply dryly as I take a sip of coffee and let the taste of hazelnut register on my tongue. I moan, closing my eyes to appreciate its perfection.

"Damn, you outdid yourself with this one." I compliment her mad coffee making skills as I do every day. Cami just smiles, knowing how much I love her coffee.

"You deserve to be happy, Savvy. Don't torture yourself by staying away from Bash. You haven't been yourself since our birthday when you made him leave after Charlie proposed. I still don't understand, but I know you will figure it out. He is a good guy when he is with you, and you light up so much brighter when you are with him. It's okay to forgive people, Sav." Cami pours out her wisdom and I take it in.

"Thank you for caring. I don't know what is wrong with me. I guess I'm still just pissed that he left me and walked away from love. It was so easy for him to do it the first time. I guess in my mind I'm asking myself what would keep him from doing it again," I reply as honestly as I can.

"Fear is keeping you from what you truly want. Fear of history repeating itself. I get it, but you can't live in fear forever. You have to choose to move past it. With or without him," she replies, patting my hand. I look at the beautiful ring on her finger and wonder how I would actually feel being someone's wife at this point in my life. I'm not ready for that, but I think I'm ready to start things fresh with Bash.

"Thanks, Cami, I always appreciate your wisdom. I'm going to go take a shower, get cleaned up, and see if I can find myself a job," I reply, finishing off my coffee and rinsing my cup in the sink.

"Good luck," she calls out as I head to the bathroom.

It's hotter than Satan's asshole today and I'm thankful I chose a cute red floral tank dress with crisscross straps along the back. I paired it with my brown boots that also showcase a cute little floral design. I wear mascara, blush, lip-gloss, and decided to put my curls up in a messy bun.

My necklace hangs heavy on my chest, still showing the world that my heart belongs to someone who may or may not break it again, if there are any pieces left to shatter.

I push my thoughts of Bash to the side and trudge on past several cute boutiques on Royal St., wondering where I should even start to put in applications. Before I know it, I'm in front of St. Louis Cathedral. I didn't even realize I was coming this way.

Without even thinking, I walk up the steps to the massive doors and I test one to see if it opens. To my surprise, it does, and it's eerily quiet inside. I let myself in and take in the beauty of the vast space. The door closes behind me with a loud thud that echoes off the church walls, making me jump. I turn back to the door with my hands flying to my chest as if my heart would leap out if they didn't contain it.

I feel a sense of peace wash over me as I take a deep breath and let it out. I turn back and walk toward the sanctuary as if something is pulling me in that direction.

I look around the amazing space in awe. Stained glass, beautiful architecture, statues, and artwork make the place look more like a museum. It's breathtaking to say the least.

"Don't make it so obvious you're a tourist, come take a seat and act like you're a good Catholic praying to the rosary or you will get kicked out," a deep sexy voice whispers in my ear, followed by stubble grazing my neck. The smell of sandalwood and cedar mixed with something I can't decipher hits my senses all at once, making my thighs clench.

I turn abruptly to see a man who looks very much like Bash but extremely different at the same time. His frame towers over mine. His hair is dark, curly, and put up in a man bun. His arms are chiseled with ink covering every inch of skin that is visible until being covered by a black V-neck tee that hugs the muscles it covers, giving away just how built this guy is. Tattoos peak out of the neckline going up his neck.

He has the same face as Bash but what I thought was stubble is the start of a beard. I wonder if he keeps it like that on purpose. His eyes are honey colored instead of the caramel I used to love so much.

"Do I know you?" I ask in a whisper as the stranger, whose hand doesn't feel so foreign in mine, ushers me to a pew to sit down next to him. I don't even try to pull away; I follow aimlessly wherever he wants to take me.

"No, but you want to, angel," he says as we both turn toward each other, not pulling our hands away from the others.

"That's presumptuous of you." I try to keep my voice low, even though I fail miserably.

"I'm Christian, and I'm willing to overlook you not being Catholic and not get you kicked out if you will tell me your name and maybe agree to lunch," he replies seductively with a sly grin.

I don't know why but I find myself blurting out, "Savannah, you can call me Savvy. Lunch sounds great," I reply before I even think.

"Savannah, your name even sounds angelic. Tell me, Savvy, what brings you to New Orleans, fun, work, or danger?" he questions as his eyes bore into mine like he is looking into the depths of my soul. His hand is caressing mine, rubbing his thumb back and forth on the back of my hand, sending little bolts of lightning up my arm. The heat between us is thick and I'm finding it harder and harder to breathe as he leans in closer until his mouth is next to my ear. "I think it's danger, little angel. If I'm right, I'm all the danger you will ever need," he whispers before breathing in at my neck and kissing it softly, making my core clench.

Fuck, who the hell is this guy. I feel like I'm under a spell and my body is on auto pilot when a soft gasp slips from my lips as his other hand snakes around my neck, lifting my chin with his thumb as he pushes my head back to look into his eyes once again. "Want to go somewhere we don't have to whisper and keep our hands to ourselves. I'm failing at that one and I'm sure I'll have to repent later, but I believe you are worth it." He finally speaks with a sly grin.

"Yes," is all I can muster.

My mind is spinning and I'm grateful once he pulls me outside and I'm able to take in a shaky breath of air. Hot, humid air, but air, nonetheless.

I almost stumble when he pulls me around to the side of the church and down Pirates Alley before pushing me up against the brick wall, crushing his lips to mine. I get lost in the feel of his need for me and let my hands snake up his back to his neck. His hands are grabbing mine and pushing them above my head against the not-so-forgiving brick. He holds both my wrists in his left hand while his right grabs my jaw a little harshly, holding my head in place. Our tongues dance like they have known each other forever. My leg comes up, instinctively trying to wrap around him to pull him closer. He slows the kiss down, pulling back a little and kissing me softly one last time, placing his forehead on mine. He releases my arms, and they drop to my sides, along with my leg, and I automatically clench my thighs to ease the heavy throbbing. The only thing holding me up is the brick wall and his hand still holding my jaw.

"You ... okay? I didn't mean to be so rough, I just needed to taste you," he explains through ragged breaths.

"I'm fine, but I need you to let me breathe and think for a minute," I reply, trying to catch my breath and my bearings.

The moment he steps back, letting his hand slip away from my jaw, I want it back. I have never felt anything like this with anyone besides Bash, kind of. I mean, we have sparks, but this, with Christian, was more like fireworks at Duck Creek back home on the Fourth of July, and this guy looks like Bash, kind of.

"How about we go get a drink and some food, and maybe get to know each other a little better before you let me kiss you like that again and again. Deal?" he asks but it sounds more like this is happening and there is nothing you can do about it kind of request as he starts to lean into me again.

"Yes, that's a good idea, but don't get ahead of yourself thinking you can kiss me like that again just because," I tease, putting my hand up to push against his hard chest. I'm rewarded with a huge cheesy grin.

"I won't kiss you again until you are begging for me to, love," he replies with a shit-eating grin and my heart stops. He notices the look of disbelief and chalks it up to the fact that he basically is claiming I will beg him to kiss me again. He may not be wrong, but I won't let him know that. No one has ever called me love like that except Bash when he was trying to be his adorable self. He did it because he knew it was a trigger for me to melt. Christian has no idea that calling me that one word will undoubtedly be my undoing.

He grabs my hand again and brings it to his perfect heart-shaped lips and kisses it softly before lacing his fingers in mine, pulling me toward the square again.

"What's the best thing you've eaten since you've been in New Orleans?" he asks, gaining a grin from me.

"Redfish Oceana," I reply honestly.

"Oh, already been to the best restaurant in town, huh?" he replies as more of a statement than a question.

"Yeah, it was the first place I ate on my first night in town. I loved the gator bites too," I reply.

My stomach growls on cue and we both start laughing.

"I know exactly where to take you to lunch. Tableau. The food is to die for, and the drinks are some of the tastiest in the whole Quarter," he replies.

I see his eyes light up when I nod my head yes and reply, "Sounds good."

We don't have to go far, and he asks the hostess for a balcony table. "You will love the view from the balcony, you can see the whole square from up there." His smile widens as he takes my hand and guides me through the restaurant, back outside to a courtyard and up a beautiful cast iron staircase to the balcony. My eyes light up at the view. He can tell he has done good just by my actions and face. I can't seem to hold in my excitement as I rush toward the railing of the balcony to take in the square and all its beauty.

"So, I take it you approve?" His smile meets his eyes and I melt a little under his stare again.

We sit down at the closest table to the railing, and he orders an Old Hickory and I settle on a Blackberry Cobbler. Gin has become my liquor of choice in the last few years. Christian raises his eyebrows at my order.

"What?" I ask, not understanding the look I am getting from him.

"That's a very grown-up drink for such a young lady." He chastises me with a slight smirk.

"How old do you think I am?" I question him with a smirk of my own.

"Probably too young for me and probably too young to even order it if I'm being honest." He runs a hand over his face before letting out an exasperated amount of air from his lungs.

"I'm twenty-one. Happy?" I announce. He seems to like that answer and allows a smile to creep back onto his face as his eyes travel down to my chest.

"My eyes are up here, and I would appreciate you looking at them instead of straight at my chest," I finally say while his eyes are still plastered to my chest.

"Sorry, I was actually looking at your necklace. It's beautiful and unique, just like you," he says as he reaches over and picks the little broken heart up, almost studying it, before he asks, "Where did you get it?"

I try to think of a lie, but the truth starts tumbling out of my mouth before I can stop myself. "The man who tore my heart into a million pieces gave it to me, and I never take it off. It's a reminder of what he did to me." I don't even feel bad for telling him the truth, I just can't decipher what he is thinking.

"His loss obviously. Want to tell me about it, along with everything else about you? I'm a good listener, and you seem like someone who has a lot to say but never allows yourself the pleasure of saying what's on your mind. Are you more of a seen and not heard kind of girl and just show up with your voice when you have to?" he asks as if he can see into my past, plucking out little details to make me crumble.

"I grew up in Oklahoma, on a ranch. My father raised cattle and quarter horses, and my mom fucked every guy that would give her the time of day. They are still happily married to this day. What about you?" I can tell he challenged me to do exactly what I just did by proving him wrong. Deep down, I know I just proved him right.

"So, a daddy's girl with mommy issues, or do you have daddy issues too?" he asks without batting an eyelash just as our waitress sets our drinks down. I pick mine up, taking a longer sip than intended and can't help the slight moan that escapes. It is really good.

"Both, I guess. I also have a brother that thinks he is my dad, acts just like him too, except he likes to shove powder up his nose instead of chasing a high on a horse. What are your issues? Since I'm throwing all of mine out, you might as well join in on the shit show. We can see how many red flags we have put together." I wink at him as I take another long sip.

"My mother died when I was four, my dad's a dick, like major dickhead status, and my twin brother likes to tell me what to do since he has a degree and I don't. He's the brains in the family business. He was always the smart one, ruthless to a fault, and up until a few years ago was a bigger dick than my dad. He turned over a new leaf, found God or some shit, and came back a changed man, or so most believe anyway. I run the side of the business that you have to get your hands dirty, while he prefers to keep his hands a little cleaner now and only handles business that requires a little more finesse when he has to. I've seen the shit he has done behind closed doors, and he hasn't changed, just changed his image. He never shows it, but he has a necklace like that. Tell me, cowgirl, is Sebastian Devereux the man who broke you?"

My heart is pounding in my chest, and I can't lie to him. "Yes," is all I say as I put my head down in shame, knowing that I just kissed Bash's twin brother. That I'm sitting here telling him things I don't talk about with anyone and feeling things for another fucking Devereux.

"I thought you looked like him, but different. I know you aren't Jake, I mean Bash, but I felt something with you in that church that I have only felt with one other person. Turns out he is your brother. Fuck my life," I mumble out most of the words, feeling like a piece of

C.R. Johnson

shit. A big hand softly grabs my chin, making me look up into his honey eyes as a lone tear falls down my cheek.

"You owe him nothing, love. He does not own you, even though in your mind he has since you gave yourself to him. Let's start over. Forget that you have history with my brother and see if there is anything between us. He doesn't matter." He says the words, but they don't register until the waitress comes to take our order.

"Two bowls of gumbo with French bread," he orders nicely, watching the waitress walk away slightly annoyed before he turns back to me. "What do ya say?" he asks with that stupid cheesy grin again.

"Okay, I don't know how to do this because I've never really dated. I'm going to be honest and tell you I'm supposed to have dinner with Bash tonight," I reply, not sure how he will react.

"Do you want to go to dinner with Bash?" he asks, and I can tell he is not being spiteful in the least. He seems genuine and not at all upset.

I sit and think about it for a second, not really knowing the answer to that question. "I don't know," I finally answer because nothing else will come out of my stupid mouth.

"Yes, you do, or you wouldn't be questioning whether you want to or not. Don't hold back, tell it like it is, love. It's the only way to be true to yourself." He speaks in riddles like Charlie and sometimes Cami, like here is your answer, now figure out the riddle.

"You're right, I only agreed to dinner so that he would stop bringing me flowers. I wanted to say no this morning when I slammed the door in his face while he was on his knees. I loved him, more than anything, and he left me. How can I trust that he wouldn't do it again. So no, I don't want to go to dinner with him and listen to all the reasons we are supposed to be together. I told him I fell in love with a lie, and I don't know him anymore. I thought I wanted to, but meeting you, and feeling what you made me feel even before you kissed me, and sitting here with you, it's where I want to be in this very moment." I finally unload and I earn another megawatt smile from this insane man in front of me.

"Well done. Now, let's forget about what's his name and enjoy a day together. I have no other place to be, and I would love to be your tour guide. Tell me what made you choose New Orleans and if there is any place that you have your heart set on seeing." He has no idea how much I laughed internally when he said what's his name. I take a drink, letting the liquor linger on every taste bud before I swallow.

"Unfortunately, something Bash said made me want to come here in the beginning, but my favorite show is The Originals, and I absolutely love the history and culture. It's a beautiful city, and I did find a little magic to help me chase my dreams. Silly, I know, but I love it here. I feel at peace in this city for the first time in my life. I would love to see Lafayette cemetery, number one. It's the most filmed cemetery in The Originals." I reply without hesitation. I don't even feel bad for bringing up Bash, I mean, he asked.

The waitress comes back with our gumbo and asks if we would like to order anything else. Christian never takes his eyes off of me and orders us two more drinks and asks for the dessert menu.

"Good call on the gumbo. What is it? It's really good," I ask, never having had anything like it before.

"Awe cher' it's a Louisiana staple. Take the French bread and put some butter on it and dip it. You'll like it. I can teach you how to make it, but just know it takes hours to get it as good as this. I like to take my time with everything that matters, and good food always matters. We can go to the cemetery after lunch."

His smile is infectious, and I can't stop myself from letting go and enjoying whatever time I have with him.

"What made you come into the cathedral today, love?" he asks, looking very curious.

"I don't know. I just found myself going up the steps and in before I even knew what I was doing," I answer honestly.

"Divine intervention then. I was praying for you, and then to my surprise, you walked into the light, and I swear you looked like an angel sent from heaven above. I had to meet you, and here we are, you, looking like an angel sitting in front of me." I'm stunned by his revelation, and a little surprised.

"You think God sent me into the church to meet you?" I bust out in an uncontrollable fit of laughter. "Christian..." A finger is over my lips to shush me before I can get another word out.

"Call me Sin, all my friends do. Before you ask, middle name is Sinclair, don't laugh. I already do enough at that one." He removes his finger from my lips, replacing it with his lips, and cupping my face with both hands. I can't help but smile at how he shushes my laughing with quick pecks. Which in turn makes me chuckle more. He pulls back and we both continue to laugh. I right myself and take another drink.

"Okay Sin, seriously, I'm no angel, quite the opposite actually. I'm a good person I think, but no saint. You seem so carefree, and I like the way you make me say exactly what I think instead of what people want to hear. Maybe there is such a thing as divine intervention, or maybe everything has literally happened in the way that it did to bring me to this very moment, either way I'm here for it. I want to know you, I don't know why, but I do. If that makes me a bad person then so be it." I hang my head, because for the first time, I don't care about anything else than what I'm feeling, and I know it's selfish. He makes me feel alive, and for the first time in a long time, heard and seen.

By the time I finish getting out what I'm trying to say and look back up into his eyes, I can see how bright they are in contrast to his thick black eyelashes. His features, although you would think would be darker than Bash's, are quite the opposite.

"I'm very happy to hear that, love. Thank you for letting me know how you feel. Let's order dessert, yeah?" he offers in the sweetest way, still acknowledging the fact that I opened up, was vulnerable, and offered dessert as almost a reward, and I like it.

"Do they have crème brûlée?" I ask, hoping I get to taste that amazing, sweet goodness again.

"Baby girl, you are speaking my language. This is the best and prettiest crème brûlée in all of Nawlins." He drawls out his words, making them sexy as hell, especially when he called me baby girl. It stung for a moment, but when he said it, it was almost a growl and I'd be lying if I said it wasn't hot as fuck.

The waitress comes back with our drinks. "One crème brûlée please," he asks while holding my hand, rubbing his thumb back and forth. The waitress smiles, nods, and takes off.

"Tell me more about you. I know you're like a drug lord or some shit, right?" I ask like it's no big deal, hushing "drug lord" while making air quotes as I take another bite of gumbo. He almost chokes on his French bread, and I can't help but chuckle.

"Yeah, I guess you could say that." He smirks as he dips his French bread in his gumbo again before putting the whole thing in his mouth and licking his fingers clean. I can't help but imagine if he would do the same after his fingers have been inside me, or would he expect me to clean up my own mess. I clench my thighs as I feel my panties drench from the thought of his fingers gliding inside me.

"Whatcha thinkin' about, love?" he asks with a sly grin and cuter-than-mine accent.

"Have you ever had sex in a cemetery?" I ask, genuinely curious, and wanting to know more than anything if it's possible. I don't know if I am actually going to fuck him tonight, but I know without a doubt there is a fifty-fifty chance that I will, and if not, then there is a one hundred percent chance it will inevitably happen, and I know we are going to the cemetery after this.

"No, I can't say that I have, or that I have even thought of it. I mean, now that you mention it, it does sound intriguing. Are you asking me to defile you in a cemetery, love? Because I would absolutely love to, but not our first time, and certainly not while you are still seeing my brother. When I fuck you, Savvy, it will be because you know that you can't live without me, and you won't ever want another man anywhere near what's mine. I don't share, love," he replies, making my heart skip a beat while my clit throbs with need. I swallow the lump in my throat and down half of my second drink.

The waitress brings out a larger-than-life crème brûlée that looks like it has been branded with a capital T and a fleur-de-lis on either side. It's stunning, and I almost hate to crack it.

I take a picture of it on my phone, and we both decide a selfie is appropriate. We actually complement each other well with our dark features and bright eyes. If I didn't know any better, I would say we look like a young couple in love dining out somewhere fun, capturing our special moment in time.

We both crack the crystalized sugar at the same time, digging into the creamy dessert, lifting our spoons to each other. We chuckle and feed one another the rich dessert. We both moan with delight at the perfectly flavorful dish, cracking up again at our similarities.

We finish as much of the massive dessert as possible without making ourselves sick. Sin pays the tab, and we leave hand in hand, running into Bash and a dark-haired woman making out on the stairway with her hand down his pants giving him a hand job while he palms one of her tits under her halter top. I start laughing while walking past them as his eyes shoot up to meet mine, going wide.

"Dinner is canceled tonight, little brother, but don't worry, I'll be her date." Sin chastises his brother and laughs along with me, slinking his fingers into mine. When we make it outside, I need answers.

"Did you know he would be there with her?" I question him, because even though I think I know the answer, I could be wrong.

"Yep, I did. This is his Monday spot because it's less crowded in the square the first few days of the week. The rest of the time, he goes to hotels or one of the condos we own around the Quarter. I didn't want to tell you, I figured you are more of a show me not tell me kinda girl, so yeah, I knew, but he could have taken her anywhere really, I just got lucky. Not sorry either," he replies without a trace of remorse.

"Thank you. You didn't have to be honest with me about your

brother, yet you did anyway, for whatever reason, so thank you," I reply, obviously surprising him.

"You're welcome, angel. Ready for your tour of the city?"

"I'm ready to have some fun. Let's do something crazy," I reply as he twirls me around as we pass by a live jazz band playing close to the river.

"Something crazy, huh? I could think of a ton of crazy things, what do you have in mind?" he replies with a sly grin.

"I want a tattoo!" I proclaim, squealing like a little schoolgirl.

"A tattoo, huh? Of what, and where?" he asks curiously as he pulls me into him, kissing my forehead as we stroll toward the French Market. I shrug in response not exactly sure yet. I love that he can't keep his hands off me, and I even love that I don't want him to stop.

He takes his phone out several times, checking messages, typing away, but his hand never leaves mine. I take the opportunity to check the buzzing beast that has been burning a hole in my purse. Thirteen messages. Twelve from Bash, and one from Cami letting me know Bash came by. I reply to Cami, telling her I'm fine and to not wait up. And that Bash is a dick. I don't wait for her reply. I decide enough is enough and turn my phone off and put it back in my purse.

"I thought we were going to the cemetery?" I quip, pouting.

"I decided it would be more fun if we went after dark. I have a surprise for you later."

"Okay, where are we going then?" I ask, only knowing the French Market is this way but never venturing past it.

CHAPTER 7
Christian/ Sin

As soon as I saw the necklace she wore in the church, I knew she had something to do with Sebastian. I've seen that exact replica around his neck for the last three years. I should have known if some higher power had sent her to me, there would be some kind of hoops I would have to jump through to make her mine. I'm watching her bounce down the street with her hand in mine, not really sure how I got so lucky. She is beautiful, sure, but she is so much more. She has a mouth on her and a backbone, which most of Bash's conquests don't. She is also funny, and honestly, I'm fascinated by her. I saw her walk into Oceana's a couple of weeks ago and swore I had seen a ghost. She looks so much like Lottie. I knew it wasn't possible, but their similarities are uncanny. I told Dave, the owner, that I got her tab. When I went to find her, she was talking to douchey Boudreaux, then I saw her leave with one of the waitresses, Cami I think. They bolted out of the restaurant before I could even get up to say hi. I didn't know her then, but I've wanted to ever since, until she walked into the church. It was literally like God himself said here's your sign, now go for it. I wasn't going to let her get away again.

I pull her close to me as I turn us toward Tough Love Tattoos. I already texted my guy Lex to do me a favor.

"Surprise number one, a tattoo as you requested, my dear." Savvy bounces giddily as I open the door for her.

"Seriously! I can't believe I'm doing this. My dad will have a heart attack." She squeals.

"Let's hope not. What permanent mark do you prefer to brand your body with, beautiful?" I ask, curious to know what she has in mind.

"Love," she replies quickly. "I want the word love on my wrist," she finishes.

"Love, why?" I ask, not understanding how she could want the word love when she just saw the guy she probably came here for with another woman.

"Love is a universal word, and it's what every soul on earth wants. It is not given as freely as one would think, and it has power over you. I guess I want what everyone else wants. It will be a reminder of what life is all about." Her words hit me hard. Love is what everyone in the world wants. It doesn't come easily, and most would kill just to have the feeling even for just a moment.

"You're a poetic little thing, aren't you, Savvy?" I ask, realizing just how precious she is. I can't say what it is that draws me to her; her looking so much like Charlotte, the fact that she came into the cathedral while I was praying for her, I don't know. Whatever it is, I hope it never goes away.

"Can I do an infinity on my wrist with the word love as a part of the design?" she asks sweetly.

"If that's what you want." I confirm, nodding my head.

"Yup, that's an easy one," Lex replies, startling her.

"I would also like to schedule another one that will take longer." She throws out as she sits in the black leather chaise lounge.

"Something big?" I ask, now very curious as to what this little minx has on her mind.

"Well, I want a fleur-de-lis on my back that comes around to my chest, with birds flying out of it like they are ripping part of the tattoo, and the words Always and Forever in cursive on my chest. Can you create something like that?" she questions Lex.

"I think I can do something special for ya, especially for one of Sin's friends," Lex replies, giving me a wink.

"Okay, do something to take my mind off of the sting please," Savvy states with big eyes as Lex starts the tattoo on her left wrist. I'm standing on the other side of her chair, so I sit on the end of her lounger and hold her other hand, pulling her wrist to my lips and kissing it softly. I place her hand on my cheek, closing my eyes as her scent of jasmine, coconut, and patchouli hits my senses. Fuck, she smells as delicious as her sweet lips taste. I look her in the eyes as I kiss her hand and wrist, keeping them soft and sweet, just like her. I place her hand over my heart so that she can feel the erratic beating as I can. She sucks in a harsh breath through her teeth but calms instantly when I lean in and press my lips to hers.

We don't even flinch when Lex hollers, "Done, pry apart and take a look cher', see if you like it."

We both chuckle as I pull myself away from my angel. She looks at her wrist in awe that she now has permanent art on her body. She runs her pointer finger over the word love inscribed into her skin and smiles wide.

"How much do I owe you?" she asks, letting her smile meet her eyes, and what mesmerizing eyes they are; the brightest, most beautiful jewels I have ever seen.

"This one is on the house. It's my gift to you as a welcome to the city. Give me two weeks to get the artwork done for your next one, then come back in and see if you want to make changes," Lex replies with a grin.

"Lex loves doing custom artwork. He has done all of mine," I quip, so she knows I didn't take her to just anyone.

We leave the tattoo shop and I lace my fingers through hers again. I almost forgot what it was like to hold a woman's hand.

"I'm sorry, but I have to find a job. I have been here for over two weeks and still have yet to put in one application. That's what I was supposed to be doing today." Savvy sighs.

"Why haven't you put in any applications?" I ask, curiosity getting to me. I want to know everything about her.

"Well, your brother for starters. I guess I can't really blame him, I broke a lamp and stepped on the glass barefoot and had six stitches. Now they are out and I can walk again, so I decided today is the day to get a job, I even wore a dress, which I think I like since it's so hot here." She chases squirrels, eventually getting to her point.

"What kind of work have you done before, or what kind of work do you want to do?" I ask, genuinely wanting to know.

"I have been a waitress and bartender for the last three years, it's all I know. You wanna know a secret?" she asks, peeking up at me through a curl that has fallen from her cute bun.

"I want to know all of your secrets." I answer honestly. Her smile brightens and those brilliant sapphire eyes meet mine, looking through me, piercing pieces of my soul long forgotten.

"I don't want to go to college to get some stupid degree, I want to open a bookstore slash coffee shop. I know if I work hard enough and save up, I can do it. I've made it this far." She shrugs a shoulder. I think of all the things that I could say and then decide against it because I can tell that her independence is important to her. I could give her everything she wants and more, but I have a feeling that she would feel insulted.

"Well, I do partly own a real estate company. We do more commercial real estate than any other company in the city. When you are ready to find your shop, I will help you find the perfect location," I reply, trying to keep surprising her. I'm rewarded with a smile and a kiss on the cheek.

"Thank you!" she squeals.

"For what, angel?" I ask, pulling her close and kissing her forehead.

"For not acting like I'm crazy for wanting to do something with my life besides go to school. For respecting the fact that I am trying to do things on my own and not trying to be a knight in shining armor, but still being helpful. You are different than I expected, especially after you practically molested me in the alley by the cathedral." She chuckles, putting her free hand up to her lips, obviously in the memory of our quick make out sesh. I have to admit, the thought of it has my dick as hard as the brick wall I had her up against.

"I also have a friend that owns The Tavern, it's a great bar and grill and he just so happens to be hiring a waitress and a bartender. Want to go check it out and get to know each other while you land a new job?" I ask, hoping she will say yes. Nick is a good guy, one that I trust, and would help keep an eye on her for me.

"Yes! Oh my God, thank you!" She jumps up, wrapping her arms around my neck, and kisses me, not hard, but not soft either, but sweet; she is something else.

I turn us to go in another direction toward my buddy's bar. "I didn't say I could get you the job, you will have to do that, but I don't think you will have any trouble," I reply, letting her know she isn't getting any freebies. I know she appreciates that, even though I know he will give her a job. She doesn't have to know that though.

"I will be on my best behavior," she teases. I full on laugh, just because I would love to see how she is when she isn't behaving.

"What's so funny?" she asks, nudging my shoulder.

"I was just thinking that I would love to see you at your worst behavior," I reply, kissing her hand still in mine.

"Maybe you will be lucky enough to see all the fucked-up sides to me." She smiles shyly as she pushes back a loose curl behind her ear.

"Angel, I want to see it all." I pull her close, stopping in the middle of the road. I raise the back of my free hand to her face, lightly stroking her cheek down to her jaw. I grab her chin, softly pulling her lips to mine, and then let her go, continuing to walk toward my buddy's bar, pulling her by her hand and laughing.

"I have fucked up sides to love, and I hope you stick around to see each and every one of them." Savvy gives a soft laugh as she hugs my arm as we walk. I could get used to this.

I open the door for her to enter The Tavern, and my buddy behind the bar gives me a wave. "Savvy, this is my buddy Nick, he owns the bar."

"Hi Nick, Sin was telling me that you are hiring. I have waitressed and bartended for the last three years back home, and I know I could do a good job at either position. Can I fill out an application?" she asks sweetly.

"I actually just hired a girl for the waitress position but have been having a hard time filling the bartender position. Show me what you've got. Happy hour will start in about forty-five minutes, think you can handle it?" he asks with raised brows.

"I know I can. May I get acquainted with the bar for a bit before?" she asks with all the confidence in the world.

"Whatever you need, girly, have fun, and start with taking my buddy Sin's order first. If you can handle happy hour, you got yourself a job," he replies, extending his hand to shake hers. She takes it and shakes firmly before letting go.

She gives him a wink and replies, "Then I guess you have a bartender." She spins around to me, and with the brightest smile I've seen so far, she asks, "What can I get you, sir?"

"Hurricane please," I reply with a grin.

"On the rocks or blended?" she quips. Oh, my girl knows her shit, thought I would stump her on that one.

"On the rocks please," I reply, granting her a smile in return.

By the time happy hour is over, Savvy has won over every patron that has been lucky enough to waltz in. She is witty yet sweet when she wants to be and has no trouble handling herself when anyone gets out of line.

"So, what do you think, Nick, did I bring you a good bartender?" I ask as he just stares at her behind the bar, happy as a lark.

"I owe you one, brother. Where on earth did she come from? It's like she puts a spell on everyone she comes in contact with," he replies, shaking his head, still reeling over my girl.

"Crazy as it sounds, God basically put her right in front of me at the cathedral this morning while I was praying to the rosary." Nick knows me, and I don't have to use my bad guy persona or name with him; he is like family.

"She is definitely heaven-sent, bro." He laughs as he takes a swig of his beer. "Hell, I don't even do this good of a job during happy hour, and it's like she is drawing more and more people in. We are always busy, but today we are getting slammed, and she has barely broke a sweat." Nick smiles, obviously as impressed with her as I am.

Savvy bounces over to our table, smiling from ear to ear, knowing she is badass. "So, Nick, I take it I have a job?" she says sassily, bouncing up to kiss my cheek.

"You're hired. When can you start?" Nick replies with a shit-eating grin on his face.

"Tomorrow, unless you need me tonight." She bounces up on her toes, clasping her hands in front of her, bringing them up to her chin.

"Take tonight and have some fun. Be here at ten a.m. tomorrow, we can talk about pay and your schedule." He pulls out a wad of cash and holds out a couple hundred bucks toward her.

She pushes it back and replies, "No need, I just made close to three hundred bucks during happy hour. You can start paying me tomorrow, that was fun. Now we do shots, boys, to celebrate me getting a job, and you for getting a phenomenal bartender," she replies with a smirk, making her way back behind the bar.

She takes nine shot glasses, dipping the rims in a red sugar, and pouring Midori mixed with Jäger, Chambord, and a splash of sweet and sour mix, puts them on a tray, and brings them over.

"May I present the sexy gator." She puts the tray down at the table and takes a seat. She grabs a shot, holds up the glass, and says, "To new friends, taking chances, and forging our own paths." We all clink our glasses, hit the bottom of the tiny glass on the table and drink. Damn, it's good. I decide it's my turn to make a toast. I pick up another shot glass and raise it to the middle of the table.

"To divine intervention, I wouldn't be sitting here right now if Savvy hadn't walked into the cathedral, taking my breath away." We repeat the ritual of taking the shot. Nick picks up his third shot and raises it.

"Thank God you walked into that cathedral today, I have tried to find a good bartender for weeks!" We all laugh, taking our shots.

"Since you obviously don't have a date tonight anymore, and you got a job, how about we have some fun. Let me take you for a night out in New Orleans, the way it should be done," I offer, hoping she will give me a chance.

"Can I wear this, or do I have to go change, because I have a feeling you know who will be there, and I don't want to deal with him tonight," she replies, making my heart skip a beat at the fact she didn't even have to think of her answer, just doesn't want to deal with my asshole of a brother.

"You can wear whatever you want. If you don't want to wear that, there are a few boutiques around that I think you would like, and if you want to freshen up, we can go to my place," I reply, happy she doesn't think I'm a creep just trying to get her in my bed. I mean, I want her in my bed, but I can wait.

"Thank God, I need to shower after slingin' drinks." She laughs, obviously relieved that I offered to take her to my place. I'm sure the three shots she just took are helping me more than her, but I won't take advantage of her if she has been drinking. Not our first time.

"Ready to go then?" I ask, standing from my seat, extending my hand to her.

"Yeah." She smiles, taking my hand, then turns to Nick. "Thanks for giving me a shot, see ya in the morning." She stands, going up on her tiptoes, pulling me down a bit, and kisses my cheek.

Once we are out of the bar, we take a left on Royal. I only live a couple of blocks from the bar, I know she will shit when she sees it. It's on the tour guides stops from being the first Mikaelson compound on The Originals. I bought the old hotel when it went belly up and made it almost exactly like the replica they built in Conyers, GA. I have to admit, I'm a nerd when it comes to The Vampire Diaries, The Originals, and even Legacies, even though it sucked in comparison. I have watched all the shows, and when she said that she loved The Originals too, and it was one of the things that drew her to the city, I have to admit, it is just one more thing about her that makes her so perfect.

I turn us left and take her through the brick walkway. We stop at the wrought iron gate with fleurs-de-lis decorating the tip of each spike. I put my hand on the scanner and it unlocks, opening for us to walk through. The gate closes a bit abruptly, making her jump. I smile apologetically and try not to laugh.

She gasps when we enter the courtyard, and she looks around. "Holy shit! Is this the Mikaelson's home! Are you fucking with me? How in the hell are we in here? Is this even real?" She asks question after question, running to the fountain, then the staircase, then back to me.

"Surprise! When you said that the show was another thing that drew you here, I knew you would love this place. I bought it a few years ago and have been restoring it to the actual house in the show. I'm about eighty percent of the way done, but it's coming along nicely," I explain.

"This is the coolest thing I have ever seen. This was on my bucket list, but I never thought I would get to see it like this, just figured it would be on a tour I take." She is still squealing, in awe of all its beauty while I'm in awe of her.

CHAPTER 8
Savvy

I can't believe I'm taking a shower in Klaus Mikaelson's bathroom! I squeal in my head, still fangirling, while washing my body with Sin's bodywash. I hold the loofah up to my nose, trying to decipher the mixed scents without cheating to look at the bottle. Cedar, and definitely a hint of lemon, and I still say sandalwood. I pick up the bottle, it's Creed Spice and Wood, sun drenched lemon, check, warm clove, apples, missed those, and cedarwood, ha check, or close enough. I finish up and step out of the massive five showerhead, walk-in, cave-like shower. It's big enough for a small party. I wrap a huge, fluffy hunter green towel around myself and decide to check all the glossy dark walnut-stained cabinets to see what I can make of this guy.

No prescription meds except an old antibiotic he didn't finish, but I did find six guns stashed in various places throughout the massive master bath. Not surprising for a drug lord, I guess. I love the darker bold shades of terracotta mixed with deep hunter green, black, and white in the marble, tile, and decorative touches. Fleurs-de-lis are intricately placed on every gold handle and fixture.

There is a large shiny black clawfoot tub with gold accents on each claw in the center of the room. I walk over to it and climb in, just to see how small I feel in it. We could both fit easily. The thought of taking a bath with Sin has me clenching my thighs. I'm curious to see what he is like all riled up behind closed doors. Will he be a dominate and get off on my pain, or is he the soft and sensual type?

Laughing at myself, I climb out of the pretty tub and grab my clothes and purse. I washed all my makeup off in the shower, so I open my purse and fish out what I have to work with. I have mascara, lip-gloss, and a few hair ties. I dry off, throw my clothes back on, redo my messy bun, add mascara, lip-gloss to my lips, and then dab just a bit on my cheek bones, rubbing it in with my finger to give a blush look. I take one last look in the mirror, giving myself a nod of encouragement and start putting everything back in my purse.

I pick up my phone, shit, I forgot I turned it off. I hold the side button down while chewing on my bottom lip, waiting for it to load my lock screen. No sooner than I unlock the screen and everything loads, the dinging and vibration begins. Fifty-seven missed calls, and thirty-two messages. I drop the damn thing and yelp when it starts ringing obnoxiously loud.

"Shit, shit, shit," I curse loudly, stomping the heel of my boot, scuffing the shiny floor.

The knock on the door followed by a worried, "Savvy," startles me again just as I pick up my phone, making me jump and throw my hands up, and I drop my phone again. "Fuck!" I continue to curse as Sin bursts through the door, looking down at me with a scrunched face, first with a look of worry, then of pure confusion.

"Are you okay? I heard you yelling and was worried."

"Yeah, just got startled by my phone and then you, and I broke it good this time," I try to explain. He takes the phone from me, giving it a once over.

"We can go have it fixed tomorrow in an hour." His eyes widen, looking at how many missed calls and messages there are.

"I have to work tomorrow," I remind him.

"Then I'll take it," he replies with a light chuckle.

He helps me up, keeping the phone in his hand. As soon as I'm upright and steady, he starts clicking through the messages, walking into the gorgeous bedroom. His face keeps getting redder, and veins start popping out in places I didn't even know veins were. This can't be good.

"Savannah, I'm going to give this back to you, and I want you to read through the messages, I'm not going to delete them, because you need to see the kind of sick bastard my brother is, but after that, we will delete them and him from your life for good. Do you understand?" His voice is colder than it has been, he is being careful with his words, and doing what he does, I need clarification.

"By delete, do you mean from my phone and just never speak to the fuck-twat again, or are you meaning he will actually be deleted from, like, ya know, earth?" I ask, not really showing a ton of emotion, because I feel like he is showing enough for the both of us at the moment.

"Read the messages, we can both listen to the voicemails together, there are eighteen, then I'll let you decide," he replies with a twisted, sinister look of amusement. Damn, he is sexy.

I let my brain defog from his sexy look, registering what he said.

"Wait, what?" I ask, confusion written all over my face.

"I'll let you choose if the fucker lives or dies," he replies nonchalantly, cocking his head to the side, like he is confused that I'm confused.

"You want me to choose if Bash lives or dies?" I ask, slightly mortified.

"Essentially, yes," he replies, checking his phone.

I contemplate what he is saying. "I don't think I could ever kill anyone; I mean, unless they were going to kill me and it was self-defense, then, and only then, would it be ethical." I respond out loud without meaning to.

"Read the messages, Savvy, and you may want to hurry. Get through about the first fifteen and you will see why." He swirls his hand around with his pointer finger out telling me to wind it up.

I open the messages app and see most are from Bash, only a few from Cami, and one from my brother. I press on Bash's name and start reading.

Bash: Where did you go? Why are you with my brother? What you saw wasn't what you think!

Bash: Where the fuck are you?

Bash: Cami said she hasn't seen you. I just want to talk.

Bash: Please talk to me.

Bash: We are supposed to have our date tonight, I will pick you up at 7. Be ready!

Bash: What the fuck, Savannah?

Bash: You better show up for our date.

Bash: You are really starting to piss me off.

Bash: I'm sorry.

Bash: I didn't mean that, I just love you so much and I don't want to lose you again.

Bash: You stupid bitch! If I can't have you, no one will!

Bash: Do you think my brother can keep you safe from me? I will kill him right in front of your fucking gorgeous eyes.

Bash: You have always been mine, from the moment I popped your cherry, you have been mine, and you will always be mine.

Bash: Don't make me hurt your friends to get to you, Savvy. I will, just to watch you cry.

I toss the phone on the bed, almost as if it burned me.

"So, death?" Christian asks. I look up at him as a tear escapes. "Shit, I'm sorry. How far did you get?"

"He said he would hurt my friends. Who the hell is that person? He is not the guy I fell in love with at the lake," I reply, sobbing at the fact I was in love with a fucking psycho.

"Bash is insane. I think he tried to change, probably for you, but he will always be a psycho."

"Oh my God, everything Mia said about him was true. I denied it for two fucking years, but he was sadistic at times. If a guy hit on me when we were out or talked to me at the gas station, he would always try to start a fight. He would always accuse me of cheating on him with other guys, but he was the one who was screwing other girls, probably at random. He never hit me, well once, but he did get rough a few times. I could hold my own and he knew it, but thinking back, he was not just dominate in the bedroom, but across the board with things." I just blurt everything out without thinking. I honestly feel like I can trust Sin.

"In the last three years, there have been six dark-haired women who look very similar to you disappear, never to be seen again. All of them dated Bash, and all last seen with Bash. You aren't going anywhere near him again. Even if you choose to never see me again, you cannot go near him." His voice is stern again, but also filled with compassion. I assume at the fact that I fell victim to his brother.

"You don't have to worry about that. I don't want to see him again, but we have to go get Cami and Charlie before he hurts them. Does he know where you live?" I ask with hope.

"Fuck no, he only knows of the condo I have in Metairie. He probably doesn't even know this place exists. He is clueless to my business dealings because I don't put them on his books. Dad and I have come to a mutual understanding that Sebastian has to be dealt with. He has become a liability since he started taking product, which is breaking our first rule. We moved funds around and let him keep on fucking up his investments with his money, but not ours. He has been so high most of the time that he started losing millions in bad investments. I thought a couple of weeks ago that he might have put the shit down again, but now seeing this just proves he is high. Threatening innocent people is just not acceptable," he replies, shocking me again.

"Wait, did you use me to out your brother so that you could kill him?" I question rather harshly, pointing my finger up in his face. He literally laughs in my face.

"No, I had no idea that you would even come into the cathedral today. How on earth could I have orchestrated it all?" he counters.

"You admitted you knew he frequented that restaurant on Mondays and that you did it on purpose," I remind him.

"Yup, I'm not gonna lie to you, Savvy. I did do that on purpose, but I had no idea he was going to go all boil a bunny, if I can't have you no one will psycho, and pull a dickhead move threatening you and your friends," he replies, seeming to be honest.

"Just promise me that you're not a psycho too. I mean, you are his twin, and you are attracted to me just like he was, trying to stake your claim on me. How do I know that you aren't the one killing all those girls and hiding them in the walls and underground like they did the bad vampires during Marcel's reign in The Originals?" I chastise, trying not to laugh at myself for asking. He holds back, only letting a slight snicker out.

"Angel, you are adorable, and I absolutely adore where your imagination is taking you, but that is the one thing I left out in the rebuild, and I am a psycho, just not a serial killing psycho. I only kill if absolutely necessary, and never women or children. We have that rule because of our mother's death, and because we do have morals. When the first girl went missing two and a half years ago, I was the last to see her with Bash. I have never forgiven myself for leaving her there in the club with him. She wanted to stay, but I still should have pushed harder for her to leave when he hit her. They said it was all consensual and roleplay." Sin bares his soul, letting me know that his mother's death wasn't just an illness, or accident, but that someone killed her, and that he knows that Bash killed that girl and probably the other five fitting my description.

"I appreciate us opening up and letting out our demons, but the longer we sit here, the longer my friends are in danger. Can we please go get them and bring them back here, then we can talk as much as you want," I ask, trying not to be insensitive, but also not wanting anything to happen to them because of me.

"Don't worry your pretty little head, love, they are on their way as we speak. I set everything in motion while you were looking at your messages." He sets my mind at ease, while also creating a ton of questions.

"How exactly do you know they are and will be brought here safely?" I ask the simplest one that will hopefully get the most answers.

"They will drop off and move to at least four locations before coming here. Bash got away from my guys. He was watching the house from a good distance and left before my guys got your friends out of the house. He did have two guards holding them at gunpoint, so they were more than happy to go with Jasper and Joe. They are walking through the casino now, heading up to a room. . ." He pauses in the middle of his sentence, looking at his phone and nodding more to himself than me, then continues, "But they'll be going back down the staff elevator and leaving out the back in uniforms from the hotel, then they will leave in a minivan that will take them to another hotel where they will repeat the process and leave out of the parking garage dressed in different clothing to help hide their identities. They'll be brought here with one of the tours to help hide them better but get them directly in front of us and in the compound with my guys without anyone noticing." He explains how all this mobster type shit works.

"Cool," is all I can come up with considering I'm still in awe.

I sit on the bed, lying back on the softest, deep green satin down pillow, watching as a little white feather puffs out in front of me, landing on my necklace. All of a sudden, I can't stand the thought of it touching my skin. Before I know it, I sit up and rip the damn thing off my neck, throwing it across the room. It lands in the corner with a loud thud against the dark wood floor. I smile and release the breath I was holding.

"I feel lighter already." I sigh with a smile, plopping back on the pillow again, slightly disappointed when another feather doesn't fly out.

"Lighter?" he questions.

"Yeah, like a weight I didn't even know was sitting on my chest has been lifted, it's easier to breath," I explain. His smile meets his eyes.

"I have wanted to rip that thing off your neck from the moment I recognized it. Thought it was best I let you do it in your own time. Now I know you are done with him," he replies, sitting on the bed next to me.

"So, I guess date night is off, huh?" I ask, looking up at him.

"Well, yeah, but we can still enjoy ourselves. How about I get you something comfy to put on, then we can have a drink and just get to know each other better. Or we can listen to the horrid voicemails I'm sure are on your phone." Christian hands out options.

"Wow, don't tempt me with a good time," I joke while sitting up on my knees and playfully pushing his arm. He doesn't budge, but in turn flips me onto my back with him hovering over me in less than a second. I squeal as butterflies rush my stomach at the quickness of movement and can't help the giggle that slips out.

I have this gorgeous man literally inches from my lips, and I giggle. He smiles in return, lowering his lips to mine. When they finally meet, I close my eyes. His kiss is soft and sweet. Much more tender than earlier. I get lost quickly as he deepens the kiss and my hands snake up his back, attempting to pull him closer. My legs instinctively open for him, allowing him to put his weight down on me. I feel his hard dick almost pulsing through his jeans. Apparently not everything about the twins is the same. Sin's bulge feels huge in comparison. He moves his kisses down my jawline, to my neck, and back up again, capturing my lips with his.

"Hello?" a female voice yells from downstairs. We both jump, Sin blocks me with his body while pointing a gun at the doorway. Where the fuck did the gun come from?

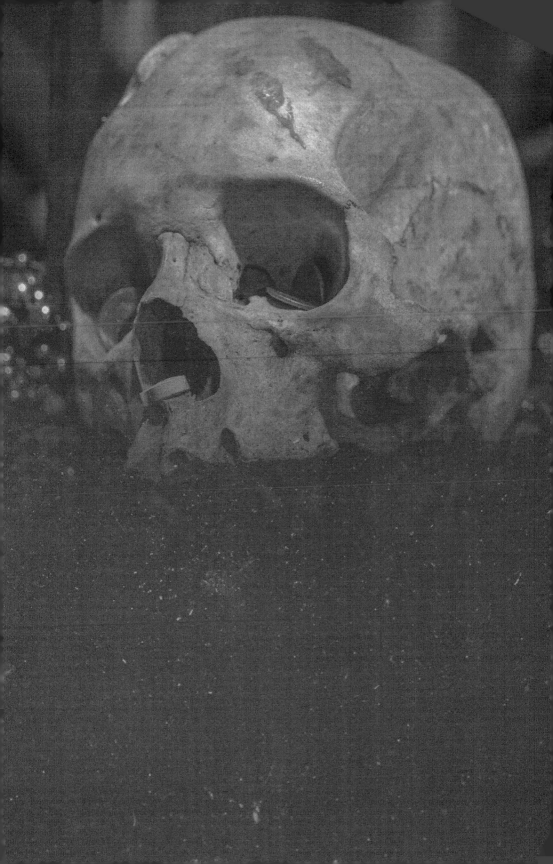

CHAPTER 9
Bash

I tip the bottle of bourbon to my lips and let the amber-colored liquor finish coating the rest of my senses as I drain the last of the liquor, wallowing in my own self-pity. My guys just let me know that they lost Cami and Charlie, my one wild card.

"Fuck!" I yell as I throw the empty bottle against the wall, watching the glass shatter into a million tiny pieces. I sit here alone in the dark, seething over the loss of someone I only truly had based on a lie. The one face I would always see as the life would drain from their eyes, always making them glaze over with a hint of blue, the color never comparing to hers. Bad pets get punished.

I think of the night two years ago, seeing Savvy with the jock from her high school. It was the first time I broke one of my family's rules since I had come back. I saw red, and instead of ending him and outing myself to Savvy and kidnapping her, I paid Mia a visit and took it out on her. She was a decent lay a few years back and didn't give a lot of lip. She would get on her knees the instant I asked, always wanting to please me like the good little whore she was. She has a similar look and build to Savvy with her dark hair, but she was a far cry from my girl. I had her meet me at the cabin, knowing Savvy wouldn't go there that night and I punished her for everything she knew that Savvy had done in my absence. I chuckle at the image of Mia tied to the bed post, standing naked and afraid, tears going down her pretty face as the fabric of the bright blue scarf I used to gag her mouth turns to navy as the moisture hits it, soaking up her tears as it muffled her screams.

I remember the sounds of my belt meeting her dark skin mixed with her muffled cries. I called her Savvy the entire night, crushing her naive thought that I actually wanted her. She was a bitch to Savvy, for good reason. I was fucking her before I ever met my girl. She was an easy lay at the time, and she was obedient. When Savvy couldn't spend time with me, Mia did, and when she didn't, I met Abby. Now that one was the real slut. She would have enjoyed what I did to Mia that night. I wasn't heartless. I filled her ass with the biggest butt plug I had in my bag of goodies while I hit her over and over again with my belt. I watched as the large blue jewel that matched Savvy's eyes would bob up and down with every slash my belt made on her ass. Hearing her beg for me to stop was music to my ears, while the tears she wept along with her sobs just made my dick harder. The mascara that she thought would make her prettier for me streaked down her face, mixed with the bright red lipstick she always wore.

I decided to leave the plug in at first and just fucked her pussy. I could feel the pressure of the plug in her ass against my dick. Then I got greedy. I grabbed the lube and vibrator off the nightstand, and then ripped the plug out of her ass. I coated my dick with lube and pushed it in her ass all the way to the hilt while her body practically convulsed around my cock.

Just remembering that night gets me hard. I unzip my jeans and pull out my dick, stroking it as I think of my cock ramming into Savvy's ass. I know it was Mia, but in my own thoughts I only see and think of my girl. I spit on the head of my dick and jack off faster at the image of me fucking her ass and adding the vibrator to her pussy. I remember the feel of the vibration in her pussy to her ass. I shoved the vibrator in all the way, leaving it there. I grabbed her neck, roughly squeezing as I fucked her harder. Her screams became silent while her body was practically convulsing as she came. Her ass tightened around my dick to an almost painful level and then the dam burst, spilling my cum into her ass. I kept pumping my dick as I came, remembering how I kept going that night until every last drop was milked and spewing out from her ass around my dick. She passed out before I even had the chance to pull out of her. I may have choked her too long, but not long enough to kill her. The thought that I might have, sent a thrill through me that I can't describe. I contemplated killing her just for the sheer fun of it but decided my DNA would obviously be everywhere. I untied her and threw a few hundred-dollar bills on the floor next to where her body was slumped.

I continue to pump the last bit of cum from my dick, pissed at the fact that I am doing it myself. I clean my hands off with a blanket left out over the chair, grab my phone and call Savvy again as I get a line of coke ready to snort.

"How's it hangin', bro?" Sin answers

"Fuck you, put Savvy on the phone," I growl.

"I think you are the only one that's fucked." Sin chuckles. Dick.

"You want my sloppy seconds, bro, have 'em, just know that she will be back in my bed within the week." I know I hit a nerve when he chuckles again and hangs up.

I decide to call the twins in to help me get my anger out. No, they are not really family, I just told Savvy that so she wouldn't question them and shut up. She had it right the first time, they are my fuck toys. I'll have my Savvy girl back within the week. She will always come back to me. Until then, I will have to find another dark-haired beauty to punish. I send a message to my middleman to get me a new girl once I know the twins are on their way up.

Christian/Sin

Once the girls quit hugging and crying, Savvy introduces me to Charlie, and I introduce everyone to my guys, Jasper and Joe.

"Detail is in place at every corner of the compound, boss. Your dad wants him taken care of sooner rather than later. He found a place in Washington for him to get clean. We just have to bring him in," Jasper reports.

"Just got a message that he showed up at the compound and was fucking up the twins pretty good when they detained him. He is already on his way to Washington with my dad," I reply, updating everyone that the night hasn't been a total waste.

"It's still early, do we all still want to go out?" I ask, knowing everyone is safe now.

"Wait, so you're not going to kill him?" Savvy asks, relief evident on her face. The guys laugh, while Charlie and Cami have their jaws on the floor.

"Not yet, angel. We are going to see if he can get his shit straight first. He is lucky he has the name he does or he would have been taken care of a long time ago," I explain with a smirk.

"Oh, well that settles that," she replies, looking at her shattered screen, her smile fading.

"What's wrong, love?" I ask, seeing her face morph to sadness as she reads something on her phone. I rush over to her and grab the phone when she doesn't respond. I look at the message, it's from Hunter.

> Hunter: You need to get your spoiled little bitch ass back home. Pops is in the hospital and we don't know if he's gonna make it. He is asking for you. Quit being selfish and get home.

"Fuck, Savvy, I'm sorry. What do you need? I'll make it happen," I ask, knowing her mind is reeling.

"I need to go home. I need to get back to my Jeep and go home. I should have never come here," she responds as she bolts into the bathroom. "Can you take me back to Cami's please?" she asks as she rushes back into the room with her purse in hand.

"I'll do ya one better, we will fly to Oklahoma," I respond, grabbing her hand and heading out the door.

"Guys, make sure Cami and Charlie are taken care of. Get them anything they need while we are gone, and y'all can stay here as long as you need. Just in case my brother has his coked-out goons looking for y'all still," I holler out over my shoulder as we head down the stairs.

"I don't have any clothes. Can we stop by Cami's to get my stuff?" Savvy asks as we exit the compound.

"No, he may still have his guys watching the place. Those guys are not on my payroll and will shoot to kill. Not chancing your safety. We will buy some new things when we get there," I respond, not wanting to freak her out, but still trying to be as honest as possible.

"I have enough saved up; I could use new clothes anyway. Why are you going with me?" She finally asks what's on her mind. I direct her over to my blacked-out Jeep, help her in the passenger side, and get in. She is laughing slightly to herself.

"What could possibly be funny?" I ask in disbelief.

"It's just that your Jeep is very similar to mine. Yours is nicer, but very similar," she chirps as she buckles her seatbelt.

"Oh, well, great minds think alike I guess." I chuckle a little at how cute she is.

"You never explained why you are going with me; you barely know me." She tries again, but I can't avoid it this time.

"I want to," I say simply. "But that's not the only reason. Ever since you walked into the church today, I have felt an overwhelming sense to protect you, to be close to you. Whether it was God himself who brought you to me in the church today, or pure coincidence, I find myself wanting to be close to you. This will give us plenty of time to get to know each other. You can show me your hometown, then I can show you more of mine when we come back home. Deal?" I lay it all out there for her to do with whatever she wants.

"Just promise me you aren't a douchebag that is going to fuck me over by fucking my friends and lying about your entire life. Do that and we should be good to go," she replies without batting an eyelash.

"Easy enough. I promise I'm not a douchebag that is going to fuck your friends or lie about my life. I also promise that I will always keep you safe and protected." I threw in the last part, hoping for brownie points. Her smile tells me it worked.

We make our way to the airport and head straight for the ticket counter. "Two flights to Tulsa or Oklahoma City please," Savvy asks the attendant. The young blonde with pin straight hair and big brown eyes keeps scanning me up and down while typing on her little computer.

"There is a flight in an hour to Tulsa, would you like to board that one?" she asks, looking straight at me instead of Savvy.

"Actually, ma'am, I'll be purchasing both tickets, so could you quit eye fucking my boyfriend and sell me the tickets before I smash your head into your stupid computer you keep tapping on," Savvy replies to her, making her head snap in her direction.

"Excuse me?" The attendant looks mortified that my angel would insinuate such a thing.

"Ma'am, my beautiful girlfriend here," I can't help but say it with a smile while my gaze goes straight to my angel, "is only stating facts, and we would both appreciate you just doing your job."

Savvy snort laughs slightly but straightens herself quickly.

"I got this, baby, you have enough to worry about right now," I tell Savvy as I give the shaky-handed attendant my card.

"Here are your tickets, Mr. Deveraux, I hope you both have a lovely flight." The attendant hands us our tickets without looking back up from her screen, obviously embarrassed. Savvy takes my hand first as we walk toward the metal detectors.

"Thank you for that, I half expected you to scold me. I got a little jealous," she admits with her head down. I stop us in our tracks, putting my finger under her chin to make her look up at me.

"You never have to apologize for stating how you feel or acting on your feelings. It's human nature. I would have done the same thing had it been a male attendant checking you out," I respond, hoping to set her mind at ease about the whole thing. She shouldn't be worrying about anything but her pops. I lean down when I get a smile and nod as a response and give her a soft peck.

We make it through security when Savvy asks to go to the gift shop. "I just don't have anything with me, and planes are cold, I'm going to get some sweats and maybe a book for the plane ride." I put my hand up, cutting her off.

"If you want sweats from the gift shop, we will go get you sweats. You don't need a reason to do anything other than you want to, and that's enough for me." She gives me a gorgeous smile as we walk to the gift shop.

Our plane is already boarding when we make it to the gate. We make it on and take our seats. I give her the window seat to be a gentleman. She sits in her Mardi Gras looking green sweats that she literally almost died over because it has a sparkly fleur-de-lis on the front. She also bought purple Crocs since she felt her boots looked ridiculous with them. I just laughed at the fact that she thought purple Crocs with matching socks were a better choice and had fun watching her pick out crazy things. I also paid for those things; she only argued a bit. I refuse to let a woman pay for anything when she is with me, so she might as well get used to it.

She looks at peace with a book in her hands, scrolling each page with her eyes. I've been watching her throughout the flight with each page she turned. I can tell when she gets to a good part, her breaths quicken and her eyes widen. I refuse to disturb her reading even though I want to, just to kiss her. She hasn't removed my hand from her thigh since I put it there. I just need to be close to her, and I'll take any way she wants to allow it. I haven't missed her little chuckles here and there with this book either.

I try to look at the cover this time when she lifts the book while flipping the page. The cover looks like it could be a horror. I feel her leg tighten, realizing by the look on her face and how her leg is pulling in, she must be reading a sex scene. Must be a good one the way she is practically panting.

We are an hour into the flight when I can't take it anymore. All her mannerisms and noises have my dick painfully pressing against my jeans and I need to take my mind off of it.

"Whatcha readin'?" I whisper out of the blue, making her jump. Most of the passengers are asleep, so I figured I would try to be quiet. I put my hand up to say sorry, and she laughs lightly.

"Sorry, I'm just in a really interesting part of the book, guess I was really into it," she replies, embarrassed.

"What's it about? Is it a horror or thriller?" I ask, my curiosity getting the better of me.

"Hmm, I guess it's kind of both, but with a shit ton of smut. It's by an indie author. I have read all of her books, except one, and this one, but this is the newest, and I don't want to be let down if it's not as good as her others. Her books were my first dark reads." She gets excited, talking a mile a minute, chasing squirrels again. It's cute, and I can't help but chuckle slightly.

Her eyebrows crease. "What's so funny?" she asks with a cute smirk, biting her bottom lip. She has done that nonstop since opening her book. I know I'm probably smiling like an idiot, but I don't care.

"What's this one about?" I ask, hoping to distract her from the millions of little squirrels waiting their turn in her head while she chases the ones she wants, changing her mind from time to time on just which squirrel she chooses to talk about. I laugh internally at the image.

"Oh, it uh, well, ya see. Okay it starts out with this chick, and her boyfriend is a douche from hell, right, then she meets his brother, who is a cop, and secretly in her mind starts to have a thing for him, but she stays with the douche anyway. That's all I got so far." She spits the words out like her life depends on it.

"Slow down, just how douchey is the douche?" I ask, really curious as to what will come out of her mouth next.

"Way worse than your brother ever thought about being if I'm right about who the killer is," she replies, startling me, knowing what my brother has done, and still thinks this book douche is worse.

"What the hell are you reading about? I liked the brother thing until you said one was a cop," I reply, slightly stunned that anyone could be worse than my brother.

"Bash, even when he was Jake, never hit me, except the one time, and I hit him back, but besides that he was dominant, he would serve out punishments, but it was never that bad," she replies with wide eyes.

"Is some of what you are saying reminding you just how much of an actual douche my brother is, and that he probably brainwashed you into being his submissive? That's probably the reason why you held on to him for so long. Girls have always thrown themselves at Sebastian, not because he was the good guy, but because he was the bad boy every girl wanted to try at least once. I'm guessing you didn't throw yourself at him?" I ask, knowing she just isn't the type. She wants a guy to fall to his knees for her, just like she did for Bash. He just never appreciated it enough to show the same adoration for her, and it's what she is missing.

"No, actually, the very first time I saw him, he was with a blonde woman. It was after a football game, and we all went out to PJ's for burgers. He was playing pool, and he was the most beautiful man I had ever seen, and although I was intrigued by him, I knew he was out of my league." She laughs at the memory. I raise my eyebrows at her innocent look.

"You were innocent before him," I reply as more of a statement because I'm now sure, especially after what Bash said in his messages about popping her cherry.

"Yeah." She sighs. Her head automatically falls down, her eyes on her hands wringing and twisting her fingers on top of her book. I raise my hand to her chin, lifting her face up until her eyes meet mine as a single tear slips out and down her cheek.

CHAPTER 10
Savvy

I think back to how innocent I was before him, making my hands red as I wring them together. Sin lifts my chin with a single finger, making me look in his honey eyes. A tear slips out. Weakness.

"Angel, tell me what he took from you," he orders softly. I can tell he is holding back the best he can considering he is shaking.

"I was a naïve little girl who knew how men could be and still let it happen to myself. I grew up around cowboys and rodeo. All the girls want a cowboy, and when those cowboys travel, they fuck every buckle bunny that is willing. I've seen it a million times, cowgirl wannabe buckle bunny hops in the back of the travel trailer, sometimes a horse trailer, which is ew, fuck the cowboy's brains out and think they are in love for the weekend, all while there are two more just like her waiting on said cowboy to come to her town and rail her the next weekend. Bash was no different, and I fell for him easily. He honestly didn't take anything from me I wasn't willing to give at the time. I can't blame him anymore than I can my parents for the choices I made," I reply, sucking it up and refusing to give that asshole anymore credit for who I turned out to be.

Sin looks at me not with sympathy, but I think maybe hope.

"What is this look? I don't recognize it yet," I say, trying to get him to speak instead of gawking.

"I'm just really surprised you see it that way," he replies, obviously stumped by my revelation.

"You told me to always be honest and tell you how I feel. I've never done that with anyone before, not even Bash. I honestly didn't know I even felt that way until you told me to tell you what he took from me. When I truly think about it, he didn't take anything. I gave it based on a lie, sure, but would I have still given myself to him had he been honest? We will never know. There is one thing I know for sure now, the past is the past and all we can do is move forward and not repeat our mistakes." I sit up a little, proud of myself for just opening up and being honest about how I feel for once instead of playing the tough girl all the time.

"I always want you to be able to speak what's on your mind and feel whatever you need to feel at the moment. You don't have to hold back or ever hold it in for me. If you need to cry, I'll dry your tears. If you need to scream, I'll find you the softest pillow for you to scream into. If you want to hit something, I'll get you a punching bag. I just want you to be unapologetically you." He kisses my hands that have been sitting in his since we started talking.

The little bell chimes over the intercom while the fasten your seat belt sign flashes ON above our heads, pulling us out of our nice quiet little bubble. "Welcome to Tulsa Oklahoma, we will be landing in about fifteen minutes. Your lovely flight attendants will be coming by with bins for your trash. Have a wonderful morning and thank you for flying with American Airlines," the pilot announces over the intercom.

We both fasten our seatbelts, locking hands as I wrap my free hand around his forearm and lay my head on his shoulder. He kisses my forehead as we sit in silence while the plane lands with my face hidden in his arm. I hate flying, but it was the fastest way to get to Pops. He never let me go until I sat up when the landing was over.

We make our way to rent a car. Christian keeps my hand locked in his while talking with the associate at the counter. It's almost one a.m. and I have to admit, I'm exhausted. "Come on, love, let's find a hotel close, and we can see your pops in the morning. They aren't going to let us see him right now anyway," Sin says as he helps me in a blue two door Jeep Wrangler. "Are you hungry? You haven't eaten since lunch today," Sin asks, and I have to admit I haven't thought about food once.

"Yeah, I could eat. Oohh! Let's find a Waffle House," I reply, excited for greasy food.

"What in the hell is a Waffle House?" he asks, raising his brows.

"Wait, do you like breakfast?" I ask, because it's mainly a breakfast place and probably not his style, but it's so good.

"Yeah, who doesn't love breakfast?" he replies, smiling.

I pull out my phone and click the maps app and type in Waffle House. "Sweet, there is one a few miles away. Turn left up here. It's greasy, yummy, goodness, and you are going to love it," I tell him, excited to share something I like with him. He just laughs and follows my instructions.

I watch him drive with one hand on the wheel and the other on my thigh. I realize just how different he and Bash are. Not just their temperaments, but everything about them. Sin's jawline is more pronounced, his nose is slightly pointier, and he has a freckle by his left eye that Bash doesn't. Even if you take away the hair and tattoos, I could tell them apart. That thought makes me happy.

I dance in my seat as we pull into the small hole-in-the-wall-looking diner. "Angel, are you sure this is where you want to eat?" he asks, looking rather disgusted by the look of the place.

"Do you trust me?" I ask with a sly smile.

"Yes," he replies quickly, giving me butterflies that he didn't have to think about it first.

"Then quit being a baby and get out of the Jeep and eat some less-than-healthy food with me in a not-so-pretty environment," I quip as I jump out of the Jeep and keep a bounce to my step as we walk in.

"Welcome in, take a seat wherever you like." A woman in, I'm guessing, her late sixties rasps out from behind the counter. I plop down in a booth, and Sin follows suit, scooting me over to sit on the same side with me.

The silver-haired woman wearing the diner dress that matches the brown and gold colors of the establishment comes to take our drink order. "Sweet tea, please," I ask politely.

She looks to Christian and smiles down at him. "And for you, doll?" she asks him.

"Coffee," he replies with a small smile. The waitress leaves and we start to look over the menu. I skim mine, but already know what I want.

I watch him in wonder. He is being so nice, even though this would never be his first choice to eat at. I tried to get Bash to go to a Waffle House once, he just laughed and kept driving.

The waitress brings our drinks back and he lets me order first. "Ham scramble bowl, a Pecan waffle, and a side of bacon, crispy, please." I give her my order and then she looks to Sin.

"Same," he says as he takes my menu, putting it together with his to hand to her. I take them and put them back behind the napkin holder, smiling at him as I do. He just chuckles at me. The waitress yells out the order to the cook who looks about the same age as her. I chuckle, while Sin looks mortified.

"Tell me something about yourself that no one else knows." I decide in that moment that he could tell me anything and I better prepare myself, he is a drug lord or whatever.

"I don't like cats," he replies with a grin. Not what I was expecting, but I want to know everything about him, so I just laugh.

"Me either, I mean, they're cute and all, but I prefer dogs. Not what I meant though. You can do better than that," I quip, hoping to get more out of him.

I watch him add cream and a ton of sugar to his coffee, stir it, and take a long sip before he responds, "This coffee sucks." I just laugh because I already know this.

"Hence why I ordered sweet tea. You will hate the coffee everywhere here. It's just better in New Orleans," I reply honestly. He chuckles at my revelation, and I see a spark light up in his eyes.

"I was almost married once. She died the day we were supposed to say our vows." He finally let me in. I know I'm gaping at him, not knowing what to say, but I can't find the words. I reach my hand over and cover his.

"I'm sorry, what happened?" I ask, not knowing what else to say.

"She was murdered. The police closed the case, saying that she took her own life, but I know they were paid to make it look that way," he says with a hint of anger in his tone.

"How long ago?"

"Six years. Sometimes it still feels like yesterday. Charlotte was beautiful and kind. Everyone loved her. She had the same spark I see in you," he responds, letting me know I remind him of his dead fiancé.

"I'm sorry, I didn't mean to bring up bad memories."

"That's the thing, other than finding her body in our honeymoon suite, I don't have any bad memories of her. I spiraled for a few years after her death, investigating what the police wouldn't. The reason I'm telling you this is because since her, I haven't let anyone else in. You are the first. I know we just met yesterday, and the circum- stances are odd, but I feel something for you that I haven't felt in a really long time. I'm not saying it's love, but I can't describe it any other way. I look at you and I feel peace. I can't explain it. You also look like her. I'm not saying mirror image, but the similarities are obvious to anyone who knew her. You both have the same eyes." He puts all his cards out there. I don't know why, but I'm not surprised by his words.

"I'll tell you a secret now. Since the moment you spoke in my ear at the cathedral, then kissed me the way you did in the alley, and everything since. I feel the same way. I can't explain the draw I feel toward you. When you touch me, I feel safe. When you remove your touch, I find myself wanting it back. Like I need it to breathe. I know that sounds crazy because we really don't know each other, yet I feel like I do know you at the same time. It's crazy. Bash had mentioned something about Charlotte before, but only said I reminded him of her and that she was just someone he once loved who had passed away." I decide to throw it all out there just as the waitress brings our food.

"Can I get you anything else?" she asks.

I shake my head no as my mouth salivates over the smell of bacon.

"Looks great!" Sin says with a huge smile on his face. She walks away with a big grin of her own.

"Angel, did you mean all of that?" he asks, taking my hand like it's his lifeline.

"Well, yeah. I mean, I probably could have been more eloquent with my words but..." Sin silences my words with his lips. God, his lips are amazing. He kisses me softly, cupping my face in his hand. He pulls back, leaning his forehead on mine.

"You have just made me the happiest man on earth," he replies.

"Ditto," I reply with a stupid cheesy grin.

We both eat our food, and I don't miss the little moans he made when he ate his waffle. "I told you it was good," I chastise.

"I will always listen when you recommend somewhere to eat, love," he quips with a grin of his own as he shoves another bite in his mouth.

"Some of the best places are the holes-in-the-wall," I reply, popping a piece of bacon in my mouth.

"Remember you said that when I take you to new places back home." He chuckles. I love how he says back home, like I belong there. I decide it is my home now. It's definitely where my heart wants to be as long as I'm with him. I shake my head at my own thoughts.

I take out my phone when I'm about to bust. I search hotels near Saint Francis Hospital. I know that is the only hospital Pops would be taken to outside of Vinita or Pryor.

"Do you prefer the Double Tree or Hyatt to stay at tonight?" I ask as I continue to scroll through the hotels on my phone.

"Double Tree is nicer. Just see which has availability and I'll get the room when we get there, angel," he replies sweetly, kissing my temple.

"Double Tree has availability, and it's less than a mile from the hospital. But I would like to pay for the room. We are here because of me, you shouldn't have to spend your money here," I reply, looking up at him from my phone.

"Too bad. You do not get to pay for things when you are with me. I'm sorry, but I was raised to take care of the most important woman in my life. It's just how I am, and you will have to get used to it," he responds, and I don't like it, but I relent, rolling my eyes.

"Can I at least pay for breakfast?" I ask, knowing he will say no, but enjoying testing the waters.

"No, Savannah," he clips and gives me a duh look.

We make it to the Double Tree, check in, and I can't help but be nervous to spend the night with him as we go up in the glass elevator, looking down as we make it to the top floor. He booked us a king corner suite with a balcony, of course. I've come to realize how much balconies make a difference after living in a place surrounded by them. I stand at the wall-sized window and decide to step out onto the balcony. I can see the big pink hospital's giant white cross surrounded by light from here.

Christian comes up behind me, wrapping his arms around my waist, looking out into the night sky full of stars. "I don't think I have ever seen this many stars before," he states, looking up in awe.

"Welcome to Oklahoma. This is nothing compared to where I grew up. We are in the city, and the lights keep you from seeing them all. You will love the stars in the pasture. I'll take you to see the most beautiful sunsets too," I state, knowing he will love those things.

"I would love that, angel," he replies, leaning down to kiss my neck.

A soft moan leaves my lips without warning. His hands start to explore my hips, pulling my ass into his very hard cock beneath his jeans. I moan again as he peppers my neck with soft kisses. The feel of his rough, stubbly beard against my skin followed by his warm lips sends a shiver down my spine. He turns me around abruptly, lifting

119

me by my ass. I wrap my legs around him instinctively as his mouth finally finds mine.

He walks us back into the room, breaking our kiss to lay me on the bed. He undresses me slowly, kissing almost every inch of me as he does. He pulls away from me, and I miss his touch already.

He makes quick work of undressing himself before he comes back to me. His lips are on mine quickly as his hands roam my body. Sin has expert hands. His lips part from mine again as he peppers soft kisses down my body until his face hovers above my glistening pussy. He hasn't even touched it yet, but she already weeps for him.

His hands part my legs farther as he rubs up my thighs, holding them in place. He darts his tongue out, licking from my ass to my cunt, diving in my tight entrance.

"Fuck," I moan as I throw my head back. He licks and sucks my clit until my legs are shaking uncontrollably. My hands go to his head as I grind my pussy on his face, pulling him in. I feel my insides clench and I can't move. I let the wave of bliss wash over me as he continues to lick softly, allowing me to come down from my high.

He moves up, cupping my face with his hands and allowing me to taste myself on his kiss. I put my hands up above my head instinctively.

"Wrap your arms around me, angel, I want to feel your hands guiding me to go as deep as you want me," he rasps out between kisses. I do as he says. The feeling is foreign, but I like touching him.

Christian peppers my face and neck with kisses before capturing my mouth with his again as he slowly slides into me, stretching me to fit his size. It takes a few slow pumps back and forth before he is balls deep, making my legs shake again. I moan, holding onto him for dear life. He is slow as he pulls out and slams back into me fast, rolling his hips. I can't help my hips bucking to meet his. I dig my nails into his back, moving down to his tight ass, and pulling him farther into me.

"Fuck, angel, you feel so good," he rasps in my ear, capturing my lobe in his mouth, sucking.

"Fuck... Sin... Please," I respond between ragged breaths.

He captures my lips with his again as he starts to speed up. He has one hand wrapped around the back of my neck and the other under my hip, squeezing my ass as he pounds into me, pulling me closer and going deeper now with every thrust.

He sits up abruptly on his knees with my legs still wrapped around him. He doesn't relent. He bounces me on his cock, thrusting his hips as I come down on him. He fucks me harder and harder, never letting my lips leave his.

He pulls out abruptly, turning me onto my stomach. I lift my ass, going on all fours. He pulls my hips back as he slams into me. My eyes roll farther to the back of my head with each thrust.

He lifts me to where my back is against his front. He grabs my neck, turning my head, pressing his lips to mine. His hands both go to my tits, using them as the leverage he needs to bounce me up and down on his dick, pumping in and out of me. He reaches one hand down to my clit, rubbing it vigorously as he pinches my nipple. My moans are muffled by his mouth as my body takes flight once again. He continues pushing in and out, faster and faster, until he finds his release in me, carrying my orgasm to new heights. His moans fill the room, matching my own as he refuses to relent until my body slackens in his arms.

We both collapse on the bed, breathless and panting. He pulls me back onto his chest, holding me there and kissing the top of my head. "Fuck, angel, I'm sorry that was so fast. Give me ten minutes and I promise to have you seeing more stars than any Oklahoma sky has ever given you." His words come out ragged and I can't help but chuckle, still trying to catch my breath.

CHAPTER 11
Savvy

I wake up to the smell of coffee hitting my senses. I slowly open my eyes to meet gorgeous honey-colored eyes and a bright smile. He leans down, kisses me softly, and says, "Good morning, love." I sit up as he holds out a cup for me.

"Good morning yourself, handsome." I smile up at him shyly, knowing I probably have that just fucked look. Oh well, if he is my one, then he will see it eventually.

"They have a Starbucks downstairs and guessed on a white chocolate mocha for you." I take the cup and take a long swig.

"How did you know that is my favorite?" I ask smiling from ear to ear up at him.

"Lucky guess 'cause it's my favorite."

I set my coffee on the bedside table and stretch my arms above my head and yawn.

"Fuck, I'm sore." My muscles tighten and feel like I went five rounds in the ring.

"I would say I'm sorry, but I'm not." He grins, cupping my face and kissing me softly. He pulls back, still cupping my cheek. "Want me to kiss it and make it better?"

My core clenches at the memory of last night. He made my body do and feel things that it has definitely never felt before. His touch alone sends delicious shivers up my spine. He wasn't even rough at all; he took his time with me, showed me what it felt like to be worshiped. There is not an inch of my body that hasn't felt his warm gentle touch, or the way his mouth feels. He made me come over and over, reminding me that I was his. He has the filthiest mouth in bed, and I love it.

"How about a shower, angel?" he asks, moving his lips to my neck. I feel his hand move slowly down my body until his fingers gently graze my already soaked pussy. My body trembles, still sensitive from all he did to me last night. I feel wetness starting to coat my thighs and he barely let his fingers touch me. I nod, unable to form words as my hips thrust into his touch, begging his hand to fuck me.

He removes his hand to grab my arms and wraps them around his neck. He lifts me off the bed with his hands on my bare ass. I wrap my legs around his waist, wanting any friction I can get against my throbbing clit. He slams his lips to mine, carrying me to the bathroom.

He sets me on the counter, breaking away from me. I pout, pushing out my bottom lip.

"You are so beautiful when you pout, angel. Do you want my dick, my tongue, or my hands this morning, love?" he asks in a deep sultry voice as he turns the massive shower on.

"Just fuck me already, Sin." I'm panting, practically begging him to touch me again.

He cocks an eyebrow. "My angel is greedy this morning. Tell me what you want, love." He growls as he rips his shirt off, exposing his beautiful, toned abs, covered in ink. My eyes trail down to the perfect V going into his jeans. I watch him unbutton them before his hand is on my jaw, pulling my mouth to his.

I wrap my arms around his back, running my nails down to where his ass holds up his jeans. I push his jeans and underwear over his bubble butt and dig my nails in, pulling him into me. He moans into my mouth, making my entire pussy throb.

"Tell me what you want, love, I won't ask again." He moans the words as he pulls back from my lips.

I don't understand what he is asking. My mind is racing for the answer when it hits me. "I don't know." I finally get the words out in frustration because I really don't know what I want.

"That's okay, tell me what you like and don't like," he tells me.

"I've never had a guy ask me what I wanted in bed. Jake always took exactly what he wanted, and I obeyed his every command. With guys from home, I usually just lay there hoping they would at least get me off. I guess I never thought about it other than I thought I liked to be dominated, and I think I still do, but last night, you didn't dominate me, and it was the best sex I have ever had." I'm honest because we agreed from the beginning that we would be. I'm waiting for him to get mad that I didn't say what he wanted me to.

He tilts my chin up to make me look into his eyes. "I'm honored to be the one to help you figure it all out, angel." He leans in and kisses me. I fall into the kiss easily, letting my body do what it wants and needs in this moment. I reach between us and grab his thick cock and slowly start to stroke him. He kicks his jeans and underwear off of his feet and lifts me up off the counter, continuing to devour my mouth with his. I squeal when the hot water hits my back before it pours down over our heads, mixing in our kiss.

I suck in a deep breath as my back hits the cold tile and he pushes into me slowly. His hands grip my ass almost painfully as he pulls out completely and then slams his hips forward. He growls, moving his lips to my neck as I cry out. He is hitting every spot just right as he repeats his movements over and over until he hits deeper, making my eyes roll back. His kiss is feral as he moves his mouth from mine, down my neck, and back up again.

He pulls out, sets my legs down, and turns me around. I press my hands and cheek against the cool white tile and push my ass out for him to claim. He runs his hand down my back, over my ass, and down to my clit, circling it slowly.

I moan his name as he sticks a finger in my pussy and his thumb in my ass at the same time, making me gasp at the intrusion.

"You like that, angel?"

"Yes, please, yes," is all I can manage to get out; I'm breathless.

He removes his finger, replacing it with his overly hard cock, slamming into me. He leaves his thumb in my ass, keeping a steady rhythm, making me back into him, craving more.

"Fuck me, Sin," I moan out between ragged breaths as he picks up the pace. I feel the pleasure mounting until I feel like I might explode. "Fuck, Sin, I'm ... coming," I mumble out breathlessly as my body feels like I have just leapt off the tallest cliff and I'm floating.

"Come for me, angel," he grunts as he finds his release as well. His movements are slow and methodical, allowing my orgasm to continue until my body feels like Jell-O.

He pulls out and turns me around, trailing kisses up my neck, back to my mouth. He kisses me like he may never get the chance again, holding me against the pristine white tile until I'm able to catch my breath and have a coherent thought.

He steadies me under the water and grabs the hotel shampoo. The scent of lavender and citrus hits my senses, bringing me out of the fog a little more. He massages the shampoo into my hair, lathering it up. I can't help the moan that escapes at his touch.

"What do you like?" I ask him, curiosity getting the better of me. I want to please him too.

"I like lots of things, angel. I'll try anything once, and if you like it, then I will too. I get off on getting you off. Close your eyes and lean your head back, time to rinse."

I do as he says. He washes the soap out of my hair as I contemplate what he just said. He gets off on getting me off. He is like the perfect man. I chuckle at the thought.

"What?" he asks, pulling me out from under the steamy water, wrapping me into his large frame. I look up at this gorgeous man and I can't help the cheesy grin that plasters my face.

"I think you just may be the perfect man." He starts laughing, unable to contain himself.

"Oh, love, I'm far from perfect." His expression grows serious, all laughter set aside. He cups my cheek, and continues, "I'm just perfect for you. Just like you are perfect for me." He kisses the tip of my nose.

I melt in his arms. No one has ever said things like that to me before and I felt they were sincere. Even when Bash would tell me I was his forever, I knew deep down it wasn't true. Bash was a great manipulator; I see that now.

We finish showering. Sin steps out first, getting me a towel and wrapping it around me, then one for my hair. Something about showering with Sin, allowing him to wash me, and him allowing me the same pleasure, seems more intimate than the act of sex itself. He wraps a towel around his waist.

I watch little droplets of water roll down his perfectly defined chest. A tattoo catches my eye, and I can't help but reach out and touch it. I trace my pointer finger around the beautiful dark-haired angel holding a fleur-de-lis to her chest. She looks like me, same blue eyes, but her hair is sleek and straight down to her waist.

"Lottie?" I ask, knowing I'm right. My eyes are fixed on her face. We could definitely be related, but how? Is this the reason he wants me? Is he imagining I'm her? Did Bash do the same?

Sin

I can see the moment realization hits her just how much her and Charlotte look alike.

"Angel, I know this looks bad, and part of me, when I saw you in the cathedral, thought I was seeing a ghost. You may look like Lottie, but you are two completely different people. Lottie was compliant, docile, and you are nothing like that. I love that you have a fire in you, and a backbone. I love your smart mouth, and that we have so much in common. I'm here with you because of those things, not because you look similar to someone from my past." I try to explain to her what I'm feeling without sounding like a psycho on our first day together. Okay, second day, but still.

"Is this why Bash is obsessed with me now and hurt those girls that look like me, because I look like her? Were her eyes the same as mine?" She doesn't sound upset, just sad.

"Savannah, you are the first person I have been with since Charlotte. I didn't think I could love again, but here you are, and I can't help the feelings that are between us. Do you look similar to her, yes, but I swear it's not why I'm falling in love with you." I cup her cheeks, looking into her eyes. A single tear spills over her watery lids, trailing down her cheek as I lift her face to mine.

"It's just a little creepy seeing a tattoo of an angel that looks like me on someone I met yesterday," she finally says.

I hug her closer to my chest, letting her have a meltdown. She sobs for a while. I just keep holding her head to my chest, rubbing my other hand up and down her back in light strokes.

"Let it out, angel," I say softly. She sobs harder, and I'm not understanding.

"Did you call her angel?" she asks, and I finally get it.

"No, love, I called her Lottie. We never shared terms of endearment because she thought they were for kids. She didn't like being called anything but her name. I was different back then too."

She starts to chuckle before a full-on laugh bubbles out of her chest. "You had to have had a hard time with that. You barely use my actual name."

"So, we're, okay?" I ask, knowing what the term and the tattoo must have made her feel.

"Yeah, we're good." She reaches up and kisses me softly. Just a peck, but it's better than nothing. I get that she is still processing everything with my asshole brother, her pops being sick, and whatever problem her dickhead brother has.

"I took the liberty of buying you a few things at the boutique downstairs so you wouldn't have to wear your sweats again." I go over to the couch by the door and grab the few bags of things I bought us and put them on the bed for her.

"Sin, you didn't have to do that, but thank you." She empties the bags on the bed, not upset with anything I chose for her. Her smile is as bright as the sun as she saunters back into the bathroom.

I run my hand over my face, feeling the scruff of my beard. Is it possible for me to actually love her already? I know I have never felt anything like this, even with Lottie. I loved her, but this is something different.

Is there an emotion stronger than love? If there is, this is it. Savvy makes my dick hard with just a look in my direction. I want to make her smile and laugh. Lottie rarely laughed and thought everything about me was ridiculous and even childish at times. She didn't know the meaning of the word fun, and yet I still loved her. I was more ruthless back then and didn't spend time with her like I should have. She more or less looked at us being together as a business transaction, but I always loved her. Since we were kids, I knew I loved her.

When Lottie died, a piece of me died with her. It had been buried deep down in the pit of my soul until Savvy walked into the cathedral. Now it's back burning bright, and I can't stop it. I love her, and I don't give a fuck who knows it. I'll be damned to the pits of hell before I let anything happen to her.

CHAPTER 12
Sin

Savvy looks stunning in the black khaki shorts and bright blue sleeveless silky top I got her. Her jet-black hair is down and wild with curls going in every direction. She smiles at me, leaning down to kiss my cheek as she grabs her purse off the bed and heads back into the bathroom. My dick bulges against the zipper of my black cargo shorts. Fuck, I can't even think straight. I go back to scrolling through my messages.

> Dad: Bash is locked up for now, but I don't know if they can give him the help he needs. Joe said that you went to Oklahoma with some girl. Have fun, son, but get back here soon, we have a business to run.

> Sin: Good to know. Let's keep him there as long as we can. You may have to come to terms with him never getting better.

> Dad: I hope you know what you are doing with this girl. Bash wouldn't shut up about killing you in front of her. I hope she is worth it, son.

> Sin: She is more than worth it.

I close my phone, able to relax, knowing my brother can't get to

Savvy or her friends for a while at least. Savvy comes out wearing the black strappy sandals I bought her. Her hair is tamed with a clip holding half of it back and out of her face. She doesn't wear much makeup, and I love that about her. She is naturally beautiful and doesn't need any of it.

"Ready to go?" she asks, bouncing on her tiptoes to press her lips to mine.

"Ready."

We stop at the gift shop downstairs in the big pink hospital. She gets a pretty vase of flowers, a cow stuffed animal, Cheetos, and a Coke. The nice cashier bags it up for her while I grab a Snickers and two Dr. Peppers. I pay and keep the soda and candy bar out. I eat the candy bar in the elevator going up to the cardiac floor and down half a soda.

"I'm sorry, Sin, you are probably starving," Savvy says apologetically as the elevator doors open.

"Not a big deal, just started feeling a little shaky," I explain.

"Why would you feel shaky?" she asks, concern all over her beautiful face.

"My blood sugar gets low sometimes, I just have to eat something to get it back up, no biggie. Promise." I kiss her forehead and take her free hand as we walk to the nurses' station.

"Stuart Barrett's room please?" she asks the nurse, who is blankly staring at her computer. The nurse Angie, as her nametag states, doesn't even look up, replying, "1302" with a huff and an eyeroll.

"Thanks," I reply for us both when I see Savvy get a little huffy at the bitch's attitude.

She lets it go and we walk down the hallway with arrows pointing 1300-1315 this way. We stop in front of his room and Savvy takes a deep breath, letting it out slowly before pushing open the door. We walk in to see I assume her pops in the bed sleeping. She moves over to the side of his bed, looking at his IV and what they are giving him. She turns and places the flowers on the windowsill and sits in the chair by his bed. I go sit on the couch pushed against the wall. He stirs a little, opening his eyes when she places her hand on his.

"Hey Pops, heard you have an issue with your ticker." She chuckles next to him. He smiles when he registers who is sitting next to him.

"I'm fine, baby, good to see those blue eyes though, I've missed them. You gonna bust me out of this hell hole?" he replies in a raspy voice.

"Where is Scarlett, or Hunter?" she asks, with her eyebrows furrowed.

"Haven't seen 'em since I was brought in Saturday. I just had a little heart attack. Gotta quit eatin' Mom's biscuits and gravy every day. I'm fine, just get me outta here. Someone's gotta tend to the cattle and horses. Your no-good brother ain't gonna do it. I'll be surprised if he ain't sold 'em all." The old man sounds livid.

"Sir, I'll go see if we can get the doctor to tell us what is going on with you and why you haven't been released," I chime in, trying to be helpful.

"Who the hell are you? Wait, Jake. Baby doll, is that Jake?" he asks, setting a fire off in me that I didn't realize was there. Of course, he met her dad.

"Pops, this is Christian, Jake's brother. I met him in New Orleans, where I've been the last few weeks."

The old man's eyes about pop out of his head when she mentions New Orleans.

"You have been in NOLA this whole time?" he asks, seeming skeptical of what she just said.

"Yeah, Pops, I'm sorry, I should have told you. I moved a few weeks ago and came back when Hunter said you were in the hospital. I'm going back once you are better, and I get the ranch back on its feet. I'll stay a couple of weeks. It will be like old times, Pops," she replies to him, and I duck out the door.

I head back to the nurses' station with my phone in my hand, texting Joe to look into a Stuart Barrett. I have a feeling her dad didn't like the fact she was in New Orleans, but why? It may be nothing, but I didn't miss the shock on his face. I smile wide at the nurse sitting on the counter, gossiping with the others wearing the same maroon scrubs as her. "Excuse me, ladies, could you tell me why Stuart Barrett in 1302 is still here? His daughter would like to take him home."

The one sitting on the counter with the blonde ponytail laughs. "We have been trying to discharge him since Sunday morning. No one will answer or return our calls. I can get his paperwork ready for discharge. I'll let the doctor know his family showed up." She bounces off the counter, grabbing a chart and popping a bubble with her gum.

"Thank you," I reply, turning to go back to his room. It must not be too serious if he was going to be discharged within twenty-four hours of being brought in. Why wouldn't they pick him up and take him home.

I walk back into the room and watch Savvy's interaction with her dad. "They are trying to keep me in here when I'm fine, darlin'," he says and she just chuckles.

"Good news is you can go home today; they are getting your paperwork ready now," I explain.

Savvy smiles wide and hugs her dad. "See Pops, we are gonna bust you out, and get you some real food."

I go to pull the Jeep around to pick them both up at the front of the hospital. I take out my phone and see a new message from Joe.

> Joe: Boss, Stuart Barrett breeds quarter horses and various types of cattle. He was a frequent NOLA goer a little over twenty years ago. He apparently did a lot of business out here back then. Rumor has it he was a high roller at the casinos and apparently pissed off a few people he shouldn't have. It seems that he also knocked up a woman who was married and left with the baby after she gave birth. Her husband wouldn't allow her to keep it. You're not going to like this, but the woman is Sylvia Bennett. Charlotte's mother.

> Sin: Keep this between us, I don't want anyone knowing about her. Who did you get the information from?

I wait for an answer, not really sure how this could be true.

> Joe: Your dad. Sorry, boss, but he was here when I got the message to check into him.

Fuck, fuck, fuck. He has been fucking Sylvia since her husband Frankie died five years ago. He worked for my family too.

Why didn't she go get her daughter when he died? Sylvia trained Charlotte her entire life to be cold, calculated, and almost emotionless, always with a smile on her face. I loved her because I was the only one who got to see who she was when no one else was around. She was witty and sexy as hell. Savvy probably wouldn't be who she is now if she had. Or she may have told her to fuck off. I'll make sure she gets that option.

CHAPTER 13
Savvy

I sit in the backseat of the Jeep on the way home as "I Only Date Cowboys" by Kylie Morgan starts playing. I lean forward, turn it up, and start singing and dancing to the song.

Pops just laughs. "Some things never change."

Sin reaches for the knob and turns it up a little more, thumping the steering wheel to the beat with his hand. I don't miss his honey eyes on mine a few times in the rearview mirror.

"I didn't know you could sing, Savvy." Sins eyes meet mine again and I melt.

"I can't, just in the car, shower, or anywhere other people aren't around."

"I'll make sure to let Nick know you are down for karaoke." He wiggles his eyebrows at me in the mirror.

"Ha, ha, very funny. Not. Shit! Did you let Nick know we left town?" I suddenly feel sick, thinking about not showing up for my first day.

"Already let him know. He said to take all the time you need. You still have a job waiting for you when we get home. Nothing to worry about, love."

Home. I love that home is NOLA now. Here never felt like home, not like my NOLA. The old saying is true, home is where the heart is, and NOLA has stolen my heart. Right along with Sin. NOLA is where the sin begins and never ends.

137

"You go by Savvy now?" I see Pops' face fall with his question as he turns his head to look back at me.

"It's just a nickname, Pops. I'm still your little Savannah girl. Just not as little anymore."

Sin pulls the Jeep onto the long driveway I remember so well. My heart starts to pound at the memories that flood my brain as we pull up to my childhood home. It looks the same. White two-story farmhouse with light yellow shutters and a wraparound porch. It's pretty from the outside looking in, disguising the evil that lives inside. It's been over two years since I stepped foot on this property.

I remember it like it was yesterday.

Two years prior

"Savannah!" I hear my brother Hunter from downstairs, followed by loud thumps from his boots hitting the stairs.

Here we go.

My door bursts open, hitting the wall with a loud bang as Hunter barrels in. "Where the fuck have you been?" He stomps toward me. I back up a few steps but am stopped when the back of my bare legs hit my walnut-stained vanity. He yells, with his finger in my face, "And don't lie to me, Savannah." His spit hits my face and I can see it in his eyes he is high as fuck. On what, I don't know, probably cocaine, but I do know I am not safe when he is on that shit. This is not my brother; this is his evil twin who doesn't give a fuck about anyone or anything except getting more.

"I've been here in my room, where you found me." I try to keep my voice even, not allowing my fear to show.

He grabs my throat, cutting my ability to breathe instantly. I feel my back hit the mirror and hear it shatter.

I *instantly calm when I feel a sting and my back getting damp. The will to survive kicks in. I reach around the vanity trying to find anything to defend myself with. I grab cold metal and know its hairspray. I position it in my hand, knowing the slanted finger grip will spray away from me. I spray it toward his face, hitting him in the eyes and mouth. His grip loosens as he coughs, inhaling the chemicals. He stumbles back as I gasp for air.*

I *realize he is recovering faster than me and throw the can, hitting him in the face. That just pisses him off more. I kick him in the chest, trying to use the leverage of still sitting on the vanity when he comes at me again, but he barrels through it and backhands me, knocking me to the floor.*

I *see stars trying to get up. He kicks me in the side, knocking the breath out of me. I hear ribs crack and instantly feel the burning throb.*

"You want to be known as the town slut? I know what you have been up to. You know what bad little whores get, Savannah? They get beaten by their pimps when they don't do what they are supposed to." He is practically snarling like a rabid dog. I look up in his eyes and try to push myself up.

"Fuck you, Hunter." I spit blood on his boots. I'm rewarded with a boot to the chest. I roll onto my stomach, unable to breathe, and try to crawl away from him. He stops me easily with a boot to my back, putting his weight down on me, making it impossible to move. I hear him undo his belt. I kick and scream, trying to get away, not knowing what he is capable of.

I *scream as his belt bites into the back of my legs. I fight with everything in me. He hits me over and over, my bare ass, legs, and back, my t-shirt and thong not helping protect my skin. I lie there helpless, sobbing with no fight left in me when he finally stops. I hear lighter footsteps enter my room. I peek from under my arm to see my mother hand Hunter a wad of hundred-dollar bills.*

"I told you to stay away from her face." Scarlett smacks him upside the head. She tiptoes over to me, leaning down closer to my ear. "Next

time, I'll let him bring his cracked-out friends if you ever get in my way again."

Once we get Pops settled into the house and I make sure no one else is here, I relax a bit.

"Pops, we are going to head to drop our things off at my place, and then we will bring dinner back for you. What sounds good to eat?" I ask, knowing he didn't eat shit in the hospital.

"You won't consider staying here?"

"Absolutely not, you're lucky I'm in this house at all. Kick the bitch and her tit bag son out and I'll consider it," I quip.

"I sent him to every rehab there is, he isn't supposed to come around anymore. I don't know what else to do with him. I cut him off, baby girl, what else do you want me to do?" He throws his hands up dramatically.

I start to respond, but Sin pulls me closer to him, cutting me off before I begin.

"I don't know what happened here, but if Savvy isn't comfortable, then, with all due respect, sir, that is the end of this conversation. We will be back in a little while with your dinner. I would suggest that if anyone shows up that she isn't comfortable around, you get rid of them before we get back. Or I will." Sin leaves no room for argument. I can't deny the butterflies fluttering in my chest right now. I can't ever remember any man ever protecting me in that way.

"Savannah, could you please go out to the car so I can speak with your father in private. There are certain values that I would like to keep intact when I'm serious about someone." I almost protest but decide to indulge him. I rise up on my tiptoes to kiss his cheek and go give Pops a kiss on the top of his head before doing as he asks.

I sit in the Jeep, wondering what the fuck they could be talking about. I've literally known him for two days. Though, I would be lying if I said I didn't have feelings for him. Feelings I can't explain. It's more than an attraction or lust. I mean, he is hot as fuck, but what I feel when I think of him, see him, when he looks at me with those honey eyes, or just barely touches me. Fuck, it's what I assume pure euphoria is like. This is beyond a good fuck or sex at all. There is a pull toward him, like a flame summoning a moth, he has me under his spell, and I don't know if there will ever be any coming back from this man before I burn.

I'm pulled out of my thoughts when I hear a car door. I snap my head around to see Scarlett stomping toward the Jeep, looking like she is ready for a fight. Typical two sizes too small jeans, boots, and a tight ass T-shirt. Fucking bitch, I've been waiting a long time for this. I jump out of the Jeep and stand with a smile on my face, knowing whether she comes at me or not, I'm gonna fuck her up.

"Savvy!" Sin yells from the door, making Scarlett whip her head around to see what man that voice belonged to. Fuck. She has seen him, so Suzie fucking sunshine is going to come out and play and act like she is mother of the year.

"Well, sweetheart, it's so good to see you." She opens her arms as she closes in on me, like I would let her ever touch me again. Yup, flip has been switched, just like clockwork.

I wait with a cheesy grin on my face until she is inches from me, then I throw a jab to her throat, making sure I pulled back before I did serious damage. I grab her by the hair, bringing her ear close enough for me to keep my voice low. "Don't ever fucking touch me again or I will kill you." I yank her head back, keeping a perfect grip on her bleach blonde hair and let go as I slam my fist in her face. She stumbles back, hitting the gravel on her ass as blood pours from her nose.

"Bitch down, angel!" Sin chuckles, coming to stand next to me.

"Sin, this is Scarlett, my mother." I sigh, rolling my eyes.

"Oh, she gets to know my nickname, but your Pops doesn't? Cold." I only know he is joking because he has the biggest grin on his face. I could see where some would say it looks sadistic, but I find it charming, because I know it's for me. I just shrug my shoulders and grin.

I kneel next to the woman that was supposed to be my safe place but instead chose to be my hell on earth and grab her hair as she wails, still choking.

I bring her bloody face closer to mine. "Tell your son if he comes near me again, I will kill him too, just so we're clear." I watch black tears fall from her fear-filled crystal blue eyes mixing with the blood still pouring from her nose as she shakes.

"Now there's the she-devil I remember, looks good on you." I love that she looks like the street rat she is, lying helpless for once, all disheveled, not knowing what's coming next. She isn't going to fight or say anything because she wants me to look crazy in front of Sin. The problem with that is, he is a ruthless drug lord who probably thinks this is child's play compared to what he could do to her.

I decide to let her go and turn my back on her. I walk back to the Jeep, get in, and shut the door. I suck in a deep breath and hold it in for a second and let it out. I realize I am completely calm, not shaking in the slightest. That felt ... amazing. Like another weight was lifted off my chest. When I said I couldn't kill someone, I was wrong. I could kill her, easily. I choose not to. She gets to live with a broken face for once. I want her to suffer the way she made me suffer. I want her afraid of me. I went easy on her. I don't know if I will next time.

I watch Sin come around and get in the Jeep. He takes his time and sits there a minute before starting it and taking off, slinging gravel back toward my mother. I chuckle a little, remembering her doing that every time she stormed off somewhere.

"Feel better, angel?" he asks, placing his hand on mine in my lap.

"You have no idea how good that felt. I have been dying to do that for, well, forever." I look down at our hands and realize my knuckles have some blood on them. It makes me smile bigger knowing it's hers.

CHAPTER 14
Sin

I'm proud of Savvy. I know she worried for a split second that I would pull her off that bitch. I enjoyed watching her slay her demons with no remorse. Just when I think I need to protect her, she shows me another side that proves she doesn't need protection. She needs encouragement.

I have to admit, I didn't expect that right off the bat. I knew she was running from something, but I didn't think it was her family. Truth be told, watching her kick her mom's ass was maybe one of the hottest things I have ever had the pleasure of watching. I thought my dick would burst when she told her mom she would kill Hunter if he ever comes near her again.

I had a nice conversation with her father to let him know that I will always protect her, whomever that may be from. He let me know what happened to her. It took her a few minutes to get out of the Jeep and even longer to go in the house. She just sat there staring up at a window on the top floor. I gave her the time she needed and didn't push her. I'm glad for that, because I'm not always the most patient man, but with her, I feel like time stops.

She is tougher than I would have ever imagined. I saw the scars on her back from the glass that cut her. They have faded but they are there just the same. Stuart told me he found her passed out on her bedroom floor in a puddle of her own blood. Savannah told him it was Hunter when she woke up in the hospital with thirty-six stitches, a cracked jaw, and three broken ribs. He told me she was in the hospital for three days and never came back to the ranch again. I can't promise after hearing what he did to her that if I see him, I won't kill him.

Savvy looks happy and excited sitting in the passenger seat. She is singing along to "Gunpowder and Lead" by Miranda Lambert. She really does have a good voice, and apparently dance moves. She almost looks like she is gearing herself up for another fight.

"Where am I going, angel? I don't know this town."

"Shit, you must be starving, it's almost four o'clock. We can just go pick up burgers from Stuff'Ns if you want. Or we can go to the Lighthouse Supper Club if you want a steak or fish. Unfortunately, there aren't many options unless we go down by the lake for something different." She is so cute while trying to accommodate what I want.

"What sounds good to you? You haven't eaten anything today."

"A greasy burger and chili cheese fries sound good, but I will eat anything."

"Stuff'Ns, I assume, is where a greasy burger is then?" I ask, just to make sure. I will always take a burger and fries over a stuffy restaurant.

"Can we stop by my trailer after we get food, then I guess we can stay at the cabin, since it's in my name too. Or we can stop after we take Pops' back dinner. Take a left here, the diner is up here on the right. You can't miss it, it's bright red, white, blue, and yellow checkered tile. It sticks out." She seems nervous all of a sudden, but I can't figure out why.

"Savvy, we can do whatever you want to do. If you want to stop somewhere before we get burgers, we can, or we can get burgers and then go wherever you want. There is nothing you could say or do to make me not want you." Her eyes pop over to mine and back down a few times before she finally speaks.

"I lived in a tiny little tin can before I moved. Bash had a cabin. I didn't know until recently that the cabin is also in my name. So, I own

146

it with your brother. If you don't want to stay there, I completely understand." She rushes the words out, obviously worried that I would be offended or get mad, but all I can do is laugh. She gives me a surprised yet unconvinced look.

"Angel, I don't care that you have a past with my brother, or that you have a cabin together. We will stay together wherever you are most comfortable. If you like the cabin, we will keep it to have a place to come to when we visit your dad." I try to reassure her the best I can. Her eyes light up and she is bouncing in her seat again.

"I just didn't want to stay there without you knowing the whole truth. I don't want us to have secrets or keep things from each other. I just think honesty is the best policy." She sighs, looking over at me with those sapphire eyes and I realize that I can't keep what I know from her.

I made her dad fess up about her real mother. He loved her but also feared her. He lied to Savvy her entire life to keep her from ever finding out. Her birth certificate is forged with her dad's last name. It was agreed between them for it to stay her mother's last name and he was supposed to tell her everything when she turned eighteen so that she could go meet her mother if she chose to. He didn't want her to get into that type of life. He knows exactly who I am and doesn't like Savvy being involved with me. Too bad. He obviously didn't protect her.

"Okay Debbie Downer, let's perk back up and we can have all the heart-to-heart talks once we settle into the cabin. We can go to the store and get snacks and veg out tonight. Tomorrow I was hoping you would show me around where you grew up. All your secret places." I get why it might bother her to stay somewhere with me that she spent so much of her time with my brother.

"It really doesn't bother you at all?" she asks, not convinced.

"No. You have a past. Everyone does, love." I honestly don't think she could tell me anything or do anything to make me feel any differently toward her.

I pull into the diner, and Savvy was right, you couldn't miss it if

147

you wanted to. We go inside up to the counter and pick up menus.

"Savannah?" I turn to see a young guy probably about Savvy's age.

"TJ, how are you?" she asks as she turns to give the blond guy a side hug.

"I'm good. Haven't seen you around much. I heard about your pops; hope he is feeling better. Me and a couple of the guys have been taking care of the ranch while he was gone. I'm sorry I had to run your brother off a couple of times trying to load up Stuart's thoroughbreds." The boy seems genuine enough, but I don't miss the way his eyes continuously travel up and down her body. Can't blame him, but I still don't like it. I wrap my arm around her waist, pulling her closer, letting him know she is off limits.

"TJ, this is my boyfriend, Sin. TJ and I went to school together. Our dads have been friends forever. We have pictures together at my grandparent's dairy farm in our diapers." She laughs, smacking his arm, before kissing my cheek. Just like that, any jealousy I had is gone. He is like a brother to her, regardless of how he feels about her.

I have a feeling I will meet several of the guys she grew up with who are more like buddies or brothers in her mind, and she is the one who got away in theirs.

"Thank you for helping out her pops. I know how worried she was." I put my hand out for him to shake. If he is a good ole boy, he will respect me for being nice.

He extends his as well, both of us with a firm grip. He isn't going to back down.

Moron.

I grip his hand fully and give him a nod and smirk. He releases my hand quickly, nodding his head and telling Savvy bye as I kiss her temple.

We watch him leave and Savvy turns to me, raising her eyebrows. "Is this real? I mean, you didn't get possessive, jealous, or act like I've fucked TJ before. I'm just asking, is this really who you are?" She asks the question with so much skepticism in those bright blue eyes.

"Yes, angel, this is who I really am. Honesty is the best policy, remember?" I ask, then kiss her forehead, her nose, and her lips. She chuckles into my mouth, and I can't help but do the same until a waitress clears her throat from behind the bar. We pull apart, but my angel stays in my arms.

"What can I get you?" the waitress clips.

"Hey, Abby." Savannah just smiles at the redhead. I can tell it makes this Abby's blood boil when she looks over to me and her eyes narrow.

"Abby, this is my boyfriend Sin. Can you believe Bash has a twin brother? Oh, oops, I forgot, you knew him as Jake right?" Savvy is being condescending and I like where this is going.

"Fuck you, Savannah. I wasn't the only other girl he fucked, get over yourself. Did we all know he was stringing you along? Yeah, we did, and we let him fuck us all just the same. You can still be pissed at me, but we all know who the victim in that whole fucked up situation was after he came back for you and took it out on her, and you didn't believe her. Mia wasn't lying. We were all best friends once, Savannah. We all lost Jake when he left, but we lost you when he came into your life, and you never came back from it." Abby hush shouts at Savvy with her finger pointed in her face before she storms off into the kitchen.

Well shit. Wasn't expecting that.

"Angel, you okay?" I ask as I pull her a little closer to me.

She slumps into me, hiding her face, and whispers, "She's right. I didn't believe her. Can we go somewhere else please?"

I usher her out the door before she can finish her sentence. She goes into a full-on sob when I help her into the Jeep. I hurry around and jump into the driver's seat and open my arms for her to let me hold her while she cries. We sit there for a while. I don't start the Jeep which is making it incredibly hot by the time she finally pulls away and starts wiping away her tears. I start the Jeep, thankful it's still blowing cold air.

"I'm sorry..." she starts, but I cut her off, cupping her cheek before she can say anything else.

"You have nothing to apologize for. You were hurting in a very different way than those girls were. You also have the right to cry, scream, pout, or stomp your feet if you want to. Whatever you need to do to be okay is what I will always give you, Savannah. Don't ever apologize to me for your feelings. I told you; you need to feel it all and let it out, love." I bend over the center console, kissing her forehead.

"Thank you." Is all she replies, and that is good enough for me.

"Now, food, I actually do need it to survive, and so do you," I tell her, knowing my sugar has been low for a while.

"Pull into that convenience store, The Woodshed, they have the best fried chicken. We can get us a bucket and sides, and same for Pops. They have all the good greasy shit we shouldn't eat but are going to enjoy the fuck out of. We can drop off Pops' food, then take it back to the cabin and have some time to talk. I need to tell you why that just happened, and I'll even admit, I deserved it. I need to shut the rest of the world out tonight and just be with you. I also need a stiff drink if I'm going to get through this. I want to tell you everything, Christian, and then you can be the Sin that brings me back to life again." She lets go and allows another wall to crumble for me. I can't keep it from her if she is willing to tell me everything.

"Let's get some food and then we can open up to each other about everything." I place my finger under her chin and lift it until her eyes meet mine.

"Angel, I will always be the Sin that brings you back to life over and over again." I bring her lips to mine, kissing her softly, and pull back before I throw her in the backseat and show her just how hungry I am. As much as I would love to have her for dinner, I need some food.

I whip the Jeep over to the tiny corner store and pull up to the gas pumps. "I'll start filling up and meet you inside." She smiles, jumps out of the Jeep, and heads into the store. I notice she has a lot less bounce to her step here than back home. I understand why she wanted to leave.

I start the gas pump and head inside. I go straight to the candy aisle and see Savvy getting several Snickers bars. She chuckles when I grab a couple of Whatchamacallits. The smell of grease is overwhelming in the small space. I follow her over to the other side where all the real food is. She wasn't joking, they have everything. She orders two buckets of chicken, broasted potatoes, and fried okra. I throw in mozzarella sticks, a few chicken Crispitos, mashed potatoes, gravy, and two corn dogs. I grab a few two liters of Dr. Pepper, and Savvy gets some red plastic cups, Sprite, Red Bull, and asks for two bags of ice once we are up at the counter. I refuse to let her pay again, and I can see it's starting to bother her a little.

"I'll let you buy the alcohol if that makes you feel better." I relent a little.

"Deal," she chirps and gives me a sweet smile.

Worth it.

We make it to the liquor store as I finish off a corndog. This is the tiniest town, everything within a block of each other. Savvy finishes her mozzarella stick and jumps out. She waits for me at the front of the Jeep and puts her hand in mine.

"Hey, umm, I'm not twenty-one. I have all the documentation that says I am, even legally, but I want you to know that I just turned twenty a couple of weeks ago and this is the first time I'm actually having to use it, so play it cool, I'm a little nervous." She rushes out the words, looking up at me to see my expression go from probably weird to a full-on laugh. She rolls her eyes.

"You went through all that trouble for just a year difference. That's comical, but cute, love." I kiss her nose and we go into the store. She goes straight for cherry vodka, then Malibu, and grenadine. She is adorable. I grab a big bottle of Crown, knowing I'm going to need alcohol to get through telling her what I know, and wait for her at the register. When she comes up to the front she also has a bottle of wine and a bottle of gin in her tiny arms. She looks like a small child trying to put them on the counter without it all tipping over and getting in trouble. The guy scans everything, bags it up, tells her the total, and she pays with her card. I carry the bags out to the Jeep and put them in the backseat. She gets in looking sad.

"What's wrong, angel?" I ask as I hop into the driver's seat.

"He didn't even ID me. No one does, not in NOLA or here. Do I look that old?" she asks, throwing her hands up. I laugh again at her.

"No, you are too cute, love," is all I can say as I pull the Jeep back out on the road toward her dad's place. She pouts as she grabs another mozzarella stick and takes a bite. I grab a Snickers out of the bag. She takes it from me and opens it, then hands it back with the wrapper pulled down around it and smiles. My heart melts at how even when she has had a bad day, she still wants to take care of me too. I know it's a small gesture, but a gesture just the same. I love this girl, this crazy, beautiful, angel of mine.

Thankfully the car that her so-called mother was driving is gone when we make it back to the ranch.

"Do you mind if I stay out here, I don't want to go back in there."

"Of course, angel."

I take the food into her pops, put it on the counter and walk into the living room. He is sitting right where we left him, staring blankly at the TV that isn't turned on.

"Your dinner is on the table. We'll be back in the morning to help out," I tell him.

"You tell her tonight, then if she comes back tomorrow, I'll know if she can forgive me. I was just trying to protect her. Instead, I put her in a different hell that she didn't deserve. Tell her I'm sorry." He sighs as he finally looks over to me.

"You can tell her yourself. If she comes with me in the morning. If she chooses not to, I will help you set up some help. Then I will take her home when she is ready. You just make sure your son stays the fuck away. If he comes near her, I will end him and anyone else that means her harm, including your fucking wife."

I leave him there with his own demons. They are not mine to

bear nor Savvy's.

I see Savvy perk up and smile when I come out of the house. I hop in the Jeep and take off. I turn the music up as "Wild As Her" by Corey Kent blares through the speakers and I sing along with Savvy. I place my hand on her thigh and keep my left on the steering wheel. She places her hand on mine, pulling it up higher on her thigh. I let my fingers brush up against her pussy through the soft fabric. Her breath hitches as she pushes her hips up into my touch. I cup her cunt, then remove my hand completely.

"Take them off," I order gruffly.

"Sin, turn right at the street after Stuff'Ns." She pants as she unbuttons her shorts, then moves them down her legs. I watch her purposely leave her little lacy black thong in place.

"Lay the seat back, angel."

She does as I say. I reach over and put my hand on her thigh again, letting it travel slowly up to her sweet pussy. I slowly let one finger move over her thong and dive into her wet lips. She gasps as I slowly move up from her tight little hole to her clit, rubbing slow circles. Her hands clench the seat on both sides as her hips buck into my hand.

"Oh God, yes, Sin." She pants as I slowly move back to her sweet little hole and let my middle finger finally dive into her. I take the turn she said as I push my palm on her clit, rubbing against it while applying pressure.

"Take the first right," she almost yells out as she throws her head back into the seat. I pump my finger, swirling it around until her body stiffens and her walls close around my hand. Her legs clamp my wrist, but I don't relent. I stop the Jeep on a curve and put it in park. Leaning over, I pry her legs apart to kiss those sweet lips and delve my tongue in, flicking her clit as she comes all over my hand. When she finally comes down, I slowly pull my fingers out of her, bring them to my mouth, and lick up every bit she offered. She watches me through hooded sapphire eyes as I lick my hand clean.

"So sweet, angel."

CHAPTER 15
Savvy

Once we finally make it into the cabin, after a long make out sesh in the car, reality set in once again and I'm hit with the reminder of what Bash did to Mia. She tried to tell me after it happened, but I refused to believe that he could do something like that. I also refused to believe that he came back here at all and didn't choose to see me.

I was a bitch to Mia. She was always pissed at me, saying I took him from her, but he always said she was crazy. He took her on one date, and she wouldn't leave him alone after. I see now that he was just as manipulative as my mother. Apparently as much of a fucking whore too.

I look in the long mirror on the wall by the bedroom door and take in my appearance. I put on the silky navy and white striped cami and shorts set he got from the hotel. I decide I'm as good as I'm gonna get and let my hair down before I go back to the living room with Sin.

He sits on the old couch, still in his shorts and T-shirt, chowing down on a chicken leg.

"Drink?" I ask, needing liquid courage to unleash all my demons on him.

"I have a Dr. Pepper, but will you bring the Crown please, angel?" He is so polite. I have to admit, I prefer being called angel rather than love now.

"Sure," I holler, bouncing into the kitchen.

I just hope he can handle all I tell him without losing his shit. He does keep surprising me with how different he is from his brother. He didn't even flinch when I told Scarlett I would kill her son. He smiled. Like he was proud of me for standing up for myself. He didn't even question why I did what I did. He has my back without even knowing why. I'm not going to lie and say this is a normal relationship for us in the last forty-eight hours, but he isn't a stranger. I don't know if he ever was.

I put ice in my cup, add more cherry vodka than I should and a can of Red Bull and finish it off with grenadine. I give it a stir before adding a straw and suck half of it down. I go ahead and refill it, knowing I will finish it quickly. I grab the Crown Royal and head back to the couch and plop next to Sin.

"You have this smorgasbord set up just how I would do it if I were having a Gilmore Girl moment." I compliment him, grabbing the fried okra and popping one in my mouth as I relax a bit.

"How do you feel being here?" he asks as he takes the bottle of liquor, pouring some in his cup. Funny, I like Crown with Dr. Pepper too.

I stop for a moment before I answer, never really taking the time to process what my heart has gone through since I was sixteen years old. When he brought me here, to the cabin, where it all started.

"I feel like I have literally come full circle. Innocence given. The sweet caring girl I used to be lost. Fell in love. Had my heart shattered into a million pieces. Got myself too broken. You know what though?" His eyes haven't left mine since I started speaking. He shakes his head, licking his lips. "I'm in the process of being repaired, not by the one who broke me, but by his twin brother who is pure sin, saving me from the devil himself. Now, back to ... falling in love. I don't know how or why, but I love you, at least, I think this is what love is supposed to feel like." I tell him exactly what I think instead of wrapping it in a pretty bow first.

"I love you too, Savannah." He pulls me onto his lap. I make the move to straddle him.

"I might need you this close to talk about all the things that have

156

made me the way that I am. I want to tell you everything, but I need to know this is real. That I'm not going to wake up to a flower and a note saying goodbye. I can't go through that again. Not with you. I won—" He stops me by crushing his lips to mine. His hands are cupping my face, moving into my hair. He pulls my head back, gently tugging my hair. I moan as our lips part.

"I will never leave you. Not until my dying breath, and even then, I will follow you in my afterlife until you are back in my arms again. When I tell you I love you, they aren't just words to me. You have my heart now too. I'm just as scared you are going to break it, angel."

I melt in his arms once again at the revelation that I have the capability of hurting him too.

"I hadn't thought about it that way. No one has truly ever given me their heart to protect. It's a gift, just like love. I promise to protect it. Always." I truly never believed a man could be hurt by love. He is proving me wrong.

He kisses me sweetly, pulls back, and whispers, "I will always protect your heart first." He lifts me up and places me back on the couch next to him.

"You need to eat, and we need to talk. I found something out today and your pops confirmed it all. I need you to know that no matter what he said, I planned on telling you tonight, away from everyone else." He is starting to worry me, but I nod and grab a piece of chicken.

"Lay it on me. What did my mother or brother do now?" I ask, not really surprised he got info about them.

"Your mother Scarlett, isn't your birth mother."

I stop mid bite into a chicken leg, shocked at what he just said.

"What are you talking about? That's impossible, my birth certificate says I was born in Vinita to Scarlett and Stuart Barrett." I shake my head at him, knowing his information is wrong.

"Angel, your father had an affair with a woman in New Orleans named Sylvia Bennett, knocked her up, and her husband wouldn't let her keep the baby girl. Your dad brought you back here, paid his doctor friend to forge your birth certificate and made Scarlett take care of you as if you were her own. He told me himself that he just wanted to protect you from that life. You look like your mother. Same eyes." He says the words, but they take a minute to register. This can't be possible.

"You're serious?" I ask, knowing the answer. He just nods. I start laughing, hysterically. I know it's not a good look, but I can't help it. "I'm not the fucking cunt's daughter? I was born in New Orleans? Now this has made my life." I pick up my drink once I calm my cackling to a minimum and take a long swig from my straw. I let it go and then decide I wasn't finished. I suck on the straw, gulping down the sweet liquid and going over the words he just told me over and over in my head. I look back up to Sin when he takes my drink out of my hand. I realize I was sucking air for I don't know how long, just processing.

"I'll fill it back up, what is it?" he asks.

"Just bring it all, I don't know what I want yet."

"Fair enough." He shakes his head and goes to the kitchen.

"Bring the Red Bull and soda too!" I holler at him. "I know I'm already buzzed, but I don't care. It's not enough."

He just laughs. "Whatever you need, angel."

He comes in carrying everything in his big bulky arms.

"If I'm being honest, I'm glad Scarlett isn't my mother. I mean, I've always wondered how the hell I came out of her." I laugh as he sits close to me, putting everything on the big coffee table.

"You said I have the same eyes as my birth mother. Obviously, you know her?" I ask, dreading the next thing that comes out of his mouth.

"Ask the question you really want to ask, angel." He already knows what is in my head. He knows me and knows what I want him to tell me, but he is going to make me ask. He wants blatant honesty all the time. So do I, but this, this is more than I bargained for.

"Who is Lottie to me? Are we related?" I ask because it's what I want to know most. I want to know who the only other woman he ever loved was, and why I look so much like her.

"She was your big sister. She was six when you were born. I remember her saying she had a baby sister that no one knew about. She said you were sent away by the evil king to a faraway land to be with your daddy and play with horses all day until you grow up and find your way home. We were all kids back then. The last time she told me that story she had decided she was going to look for you. It was the day before our wedding. We were watching the rain from our breakfast nook, having coffee and beignets before we had to say goodbye until we said I do. She was adamant that the story was real, that she got to meet you and kiss the freckle below your lips. She said you had her eyes, and it was like looking at a picture of herself when she was a baby. She kept one that was her mother's. She hid it from her father, just like her mom did, saying they were pictures of Charlotte as a child. He never questioned it. I have a few of them in a box back home. You can have them if you would like. Your dad sent some that they really hid because you were always on a horse. Charlotte found them about a month before our wedding. She had forgotten about you as she grew up and questioned her mom first, thank God. She waited until that day to tell me. I think she wanted to make sure that I would help her. I didn't think much about it after I found her body. I guess I blocked it out until now. I couldn't remember our last conversation until earlier. I'm sorry I didn't find you after she died. I feel like I failed you both." He lays it all out there.

I decide a shot may do the trick and help me process the information. I grab two more plastic cups and pour us both a shot of Crown.

I take a deep breath and let it out before I down the harsh taste of liquid courage and chase it with a Sprite. I pour myself another drink as I watch him down his shot, never making a face or needing a chaser. Just watching me.

"Well, I have to admit, what I have been worried about telling you all day doesn't really hold a candle to the shit bomb you just dropped." I laugh. I just laugh, because if I do anything else I might lose it. I decide jokes are the way to break the ice.

"I guess it's only fair that you fucked my sister since I fucked your brother. Wait, Bash was fucking Charlotte too. He said it, I don't remember the specifics, I was drunk and in and out of it. He was wasted too, telling me all about his perfect Lottie. I don't remember much, but I remember how he looked when he spoke about her. It made me jealous each and every time he did it. He called me Lottie a few times in the beginning, but I brushed it off. Then he just started calling me baby girl. He apparently called all of his whores that, that way he didn't mix us up." I tell him the truth, knowing it sucks to hear, but I won't lie to him. Even if my words are starting to slur.

I grab a roll and mashed potatoes and gravy. I dip the roll in the potatoes, then the gravy, making sure I pile carbs on top of carbs and shove it in my mouth.

"I found out about the affair about six months before she died. You're not telling me anything I didn't already know, angel." He kisses my temple. "Tell me something that I don't know about you. Let me in. Tell me your deepest darkest secrets, angel. I will help you chase your ghosts to hell if it will help you heal." He cups my face, looking into my heavy eyes.

I lick my lips, trying to find my voice over my heavy breathing.

"Bash hurt Mia because of me. He brought her here after he saw me with a guy in my Jeep, back at the yacht club where I worked. No one was around, or I didn't think so, Christ, it was one thirty in the morning and the parking lot was bare, and pitch black. He called Mia and got her to meet him here at the cabin. She thought he had come back for her, just like I would have. She met him here with the expectation that he missed her and couldn't wait to see her. She told me that he tied her hands to the bedpost. She said that before they went to the bedroom, he kept asking her questions about me, that he was angry, but wanted to know everyone she knew I had been with. Once he tied her up, he gagged her and started calling her his sweet Savvy girl before he beat the shit out of her. She said he forced a butt plug up her ass, fucked her as he hit her, then fucked her ass until she passed out. She said she begged him to stop a million times but that her crying and screaming just made him get off more. She said she woke up to four one-hundred-dollar bills laying around her. She said she was bleeding pretty bad but went home and showered and tried to pretend it never happened. When she told me, I threatened to kick her ass for lying about him. I didn't think it could be true. Not about the guy I fell in love with. I was wrong. I think back on that day a lot. She looked awful, scared. She tried to warn me to stay away from him, not because she wanted him, but because she knew what he was capable of. I should have believed her. I have to live with that regret."

Sin just stares, listening, no judgment showing at all.

I take another long drink from my straw. "I remember Mia in sweats, black circles and puffiness around her eyes. She looked like a shell of the girl I remember before him. I did too, for months after he left. Then I woke up one day and became the slut that bounced from guy to guy, trying to feel anything again. We were all innocent before him. I wouldn't doubt it if he didn't play us all the exact same way. Taking our virginity, making us all fall in love with someone who didn't exist. I'm not the only girl in this town that changed after him." I'm honest with him and myself for the first time since he left not just me, but all of us. I hate him, not just for me, but all the girls he ruined in this town.

"I'm sorry that you had to go through all of this, angel." He holds my hands in his again, letting me know he is right here with me.

"I'm not sorry, Christian. If Bash hadn't shattered my world, I may have never found you. I think it all had to happen, maybe not like it did, but something had to happen to get me to New Orleans. Fate, or whatever, but I wouldn't change it if it meant I would never have this, with you." I look up into his honey eyes.

His lips crush into mine. His hand cups the back of my head, laying me back on the couch. He presses his body into mine as I spread my legs and pull him down on me. I want to feel him. I need to feel him. He grabs my legs, wrapping them around his waist. He pushes his hips into mine, creating the perfect friction with the silky material of my shorts. He moves his mouth from mine to my jawline, then to my ear, peppering me with soft kisses.

He whispers in my ear, "Hold on, angel." I do as I'm told, wrapping my arms around his neck. He lifts us both from the couch in a swift motion, cupping my ass once we are standing. His mouth moves along my neck, rubbing his stubble and then nipping at the now sensitive skin. My core clenches as my pussy throbs, begging for the stupid fabric between us to get the fuck out of the way. He places me on the bed, moving his kisses down my neck to my nipples poking through the thin material.

He sits me up. "Raise your arms," he orders softly. I do as I'm told, biting my lip as he removes the cami. "Lie back, angel." His voice is softer. I lie back and place my hands above my head, not knowing what else to do. I close my eyes as his hands move my shorts and black thong down my legs, slowly, too slowly. He isn't touching me anymore, and I need his touch.

"Please, Christian, I want you, I need you."

His naked body is on mine quickly. I open my eyes when I feel him at my entrance and then his hands snake into mine above my head. His lips are on mine as he pushes into me ever so slowly. My hands tighten around his when I feel my pussy quiver, adjusting to his size. I moan into his mouth as he pulls back, then pushes in deeper and deeper until I feel his ballsack against my ass.

"Fuck, angel, so wet, so tight for me." I can't help all the sounds and blubbering that flies out as he pulls back and slams back into me. He hits that spot again that only he has ever been deep enough to hit. I moan, spreading my legs wider for him. He releases my hands, finally allowing me to touch him. I reach around to his ass pulling him farther into me, lifting my hips to meet his. He snakes an arm under my leg, and pushes it up toward my head, allowing him to get deeper. He slows his pace again, circling his hips with each thrust.

"My sweet angel," he whispers as his mouth finds mine. He moans into my mouth as he thrusts over and over. He pulls back from my lips, moving down to my nipple. He cups one breast as his tongue swirls on the other. He lets my leg down as he pulls out of me.

"Roll onto your stomach." His voice is as ragged as his breathing. I do as he says. "Ass up in the air, love." I bring my knees up on the white satin sheets, laying my face flat to the side.

"Good girl." He sits up on his knees behind me with his palms on my ass cheeks. I jerk when I feel his tongue hit my pussy. A yelp escapes as his hands squeeze my ass, pulling my cheeks farther apart as his tongue travels to my ass. I tremble when he puts pressure on it with, I assume, his thumb. His tongue dives into my pussy, and I feel wetness coating my thighs. I suck in a breath when his tongue meets his thumb at my ass. He probes his tongue in and out of my tight hole, making my entire body jerk. He moves his fingers in and out of my pussy, moving my juices up to my ass. He slowly slips a finger in my ass as he adjusts his dick to slip in my pussy. I push back against him, wanting more. He adds another finger in my ass.

"Oh fuck, Sin." I bury my face in the sheets, moaning, unable to take much more. He fucks both my holes at once. I can't even have a coherent thought. My body is opening up for him in ways I never thought possible.

"I'm going to fuck this sweet ass, angel."

"Please!" I yell out the word, begging him to do it. I want him to take everything my body can give, and then take more. I feel him pull out of both holes, leaving me completely empty.

"Please, Sin," I beg, lifting my face from the sheets as tears start to fall. I feel his hard cock move back and forth between my holes, slipping slowly in and out of each one. He is only letting the tip in my ass, while he still pushes into the hilt in my pussy, teasing my ass, making it beg for more. I moan when he is in my ass again and push back against him. He lets me move my ass back and forth, allowing him to go deeper with each movement. I still, holding in a breath when it gets to be too much.

"Relax, angel," he tells me as he reaches around, rubbing slow methodic circles around my clit. I let out the breath I am holding in

163

and push back on his dick again as the tidal wave builds. He starts moving with my hips, slowly fucking my ass until my hips start to buck and I feel him slide all the way in.

I grip the sheets, moaning. My body convulses under his, wanting more and more until he is slamming into my ass, over and over, making the wave crash over me. Wave after wave of pleasure ripples through my body. His moans mix with mine, his motions slowing as I feel him still before pumping slowly again, rubbing my clit and making me soar higher and higher again, until I fall. My body finally flattens to the bed with his as he slowly pulls out. He wraps me in his arms, pulling me to his chest. Kissing my hair, over and over. The euphoria starts to wear off. My chest tightens, and I can't help the tears that come when the sobs finally come out.

Sin holds me like that for a while, letting me get it all out. He rubs his hand up and down my arm. "Shhh, angel, it's okay. I've got you. Let it all out. I'm right here with you." He reassures me every chance he gets. I turn in his arms to face him. He kisses my forehead, softly pushing my hair out of my face, cupping my cheek. "I love you, Savvy." His raspy voice lets me know that my hurting is in turn hurting him.

"I love you too, Sin." I smile through the tears, knowing now that I can love again. That I am worthy of his love. That I deserve to be with someone who cherishes my heart as I do theirs.

"Bath, angel?"

CHAPTER 16
Sin

I watch my angel sleep as the sun starts peeking through the back wall of windows facing the lake. I have to admit, it's beautiful here. I can see why she loves this place so much. I watch the sun rise over the lake, creating a masterpiece of colors I know only God could create. I look over at Savvy in wonder.

We stayed up talking until three o'clock this morning. She opened up more about her mom and the role she played in her brother putting her in the hospital. I opened up about my family, letting her know what happened to my mom, how Bash changed, and even Lottie and how broken I have been since she died.

I think we both realized just how similar we are. We ate until I thought I would bust, drank way too much, and passed out watching The Originals. I woke up when I heard a noise outside. It was just a family of deer passing through. It's so peaceful here.

I decide to let Savvy sleep and go get us some groceries so I can make her breakfast. I noticed that convenience store yesterday had eggs and breakfast meats. It's not like there is a McDonald's on the corner here. I find a note pad and pen in the kitchen drawer and write,

Angel,
I'm just getting breakfast and

will be right back!
I love you!

Your Sin

Just in case she wakes up, I don't want any other ridiculous thoughts going through her pretty little head. I throw on my shorts from yesterday and a grey V-neck. We need to go find clothes today. I head out the door with my keys in hand.

I didn't think to check if the kitchen had any pots and pans or utensils to cook with as I grab a package of bacon out of the cooler. Shit. I put it back and head over to the diner side. Thank God they have an assortment of breakfast foods. I get us two bacon, egg, and cheese biscuits, two ham, egg, and cheese croissants, four hash-brown patties, a gallon of apple and a gallon of orange juice. This place is made for lake life. Easy in and out shops with all the bad foods you swear you can't eat but indulge in here. We have places like this in NOLA, they just happen to sell daiquiris and crawfish pies.

I see a flyer on my way out for boat rentals at Ugly John's. I take the number down in my phone and call it once I'm back in the Jeep. I rent a ski boat with all the bells and whistles for the next week.

I decide to text Jasper and have him set up a little surprise for Savvy. She had a rough night letting everything out. She needs a vacation, and that is exactly what I'm going to give her.

She already told me she isn't going back to the ranch. She is upset with her dad, but she still loves him. She is just going to need some time to let it all sink in and forgive him, not just for lying but for raising her with such a demented woman, knowing how bad she was. The fact that Scarlett was as abusive as Savannah described, I'm amazed that she is still here.

My angel is tough, and I respect the hell out of her for turning into the beautiful person she has become, inside and out. She hasn't let the bad things that happened in her past define her. It was difficult for me to hear her describe her tormentors, but it was more difficult for her to release them all.

We talked about everything we could think of. I found out her favorite color depends on her mood, and even though she doesn't like chocolate that much, she loves white chocolate covered pretzels. She would also rather have a bouquet of weeds picked for her than store-bought flowers. She likes gifts with meaning and always puts thought into the ones she gives. I pull into the circle drive and see my angel waiting for me on the porch with my note in her hand.

I see her face light up when she sees me coming. I would never leave her. I get it, it happened, but she has to realize I'm not Bash. I put the Jeep in park and grab the bags out of the back. She reaches up on her tiptoes to give me the sweetest kiss as I come up the steps. She is pure sunshine this morning, looking ravishing in my T-shirt that hangs below her mid-thigh. Her jet-black curls bounce as she opens the door for us and skips to the counter, pulling out the two barstools for us to sit.

"Hey, love," she says sweetly as I sit next to her.

"Good morning, angel." I chuckle at her choice of pet name for me. I lean in and kiss her, not able to contain myself.

She pulls back, giggling. "I'm glad you like it because that is what your name is in my phone now." She giggles again.

"I love you, angel." I kiss her forehead, nose, then lips, swallowing her chuckles. "Let's eat, then we are going shopping. I need some clothes, and so do you. Anywhere around here have swimsuits?" I ask, then start unloading the bags.

She goes for the bacon, egg, and cheese biscuit and starts chowing down while I grab cups and open the juice.

"Apple please," she says sweetly. She starts opening all the bags of food, laying them all out for me to choose from.

"I figured we could have a Gilmore Girls breakfast." I joke with her as I take a drink of juice and sit down with her.

"This is really how our lives can be every day. I would prefer to wake up in your arms tomorrow, and every day after that, but I'll forgive you this time since you brought food." She picks back at me. I can't remember the last time I smiled this much or felt this happy. She is the light my heart has been missing.

"That sounds like the perfect life to me."

I let Savvy drive us around since she knows where she is going, and I can pay attention to all the things she loves. We took the top and doors off the Jeep, letting the wind blow through our hair as we drive across a mile long, very narrow, stone bridge. I look over the side of what she calls the DAM.

"That's the golf course, but up here, you'll see Jeeps down on the rocks, where they open the gates when the water gets too high," she explains, and I see exactly what she is talking about. Jeeps line the rocky cliffs.

We finally make it over the bridge and she turns abruptly, stopping in front of an old stone building with the words The DAM Hotel painted across the top. There are racks of swimsuits and cover ups on the porch by the entrance. We both hop out and go hand in hand into the cute little boutique. Savvy goes straight to the bikinis, dragging me with her.

"Pick which ones you like, and I'll try them on for you. I'm going to look at a few things for you." She squeals and bounces up on her toes, giving me a quick peck before she practically skips to the other side of the shop.

I'm left standing in front of a wall of bikinis that all would look amazing on Savvy. This is going to show how much we were listening to each other last night; she is testing me.

I like it. I pick colors that I know she will like, blues, greens, reds, and oranges. I see a simple electric blue sundress that I think would look amazing on her. I find her several pairs of shorts, tops, and dresses. I put them all in a dressing room for her and make my way to find her. She has piles of clothes in her arms and two straw hats on her head.

I come up behind her, poking her in her sides, making her squeal and jump. She turns around quickly, giggling. I take most of what she has and kiss her temple as she describes all that she picked out and why.

"I put all of my choices in the dressing room. I'll take this one next to it and we can show each other as we try them on." She gasps when she sees everything in the dressing room.

Over an hour later, we leave with two big bags a piece and load into the Jeep. "Ready to see my favorite place?" she asks as she pulls back on the road.

"Little Blue?" I ask with a huge grin on my face. Her smile meets her eyes and I swear they sparkle. "Take It Out On Me" by Florida Georgia Line blares through the Jeep as she takes us across two more smaller stone bridges and then down a backroad that curves around until she decides to take us off roading, turning down a trail and coming to an immediate stop before the tires hit the water. She turns the Jeep off, cutting off the end of the song.

Damn, I liked that one.

I get out of the Jeep when she hops out and twirls around. She kicks the shallow water with her foot toward me.

"Shit, that's cold." I take a couple of steps back. "Wow, it is clear, it's not deep either, but it's like looking through moving glass," I tell her, mesmerized by how perfectly she described this very spot as I look around.

We are almost directly under a stone bridge littered with graffiti, and the creek goes in both directions, one slightly more enticing than the other. I get what she meant when she said I would know which direction I would want to go when we got down here. I was listening, angel.

"I told you! It's a spring! Cold all year round. We can walk it all the way back around in either direction we go, you choose, and I'll show you things along the way." She is bouncing with excitement to share a piece of herself with me, places not even Bash knew about. She said she never took him past this spot, because she knew deep down that she would need a place to get away from him at times too. She just never made this place a big deal to him. She said he didn't like it much. I can't imagine not being fully invested in anything that makes her happy.

I slip off my HeyDudes and get the water shoes she insisted we needed no matter how ugly I thought they were. I slip mine on and take hers over to her, helping her change from her sandals. She grabs both of us a suit out of the bags, handing me mine to carry. Looks like there are people down a ways to our right, and I want her to myself for just a little while longer, so I lace my fingers through hers and go left.

"Good choice," she says sweetly. She lifts on her toes again and kisses my cheek.

I always hear women say they get butterflies when the right guy kisses them or is just near them.

It's not a sexual thing but a feeling of pure happiness that just takes over your entire body. I feel that with her.

She proves that there are, in fact, crawdads, throwing one at me. I catch it, holding the poor little thing out to her. "See, angel, I told you they were mud bugs. They hide under the rocks here to get to the mud," I tease her. I kept telling her it was impossible to have crawfish here. She kept arguing that a crawdad is the same thing, just smaller. I teased her, telling her we call all the bottom feeders mudbugs back home.

We stop at a few places along the way, letting me know that it is special to her in some way. She showed me the log she was sitting on for her first kiss in the eighth grade. She admits it was TJ and laughs at how awkward she felt kissing him but was happy to just get it over with.

She stops us when we make it around a bend and pulls me toward some rocks on the other side of the creek. She pulls back some vines with little yellow and white flowers on them that smell like heaven, and ushers me back behind a tree going into the side of a cliff. We walk farther into the cave-like place, coming to an opening. We make it back out, having to duck down so we don't hit our heads on the sharp rocks forming the small exit. There are large rocks scattered around a crystal-clear pool of water. The sun beats down through the large opening high above us. It's literally a spring creating a waterfall from one side of the large area.

"Welcome to my secret place. I can only come here when no one else is around to see me sneak back here. I found it one day when Scarlett was camping down here with one of her boyfriends. I ventured off away from them to give them their adult time, as they put it. I think I was ten. I knew when I found it that it was special and untouched. No one really walks the creek anymore. They just stay in the park area." She shares more of herself with me. I'm in awe of the pure beauty of this place. The water is ice cold and feels good on my feet.

Savvy starts stripping her clothes off and slipping the tiny black string bikini I picked for her on. I stand and watch her, remembering every inch of her, clothed or not. I remove my clothes, letting my dick spring out of my boxer briefs at attention to her. She licks her lips, disappointment showing on her face, pouting out her bottom lip, when I slip my black trunks on that she picked for me.

She sighs, then takes my hand, ushering me into the freezing water. The second my balls hit the water I swear they suck up inside me, trying to escape the harshness of it after walking in the hot sun.

Problem solved. My dick may be MIA as well.

Her bottom lip quivers and her teeth chatter. We make it over to the waterfall, and I follow her, climbing the jagged rocks. She pulls me behind the small waterfall once we are on a big flat area that we both fit on. The sun is shining straight through, letting us feel warmth as steam billows around us from the cold water hitting the hot rocks surrounding us.

I feel my balls drop back down as I thaw out.

Savvy stands close to where the water goes out over the rock we are standing on. I wrap my arms around her, pulling her back to my front, and kiss her neck. She leans her head back on my shoulder, letting out a slight moan.

"This is where I would write my deepest darkest thoughts, and then wad them up and throw them over into the water. My thoughts were never safe to keep on paper when I lived on the ranch. I started keeping journals when I moved out to the tin can. I really don't need to go by there, I took everything I needed the day I moved to NOLA."

I love learning new things about her. I'm glad she was able to find a way to get her thoughts out back then.

"I started keeping a journal after Lottie died. It was my way of getting all the things out I needed to, without having to talk about it. I get it, angel." I kiss her head and just let her have the time to get whatever she needs from her safe place before we walk back out into the creek.

We make it around by the park area. She shows me where the water will rush out from when the gates open. Apparently, noodling right after they close them down here is a thing.

Kinda sounds fun.

We put our things on the rocks, and she takes me to a literal blue hole with a tiny waterfall coming out of it. The water is a complete contrast to the cold creek water. This hole is warm and much more inviting. Too bad there are children playing up the creek aways or I would remove that tiny bikini with my teeth and give her some new memories of this amazing place.

We head back to the Jeep after playing in the water for a bit and just talking again.

I realize we have been here a while and we need to get back to the cabin for her surprise.

"Ready to go get some lunch before we head to the grocery store? I want to pick up stuff for us to cook together tomorrow. Tonight, I want to take you out somewhere fun. We can go back to the cabin and get cleaned up."

"Yeah, I want ice cream! Pistol Pat's has the best dipped cones.

They have a drive-through so we can eat on the way to the store." She seems to be in a hurry to get back to the cabin too. I know what she wants, I want it to, especially after seeing her in her special place. I refuse to fuck her on rocks. Doesn't mean I didn't want to.

Savvy

Sin has been weird and cryptic since we left Little Blue. Truth be told, I was expecting him to fuck me at the spring. I know he wanted to, at least his dick did. He keeps checking his phone and just seems like his mind is somewhere else. We are getting way more than we need at the grocery store.

"We could feed an army with the amount of eggs you just put in the basket," I tease him.

"What? I like omelets," he retorts with a grin. I just shake my head and laugh.

Of course, we run into at least ten people I know and exchanged fake pleasantries. Sin is a perfect gentleman but doesn't say much. He just keeps rushing around the store, getting more stuff every time he checks his phone. Reasor's is not that big of a store, and I swear we have circled the entire thing twenty times.

When we finally check out, our basket is full enough to feed us for a month. I can't help but think that all of this food is going to go to waste. We can't stay here that long. I already want to go home. I left this place for a reason. I love being able to share a part of me with Sin, but I'm ready to see more of what makes him, him.

He pulls the Jeep onto the circle drive of the cabin. There is a truck that I have never

seen parked by the door. I look over to Sin, who just has a huge smile plastered on his face, which tells me I don't have anything to worry about. I relax a bit when his buddy, I think, Jasper comes out on the front porch.

"Surprise, angel."

I look from Sin back to the front porch. My eyes go wide when I see a familiar face peek out from around Jasper's back.

CHAPTER 17
Bash

It only took me two days to get my therapist, Allison Hawthorn, on my dick. Now the meek, sweet, innocent little slut is wrapped around it and will do anything for me. I just had to give her my sad story of my girl cheating on me with my brother and that's why I relapsed. I just want someone to love me back. Blah. Blah. Blah.

Stupid bitch isn't a very good therapist if she can't see past her own lust that I'm a fucking nut job.

She got me a burner phone to use while I'm here. Mike informed me that my little Savvy girl is having the time of her life at the lake with my fucking brother and their friends.

They all just left the cabin looking like they were going clubbing. The picture he sent of Savvy has my dick getting harder as I push Doc Allie's head farther down on my cock to choke her, until I feel her chin hit my nuts. This little cunt doesn't have a gag reflex. I wrap her dark brown high ponytail tighter around my fist, bobbing her head up and down as I flex my hips, feeling my dick slide down her throat and back up. I keep my eyes focused on my girl in a simple electric blue sundress that I know she picked out just for me. Her hair is down, her curls wild, just like her. She is genuinely smiling at me. I love that smile. I can't wait to punish that beautiful filthy mouth of hers.

I yank the doc off my dick, lift her up by her hair, and turn her around so I don't have to look at her.

"Drop your panties and lift your skirt."

She looks back at me, blinking the tears from her eyes, taking in deep breaths, but does as she is told.

"That's my good girl, now bend over your desk and lie flat." I take the phone over to the mahogany desk, and when she is facedown, I prop it up on her little green lamp so I can see my girl's face.

"Spread your legs."

"Yes sir." She pants. Her legs tremble as I watch her black stilettos part, showing me her already wet pussy. This bitch thinks I'm Christian Grey. Laughable. I'll be whatever I have to be so that I can get the fuck out of here.

I stroke my dick a few times, getting it hard again as I look into Savvy's gorgeous blue eyes. I slap her plump ass, not too hard, but just enough to make her yelp. I put a finger in her tight little cunt and feel her tighten around it. She is soaked. I pump it a few times, making her moan, and then pull it out.

"I'm not going to go easy on you this time. I'm going to make it hurt, baby," I growl out as I slam into her. She cries out and tries to move forward, but there is nowhere for her to go. I like having her pinned to the desk.

I pull out slowly and slam into her again, rocking the desk as my balls slap her clit. She cries out again. I slap her ass again, spitting on her tight little asshole, wanting to fuck it. I hold myself back and stick my thumb in her ass as I start pumping. I grip her hip with my left hand, fucking her harder. She tilts her hips, pushing her ass farther into me as both her holes tighten around me.

Our moans fill the soundproof room as I almost start to come, looking at my Savvy with a just fucked smile on her gorgeous face. Her whiney moans pull me out of my fantasy. I pull out of her without warning and shove my dick in her ass, trying to drown out her noise by focusing on Savvy's eyes. She cries out, sounding more like my girl. She is still coming, her ass tightening around my dick at an almost painful level. I close my eyes and picture Savvy coming on my dick. I slam in and out of her until I finally explode in her ass. She is a writhing mess beneath me. Her legs give out a bit before I come, the desk and my dick the only things holding her up. I pull out and zip up my pants, sitting back on the couch, phone in hand.

"You did good taking it in the ass your first time," I praise her, then go back to my phone. I pull up my messages and see a pic of Savvy, walking hand in hand with Sin, going into the club on Monkey Island. It makes my blood boil, but I smile and reply.

> Bash: Keep an eye on them. Shake things up and have some fun. I should be out of here by the weekend.

> Mike: Consider it done, boss.

> Bash: Don't let anything happen to my girl. I will hold you responsible for even fucking up her hair. Everyone else is fair game.

> Mike: Understood. We got this, boss.

I smile as I watch the doc in amusement as she tries to straighten herself up. My dick gets hard again watching her wipe away fresh tears. I can't wait to see those blue eyes cry for me again.

"I didn't say we were finished. On your knees, naked. Now."

Savvy

181

. . .

I grind my ass against Sin's crotch on the small dance floor to the beat of "Last Night" by Morgan Wallen. This man can dance. He can two-step better than anyone I have ever danced with. He leads me perfectly, letting me know every move he is going to make with his hands. I'm honestly having a hard time keeping up.

He pulls me close, whispering in my ear, "I like this song, angel, but this will not be our story." He spins me out with the biggest smile on his face. He pulls me back, dipping me at the end of the song, kissing my lips softly.

"Porch Swing Angel" by Muscadine Bloodline flows through the speakers as he lifts me back up, pulling me close with his lips still on mine, continuing to dance.

He pulls away and says," This is more like what I promise our lives to be like."

I smile up at him, knowing this man will stand true to his words. He doesn't say them lightheartedly. He knows exactly what he wants, and I know in my heart that I want all the same things. I wasn't sure I could love again, let alone so fully. Now, I realize I never really knew what love was. Until he showed me.

He keeps surprising me with how aware of my feelings he is, and he wants me to express them. He doesn't see me as weak, or broken, but strong because of who I turned out to be, despite everything I went through to get here. Dancing in his arms makes it all worth it. I would do it all again if it meant making it to this moment with him.

"I need a break. Can we go sit for a bit?" I ask, before he spins me again. He stops, pulls me under his arm, and escorts me off the dance floor over to our table with Cami, Charlie, Jasper, and Joe. Lucky for me they already ordered drinks. I sit down, taking a long swig of some blue fufu drink. Definitely has Malibu. I like it.

I relax and start catching my breath as Sin pulls me close.

"I have missed you, girl. Oklahoma is just like you described it." Cami smiles, looking from me to Sin and back again.

"Honestly, until you got here, I was ready to go home," I reply.

I see the looks of surprise on everyone's faces.

"What?" I ask, giving them all weird looks.

"We just thought that you would have wanted to stay, because of your pops," Charlie pipes in.

"Nope. Turns out, he is fine, and they just left him in the hospital to try and steal his horses. A few neighbors have been helping him out. I already texted TJ to work out a deal with my dad to be a ranch hand, along with a couple of his friends. He is taken care of. Now we are just here for a vacay, according to Sin." I reach up and give him a sweet kiss.

Cami is grinning from ear to ear sitting across from me. "Girl, I haven't seen this aura on you before. You are literally glowing like a sunrise. Sin, you have a kind soul. You are completely unguarded with her, your auras fit perfectly together. He is the blue backdrop to your hurricane of colors." She is doing her witchy thing again. Not gonna lie, I love it!

"You're a witch," Sin says as a statement instead of a question. I guess it is normal for people who grew up in NOLA to not laugh at the idea.

"Yeah, Charlie and I both are." Cami smiles at her fiancé. I get the hearts that she has in her eyes now. I have them too.

A waitress brings us another round of rattlesnake shots. I feel tipsy, but not drunk yet. Funny, for the first time in a long time, I'm not drinking to get drunk. I would normally be three sheets to the wind this late in the night. Usually when I drink, that's the goal. To numb the pain. With Sin, there is no pain to numb. I don't want to be numb with him. I want to feel it all.

"What's wrong, Jasper? Do you not like the shots? You can get something different," I offer, noticing his eyes across the room and I haven't seen him drink anything all night.

"I'm not drinking tonight," he replies, eyes still across the room. I look back at whatever has his attention.

183

Abby Scott sits across the room at a small table with a couple girls I went to school with.

"Would you like me to introduce you to the redhead you can't take your eyes off of?" I ask, finally getting his attention, his eyes going wide, landing on mine.

"You know her?" he asks, almost mortified.

"Her name is Abby. She used to be my best friend. She is a really sweet girl; you would like her. From what I remember, she likes pink panty droppers to drink. The best part is, they actually work on her. Oh and yeah, the carpet matches the drapes." I chuckle as I take Jasper's shot and slam it down.

"I prefer to be a gentleman and get to know her first, but thanks for the heads up." He chuckles, shaking his head at me.

"Look, we are used to the cowboys who grew up here with all their manners and bullshit. That girl needs a man to show her how she wants to be treated. She is like me and doesn't realize there are good guys out there, and that she deserves respect. Tell her what she can get from you, as a man, not a boy trying to just get laid. Come on, I'll introduce you." I grab Jasper's hand and yank him up from his seat, practically dragging him behind me as everyone at our table cheers us on.

"Oh, let me speak first, I owe her an apology," I tell him just before she sees us coming.

I stop in front of her table. Abby looks up at me like I've grown two heads. I take a deep breath and let it out. "Abby, I'm sorry. I'm sorry that I let a guy come between us. We have been best friends since we were in diapers, and I miss you. I'm also sorry that I didn't believe Mia. You were right, I never came back from Bash, and I'm sorry I ever dropped y'all for him. I just wanted to tell you that. Also, this is Jasper. He is from New Orleans, and a really good guy who hasn't been able to take his eyes off of you all night. Give him a chance, even if he seems cringe with all his manners, he is worth it." I spit all the things out that I needed to, watching her face morph into surprise, then a sad smile, to utter amusement.

"Thank you, Savannah. We have all missed you too. Now, Jasper, is it. I have heard that men from Louisiana can go for hours on end, it's in their blood. Is that true?" she replies with a shit-eating grin on her face.

"Yeah," is all Jasper can respond, with a sly smile. I hadn't realized how good looking he is. Hmm. Probably didn't need my help, but I feel better.

"Why don't y'all come join us at our table." I motion for the girls to follow us. There are only three, but we lost one to a guy on the dance floor by the time we make it to the table. I sit on Sin's lap and give him a slightly more than PG kiss, staking my claim so that the other girl, Jill sees not to touch. Her eyes widen as I pull away from Sin. I see her mouth the word Jake.

"Twin brother, weird right?" I ask, realizing that Jill probably fucked Bash too. "Seriously, are there any of my friends that were off limits to that douche bag?" I ask, seeing the embarrassment on Abby and Jill's faces.

Shit.

"Guys, not what I meant. I'm not even upset anymore. Neither one of you has anything to be ashamed about. I can't say that I wouldn't have stayed with him had I known about y'all at the time. No judgment here. We were all his victims." I hold up my pretty blue drink, hoping to get them to lighten up and realize I'm not the raging bitch I was before. I guess it would be hard for anyone to believe who knows me here.

"For the record, I'm not my brother, and I'm completely and utterly in love with this amazing woman right here, so don't compare us please." Sin jumps into the conversation as he kisses my shoulder.

I swear the girls swoon a little.

So do I.

"I'm Joe." He sticks his hand out to Jill.

Oh, didn't see that one. I like it.

I lean into Sin, smiling, proud of myself.

"You are just full of surprises, angel."

I take out the phone Jasper brought me. Sin had him bring me a new one since we never got mine fixed. I take a selfie of us as I kiss Sin's cheek, then pull him back to the dance floor.

We all dance and drink until they close the place down. I have never had this much fun at Monkey Island. Joe quit drinking a couple of hours ago, so he drives half of our party in Jill's Tahoe, and Jasper drives the truck with the rest of us back to the cabin.

The front door is visibly open when we pull into the circle drive. I sit up out of Sin's arms, jumping out of the truck and running inside. Fuck.

See You Soon Baby Girl is painted in bright red across the rock of the fireplace. The house is completely trashed.

Everyone comes into the house quickly, gasping once they see the place.

I feel strong hands on my shoulders. I brush them off.

"Fuck this," I say as I storm out the back door, heading straight for the shed. I open the little grey barn-looking door and go in, grab what I need, and storm back out toward the house. Sin is fast on my heels, not stopping me or telling me to calm down. He knows what I'm about to do, and he is just watching me go through the motions with a smile on his face.

I stop before I go in and face this amazing man I get to call mine. "Get our things out, tell everyone to take everything they brought and load it back up. Can you get on your phone and get us a room or cabin on the lake or something please while I take care of this," I ask him, like what I'm about to do is perfectly normal.

"Of course, angel. Do what you need to do." He leans down and gives me the sweetest kiss.

Once in the cabin, I start pouring the foul-smelling liquid over every surface. It takes me a bit, but when I run out of gas, I'm out the front door, making a trail.

"Move the cars back away from the house," I yell.

Shit.

"Anyone have a match or a lighter or something to light this with?"

I obviously didn't think this through.

Charlie climbs out of the SUV and jogs to me, holding out a lighter. He seems to be enjoying himself.

"Here you go, Savvy. Are you sure..."

I cut him off. "One hundred percent. Go back to the car, Charlie. Thank you." I figured someone would ask that at some point. Lets me know I'm acting just crazy enough. I know whoever Bash had do this is here still, out in the shadows, watching. They want a show of me being scared to send back to Bash. I'll give them one, just not the one they are expecting.

I light the edge of the gasoline on the ground and jump back when it catches easier than I expected. The flame moves quickly to the cabin. I stand there with a gas can still in my hand, watching as the entire thing lights up like the bonfires we used to have below the dam. I toss the can into the flames and turn around with a sinister smile on my face.

"You fucking want me. Come and get me motherfucker!" I yell out into the woods, flipping them off with both hands, arms going in all directions. I'm sure I look insane. I walk toward the truck with my head held high. I climb in next to Sin in the back seat.

"He may not be here, but his little fucking bitches are. Let him see how that backfired on his ass." I laugh.

"That was hot, angel. It was also very smart to let him see that you are anything but weak or scared. Although, you did challenge him directly. He will come for you, but he will not get close enough to touch you," Sin whispers in my ear. I feel the heat go straight to my pussy. I smile wider, knowing he understands why I did what I did.

I realize that we will never live in peace until Bash is gone. I made up my mind the minute I saw the literal writing on the wall. I will not hand over any more of my happiness. I want him to come after me.

So that I can be the one to kill him.

"I love you, Sin," I reply, whispering in his ear as he did mine. He presses his lips to mine, cupping my cheeks in his hands. He pulls back.

"I love you too, angel." He kisses my forehead, nose, then lips playfully, making me giggle.

CHAPTER 18
Sin

The guys and I agreed last night to get up early and sneak out to get the girl's breakfast. We all come out of our rooms looking disheveled and make our way to the elevator. Jasper and Joe both have a pep in their step this morning. Joe is actually whistling. I can't say that I have ever seen either of them like this.

"So I take it your night with the girls once you left my room went well?" I ask, with the same pep they have.

"Dude, your girl burned down your brother's cabin to prove a point. Then literally told the motherfucker to come and get her. Like a challenge. It was awesome, but aren't you concerned about whoever Bash sent?" Jasper questions, stating the obvious.

"Yeah, she is something else. No, I rented us all a big cabin that is at the end of a dead-end road on the lake. It's secluded and private. They won't be making it back to New Orleans." I let them know exactly what is expected.

"Can I just say that I might be in love with Jill. She is amazing! We stayed up talking about things I've never told anyone. Yeah. I'm sure. I love her." Joe spews out like a lovesick idiot. I can't blame him, I'm in the same boat.

"What is it about these Oklahoma girls? I think I love Abby too. She is a bit broken, but she is so much more than that. She overcame your brother too. They all did," Jasper admits.

The elevator dings and the doors open to the first floor, bringing us out of our daze.

"Shit, where is Charlie?" I ask, feeling like a dick for forgetting about him.

Joe pulls out his phone, "I'll text him."

We are standing in front of the elevators still when they ding again before the doors open.

"Hey guys, sorry, Cami woke up, and well, I already had breakfast," Charlie says, waggling his eyebrows and licking his lips.

"Dude, we don't need to know, but good man. I would have been late too if Abby had woken up." Jasper chuckles, giving Charlie a fist bump.

"Alright, let's go get breakfast and get back here so that we can wake them up the right way," I finally say after the third fist bump so we can get going. I want to get back before she wakes up.

"Keep your eyes open for Bash's jackwads. I'm pretty sure Mike is one of them. We need to know how many we are dealing with. I'm guessing just his two normal lackeys, Mike and Blake. They are the only ones not on our official payroll he gets to do all of his dirty work," I explain.

"They come into the restaurant all the time. I know who we are looking for. I thought I saw a guy that looked like Blake at the club but figured that was impossible," Charlie pipes in.

"Hey, there is a café right here we can get breakfast from. It's just breakfast," Joe whines. He looks tired.

"Shit, we could have ordered room service." Jasper points at the sign in front of the restaurant. In our defense, we were all wired for sound when we got here at three a.m. We weren't paying attention to anything but our girls. I swear Savvy is a witch who has put me under her spell. I feel like I can't breathe without her.

"Let's just order it at the front desk and see what their spa packages look like for the girls. I want to handle these assholes without them getting involved. Let's get them pampered while we torture a couple of idiots. Once we are done, we can get the girls and take them to the cabin. We can take them grocery shopping when we pick them back up." I just want to get back upstairs with Savvy.

"It may not be as easy to find them and get rid of them here. We don't have access to anything to take out the trash. We may need a little help on this one. We aren't in NOLA, guys," Jasper whispers as we make it to the front desk. He is always the levelheaded one, keeping us all in line.

"The girls may actually be able to help, since they are from here. Savvy's parents have a farm, right?" Charlie asks.

I whisper, a little too loud, "Yeah, but I don't want her involved."

"How can I help you?" a bubbly blonde with pink lip gloss and a sleek ponytail asks, eye fucking each one of us, not even being shy about it.

"We need to order room service for our girlfriends, and can we see your spa packages? We want to spoil them," I reply, clearing my throat to get her attention off of Joe's crotch.

"Yes, sir, lucky girls." She nods her head and smiles wider.

We look over the large pamphlet, none of us knowing what the fuck we are looking at.

"What would you want if you could have any package you wanted?" Jasper asks, raising his eyebrows.

"Well, there are only packages in each section of services, and it depends on how much time they have," she replies, not sure how to respond.

"How about we just put my card on file, and they can pick whatever they like that will take half the day," I offer.

"Very lucky girls." The girl swoons as she takes my credit card information for the spa. We order several things off the menu for breakfast and give the rooms they go to. We all seemed to know exactly what to order our girls, which surprised me a bit, considering they just met the girls last night. Well Charlie should know; he and Cami are engaged. We stop in front of the elevators as I get a crazy idea in my head.

"Jasper, call our jeweler. I'm picking a ring when we get home.

Platinum or white gold, antique looking, but new. Nothing too flashy though," I say as we get on the elevator.

"You got it, brother," he replies with a huge smile and slaps my shoulder.

I enter the room as quietly as possible, trying not to wake Savvy. I undress and slip back in bed next to her, pulling her close to me. She rolls over, facing me. I kiss her forehead, happy just to have her back in my arms. She starts to stir slightly. I do have about fifteen minutes before breakfast shows up.

I roll her onto her back and she whines lightly in protest. I kiss her neck down to her collar bone. Her little whines turn to moans quickly as I travel farther down her perfect little body. I pull the cover over my head when I get down to her already wet pussy. Lucky for me, she slept naked last night. I move between her legs, pushing them apart. Her back arches as I bury my tongue in her sweet little cunt.

"Oh God, Sin," she moans out, bucking her hips. I push her legs up, spreading them wider, showing me her cute little rosette. I dive into her ass, eating her out like my life depends on it. I move back up to her sweet pussy, circling her clit with my tongue as I push in a finger. She grinds on my face, and I can't get enough of her. I add a finger to her pussy as I push my thumb in her ass. I jackhammer my hand in both her holes while I suck on her clit, making her shake beneath me as she clamps her knees around my head.

"Fuck... Sin... Oh God, fuck me, Sin. I need your cock." Her words are breathless, but I don't have to be told twice when she wants something. I remove my hand, peppering kisses up her body slowly.

"Please, Christian," she begs. That's all it takes. I crush my lips to hers as I slam into her in one swift motion.

"Fuck, angel, I love it when you beg for my cock." I growl when my balls hit her ass. She bites my bottom lip as she moans in my mouth. She wraps her legs around my waist as I pull back slowly, letting her body adjust to mine, and slam into her again. Her hips start to move as I circle mine when my balls hit her ass again. Our moans fill the room as I start to move faster, never parting from her perfect lips. I swallow her moans as she comes. I feel my balls tighten as I continue to pump in and out of her, our arms wrapped around each other, never able to pull her close enough, to get deep enough inside her. I come hard, over and over as I keep pumping in and out of her, slowing down as we both come down from the longest orgasm I've ever had. I roll over, taking her with me, holding her on my chest. I keep kissing her, moving down her neck to her shoulder. She trembles in my arms.

"That is the best alarm clock I have ever woke up to." She smiles, looking perfectly fucked with her wild black curls around her face, still catching her breath.

"I can wake you up like that every day for the rest of our lives if you let me." I smile back, kissing her forehead.

"Deal," she squeaks, just as there is a knock on the door with a guy yelling room service.

"When did you order room service?"

"While you were sleeping, angel."

I get up and grab a robe, putting it on as I go over to the door. I wait to open it until Savvy gets in the bathroom and closes the door. A tall slender guy dressed like a bellboy pushes in a cart with two large silver trays and several smaller ones. There is also juice and coffee as I asked. I tip him a twenty and close the door as he exits.

"Breakfast is here, angel."

Savvy comes out in a plush white robe matching mine. We both sit on the terrace overlooking the golf course while we eat our breakfast.

"It's really pretty here," I say as I take a bite out of a strawberry. Savvy sighs.

"Yeah, too bad dipshit ruined our vacay. What are we going to do about the asshats Bash sent?" She doesn't beat around the bush.

"Angel, the guys and I are going to take care of them while you girls have a spa day. I would prefer the other girls don't get involved with this," I explain.

195

"What about this girl? I am already involved. I provoked him and them to give me their best shot. That may have been dumb on my part, but I'm over this. I want them all dead." She lets me know quickly that she will not back down. God, I love her fire.

"How about you let me handle this one, and you can help with Bash when the time comes. Deal?" I try to bargain.

"Fine, but what do you plan on doing with the bodies? If I was smart we would have found them and let them burn in the house. I was a bit irrational, but I won't be from now on." She acts like she has done this before.

"How long have you planned to kill someone?"

"Since I was seven, and I met my mom's first boyfriend. I had an entire plan drawn up by the time I was sixteen on how to kill someone on Grand Lake and get away with it. Can you get access to a woodchipper?" she asks, making me laugh.

"Okay, you have my attention. What would you do with a woodchipper, angel?" I ask, amused.

"Well, after you kill whoever, wait for the gates to open, take a woodchipper to the falls and throw in the body parts. Fish food, also no body, no crime." She huffs, proud of herself. Not gonna lie, it's smart.

"Oh, how would you get power to the woodchipper?" I ask, genuinely curious what she will come up with next.

"There is a regular plug in your trucks backseat." She sighs.

"How would you clean the woodchipper?"

"Bleach, duh."

"When will the gates be open again?"

"I don't know, when it rains enough, I guess. That could be a month from now." She looks bummed.

"What about hogs? Do you know anyone who has hogs?" I ask, not believing I'm considering it.

"Yeah, Pops has about fifty on the back west side of the ranch. Why?"

"Because hogs eat everything, bone and all."

"Yeah, but that would take time. Wild boars up on the bluffs of Lake Mont Shores would be better, no one would be up there looking for anything. You could just dump them and walk away without worry; they'll be gone within a couple of days." I'm beginning to think my lifestyle is just in her blood, because of who her mother is. She doesn't even act like we just talked about murdering people as she takes a bite of French toast. I have hit the jackpot with my angel.

"Where is Lake Mont Shores?" I ask, not knowing if it's on the map and I don't want to have it on my GPS.

"It's past the turnoff to Little Blue, about ten miles, you'll see the signs, follow them to the bluffs. Let's talk about something less morbid with breakfast, yeah?" She smiles at me, then starts laughing as she pops a grape in her mouth.

Shit, maybe I pushed her too hard to let it all out. Is she losing it, or is this really her being okay?

"Angel, are you sure you are okay with all of this? I can get it all done and over with to where you won't even know it happened."

"No! I'm not fragile. I need to know they are taken care of, then I want their phones. We can fuck with Bash a little bit too. Then we head home on Friday instead of Sunday. We send him pics of us here, letting him think we are still in Oklahoma. It will buy us a few days before he realizes we are back in NOLA. You have a lot more leverage there than you do here. I want to be smart about this. We can enjoy the next couple of days, knowing exactly what is coming next and be ahead of him. I have thought a lot about this, and I know what we have to do. We just have to be smarter than him." Savvy is not fragile at all. She is strong and has brains. Fuck, I hadn't thought past taking care of the fuckers working for Bash.

"You're right, my savage angel. We do need to be smart, and luckily, you are smart enough for the both of us."

"Thank you for seeing that I'm more than just a pretty face and a great lay, love." She chuckles, giving me shit. I love that she is smart and sassy. I even love the power she has over me. There is nothing I wouldn't do to protect this woman. Including killing my brother.

197

Luckily the girls didn't give us too much shit about getting them a spa day without us. I could tell they were shocked and appreciated the gesture. They even have a full salon, so the girls can get their hair and nails done. Savvy was upset about missing out on taking out dumb and dumber but was over the moon about a spa day once she realized what a spa day actually is.

"Where the hell do we start to look for these idiots?" Jasper asks, smiling from ear to ear as we walk out of the hotel to the parking lot.

Charlie starts laughing. "Well, won't be too difficult since they are obviously staying here too." He points to a blacked-out Hummer.

"Shit, that's Bash's Hummer. Good eyes, Charlie." Joe slaps his shoulder.

We all walk over to the vehicle. I open the driver's side door to see both idiots passed out in the front seat. White powder is spread all over the dashboard. They actually look kinda pale. I reach up to feel for a pulse as his head falls to the side in my direction, his dilated pupils clouded over.

"They overdosed. Joe, check the other guy." He does as I ask, opening the passenger door. I already know the answer. There is a baggy laying in the center console with a fleur-de-lis and a skull in the center imprinted on the baggy. That's our brand.

"Load up, boys. Throw them in the back. We're gonna have to go straight to the cabin, drop them, then go buy some ice chests."

We pull into the steep driveway to the log cabin. It's huge, and there are no neighbors for miles. There are even paddle boats on the bank. The dock out back already has the boat I rented in the slip ready to go. We are tucked back into a little cove area where people who pass by on the lake in their boats probably have no idea this is even back here. You can hear the sounds of all the boats and jet skis in the distance, but you can't see them.

"Let's get this shit over with and enjoy the rest of the week with the girls," I tell them, knowing they feel the same way. Everyone nods, except Charlie. He just smiles. "You can take a walk if you need to. We get it, but you also know never to talk about it," I explain, wondering how he feels about this.

"No, I'm good. These assholes held us at gunpoint, telling Cami all the bad things they were going to do to her if she didn't get Savvy there. I know who you guys are and what you do. I'm also getting married soon and know that I have to provide for the family we create in NOLA. It's our home, and I would rather be on the good brother's side," he replies, letting us know he is all in. I will make sure he and his family will always be taken care of, just like my guys.

It takes us an hour and a half to go to the store and get what we need and come back. We decided to get all the breakfast stuff to make it ourselves in the morning, using the four coolers to store our beer and food on the way home.

We put Mike and Blake in the shower with the curtains drawn while we were gone, just in case. There are four bathrooms and five bedrooms.

"Me and Jasper can take Mike in the shower he is in. Joe, you and Charlie can take Blake's skinny ass to the master bath downstairs to chop him up," I tell them. They all move except Charlie.

"I have to cut him up? Why can't we just put the whole body in with the wild hog things? Have you actually googled what we need to do or are you just assuming?" He is hyperventilating at this point.

"I just assumed. Charlie, get one of the two phones we found in the Hummer and google it. If they are traceable, at least it will be to them or Bash," I tell him. He does as he is told. He is too good for this line of work. He can help with the real estate side of things when we get home. I would prefer to keep them on the legit side of my business, being Savvy's friends. Now Jill and Abby will just have to be able to accept it like Savvy has. It's who we are. We were born into this life; it wasn't a choice.

Four hours later, the bodies have been dismembered and dropped in the thick woods where we spotted nothing but wild boars. Savvy was right, there are really steep cliffs up there. It wasn't easy to get to.

"Time to clean up, boys," Joe hollers as we walk back to the Hummer.

Charlie visibly gags again. He only passed out once and threw up twice but refused to quit helping. He is a good guy.

We only bought three bottles of bleach, not to look suspicious. Another hour and a half of cleaning up our mess, and ourselves, we are back at the hotel picking up the four most beautiful girls in all of Oklahoma. We found them at the bar, sipping cocktails.

My heart drops when Savvy stands up in a beautiful yellow satin dress that ties around her neck, leaving her back almost bare down to just above her ass. Brown wedges help accentuate her toned legs. Her hair is done in soft curls instead of her wild ones I'm so enchanted by. Her makeup is soft and natural with just hints of color on her lips and cheeks. She looks stunning. I feel my dick twitch when her eyes meet mine.

CHAPTER 19
Savvy

I have had the most relaxing day knowing that I don't have to worry about anything besides what I'm doing at the moment. At this very moment, I'm sipping the yummiest Moscato I have ever tried. I had a massage, facial, mani, and pedi. I have been dusted, scrubbed, waxed, and polished to perfection. Even my hair is fucking sparkly and pristine. I do feel pretty. I just hope Sin likes it. All the girls went all out, getting several treatments that would be the most beneficial to their needs. The guys were smart to let us choose what we wanted to do.

I hear Cami squeal first, jumping out of her seat to go greet Charlie. I smile wide when I see Sin's reflection in the mirror behind the bar. I turn in my seat and stand, purposefully showing him my back first. I turn toward him, moving my chair out of the way. He looks delicious in his black shorts and white V-neck tee. When I look up and meet his eyes, heat runs straight to my pussy. That's my Sin.

"You look gorgeous, angel." Sin cups my cheek and gives me a sweet kiss. He looks normal. I can't tell if the asshats have been taken care of or not. All the guys look like they went out playing golf all day.

"You look pretty handsome yourself. Have a nice time with the guys?" I ask, eyeing him. He gets it and smiles wide.

"We killed it on the golf course. Charlie did a hack up job on the first few holes but got the hang of it quickly."

My eyes go wide as I look at sweet, innocent Charlie. He smirks then gives me a wink. "Yeah, it wasn't that bad. I don't think I'm going to make a career out of it or anything, but I wouldn't mind playing a round or two back home when y'all feel like it." I get what he is saying and can't believe he helped. He is such a peaceful soul; I can't imagine him harming anyone.

The guys slap his shoulder and they all bump fists.

Sin leans down to my ear and whispers, "It's done, angel. You can relax." I let out a breath I didn't realize I was holding. I wrap my arms around his neck, hugging him. I pull back and reach up on my toes to kiss him. He puts his hand on my bare back, sending shockwaves to my core. My body reacts to him on every level.

"I want details later," I whisper to him as my pussy clenches at the thought of this man killing for me. I can't wait to do the same for him.

"Ready to go to dinner, or do y'all want to have a drink at the bar first?" Sin asks the group.

"I could use a drink." Charlie speaks first.

"Yeah, I think we could all use a couple of drinks first," Jasper pipes in.

"Okay, we just got our second round, we should finish those first anyway," Jill says sweetly. She has her arms wrapped around Joe's waist, while he has one arm wrapped around her tiny body. They look good together. I notice Abby and Jasper are just as close. The way we all gushed over our guys all day, you would think we have all been together forever, like Cami and Charlie. They are couple goals! Cami is in full wedding planning mode. She wants a Christmas wedding which doesn't give us a ton of time to plan. She already asked me to be her maid of honor and she asked Jill and Abby to be her bridesmaids.

Apparently, Joe asked Jill last night to come back to NOLA with us and Jasper asked Abby this morning. Cami and I have been begging them to just come and see if they like it. Sin's place is huge, and Joe and Jasper already live there with him from what they told the girls. Cami and Charlie are going to continue staying there until she feels comfortable going back to her house. I don't know if she will ever be able to stay there with what happened. She is still having nightmares.

I will make Bash pay for what he did to her and Charlie. He may not have physically harmed them, but the emotional damage he caused is just as bad. He will pay for what he has done to all of us.

We finish our drinks and all take a few shots to get the night started. We had an amazing dinner at Arrowhead Marina and decide to just go to the liquor store to get what everyone likes so we can make our own drinks at the cabin. I have to remind myself that I burned down the cabin that, of course, comes to mind. I don't feel bad about burning it to the ground. I smile at the thought of it in flames. Like Sin said last night, we can rebuild a new cabin to make new memories in. In a way, I think burning down the place that was once so precious to me actually helped me close the chapter of Jake here. I know Jill and even Abby watched it burn with smiles on their faces, remembering all of what they had been through there as well. I think of Mia and hope that when she opens the video that Jill sent her of it burning down, it helps her heal a little too.

We let the guys go into the liquor store as we shout all our wants through the window.

"I've decided I'm moving to NOLA! I know it's crazy, but I can't imagine not being with Joe. Maybe he's the one. I have never felt like this. Am I crazy?" Jill spits the words out as soon as the guys are out of earshot.

"No crazier than me! I'm coming too! I want to be with Jasper," Abby squeals.

"We are going to have so much fun! You guys will love NOLA!" Cami is bouncing in her seat smiling.

"I love NOLA, and I can't imagine living anywhere else now that I've been there. There is art, music, and dancing on every corner. People are happy and live the way they want in the Quarter with no judgment. You can feel the magic buzzing through your veins as you

205

walk through certain areas, especially the cathedral." I giggle, now excited to go back home with my friends.

The boys come back out with several big brown bags and get back in. When we pull up to the cabin, I'm in shock. I've never been to this area before. It's perfectly secluded. There is a giant wood-carved black bear wearing a baby blue studded fishing hat by the steps to the front door holding a sign saying "Welcome Glampers". I inwardly chuckle.

We all unload everything and head in. The cabin is decorated beautifully in all shades of blue, white, and cream. It has a rustic feel with butcher block countertops and cedar beams stained a nice pecan color while the wood floor is natural pine, showcasing all the natural colors of the wood through a clear gloss shine. There is a large dark brown leather sectional facing a huge river rock fireplace with a mantle matching the beams and at least an eighty-five-inch TV is showcased above it. It's very open and natural light flows through the floor-to-ceiling windows, giving a perfect view of the cove. It's stunning.

"Our room is this way, angel." Sin grabs my hand, pulling me into another just as equally stunning room decorated in the same colors.

"This will be our room for the rest of the week. What do you think?"

"It's beautiful. I'm sorry you had to rent this place. I know it must have been expensive, and the spa day. It's too much and I don't need all this. I just need you." I feel awful he spent so much on something he shouldn't have had to. I don't deserve all this.

"It's nothing. I'm actually thinking I like this location and was hoping you did too. I called the owner, and if you love it, it's ours. I just have to email the docs and tell him you agreed. If you don't, and want something different, we can look some more. If you would rather rebuild where your cabin was, I understand that too. It's up to you, angel." I am in shock at what he just said. I don't know what to say.

"This is all too much right now. It's beautiful, and, of course, I love it, but why? Why are you doing all of this with me? For me?" I can't help but think that this is all going to end at some point when he figures out that I'm not that special. I know part of it is the alcohol making me think about this more than I should. Remembering how I had my heart ripped out of my chest and stomped on.

"Savvy, I love you. Don't start doubting us now. We are just getting started, angel. I want us to have our own place here to come whenever you want. If you want to come for a few weeks and spend time with your dad or if we just need a weekend to relax and come to the lake. It's plenty big enough to bring all of our friends, and if we have littles someday, it's big enough for them too. The question is, why not."

My mind is spinning at the idea that this man is trying to plan a future with me.

"You just said littles, like in kids?" I ask wide-eyed. I know that he is all I have ever dreamed of, and he is saying all the things that I actually want to hear but is it real.

"Yes, do you not want kids?" he asks, as if he doesn't have an opinion on the matter when he is the one who brought it up.

"I think I do, but I don't know. I have always thought that if I did have kids, it would just be later, ya know? I guess I really hadn't thought about it. It's not like I have had steady relationships. Bash brought it up once a few weeks ago and the idea honestly repulsed me," I admit.

"Does the idea of having a baby with me repulse you?" he asks. He is showing no emotion to say whether my answer will affect him either way. I think for a second before I answer, trying to imagine having a baby with Sin.

"No. Actually, I can picture what they will look like, how you will rub cocoa butter on my belly every night before bed as you talk to our little like he can hear you. I'm not saying I don't want kids, just not yet. I want to live a little first and enjoy us. In a few years, we will see. Plus, with your line of work, I don't know what that would look

207

like with children. I'm just surprised you are thinking about it already."

"I actually hadn't until I was trying to talk you into the cabin. I pictured a couple of dark curly-headed boys and the tiniest little girl chasing each other around the island in the kitchen. I want us to have a normal life, together. Kids. No kids. It doesn't matter as long as I'm with you. I know I have fallen hard, Savvy. I know it's fast, but I don't care, I love you. I want to be with you forever, angel."

"I love you too, Christian. I don't understand it, because it has all happened so fast, but I know it's right."

"Of course, it's right, angel. You were made for me, and I you. Okay, enough heavy talk for tonight. Just think about it, please, angel. Let's go back with our friends, have some drinks, and then I will bring you back in here and worship your body the way it was meant to be." Sin wraps his arms around me, lowering his lips to mine, giving me a sweet kiss.

"Deal, but I plan on worshiping your body this time. I'm feeling a little dominant tonight." I look up into his eyes to see his reaction, giving him a lustful smirk as I bite my lower lip. I have never acted as a Domme, but the thought of having complete and total control over his body is making my entire cunt throb.

"If that is what you want, angel, I'm yours to play with however you like," he replies in the sexiest almost growl. Fuck, a blissful roll of lust sweeps through my core just by him saying he is mine. He has no idea the kinds of things I would let him do to me. I'm curious to see just how far he will let me go.

"Baby Outlaw" by Elle King flows through the surround sound of the large cabin. It's one in the morning and we are all dancing and having fun. Sin is dancing with me, making me want him more.

"Shots!" Cami yells from the large island. I can't help the thoughts of Sin bending me over the thick butcher block, fucking me senseless. I decide in that moment that I need to just let go and let whatever will be ... be.

I turn to Sin. "I want us to buy this place. We can sell the land that the other cabin was on and use the money for it so that I feel like I contributed. If you will agree to that, then I want it to be our family vacation home. We can VRBO it out and it will pay for itself within a few years. What do you say?"

His smile reaches his eyes. He picks me up, twirls us around, and kisses me. "Deal, angel, but only if you are sure. Let's sleep on it and decide in the morning."

"Nope, send the email. I don't want to overthink this. I always overthink everything. I love you and I'm tired of trying to find reasons that you will leave me and never come back. I would rather enjoy every minute I get with you in this lifetime than second-guess it because it might not happen. I want to take this risk with you, because if I don't, I will regret it for the rest of my life. I'm all in. With you." I try to explain how I'm feeling, and I know I'm probably not making much sense, but I don't care. I want to shout it from the rooftops that I am in love with this man. My Sin.

Sin moves toward me quickly, picking me up, smashing his lips to mine. He pulls back, kisses my forehead, nose, and lips again, making me giggle, before putting me down. "As you wish, angel." He pulls out his phone, and within two minutes has sent the email, closed his phone and is picking me up again, twirling us around. I giggle at the fact that this will now be our home away from home. I look at our friends around the island in their own little bubbles and smile, knowing this is my family now.

"I'm getting tired." I stretch my arms above my head and wink at Sin, hoping he takes the hint.

"Yeah, me too. We are gonna go to bed, guys. Goodnight." Sin tries to act tired but fails miserably with the cheesy grin he has plastered on his face.

"Go on, we all know y'all are just a couple horny toads," Cami yells out at us as we close the door to our room and burst out laughing.

"So, angel, you want to play with me tonight?" he asks in a low husky voice as he rips his shirt off and starts coming closer, taking slow purposeful steps toward me.

I nod my head as this perfect man undresses in front of me. He stands directly in front of me naked. He drops down to his knees and bows his head. "I am yours, angel."

I start to undress as I circle him. I don't want to actually hurt him. I want to be in control. I want to say what goes for once. I let the silky dress hit the floor in front of him. He keeps his eyes down. I step out of it and stand in front of him in only a thong and my wedges. He still keeps his head down.

"Look at me," I order. He does as I ask. I see the lust in his eyes, but the fire is gone. I realize that I am not this person. I don't know what I'm doing.

"I'm not a Dominant, Sin. I just want to be in control. I never have been." I try to explain and see the light in his eyes again.

"You are always in control with me. I want you to have control if that's what you need. Trust me?" he asks.

"Of course, I do."

He gets up and goes over to his bag, pulling out one black and one bright blue necktie. He lies on the bed with his arms above his head. "Come tie me up, angel. You will have total control."

I do as he says and tie both wrists pretty securely to the bedposts. I remove my wedges as "Wildest Dreams" by Taylor Swift comes through the speakers in the bedroom. I'm sure Cami made that happen.

I remove my thong and watch Sin's already hard dick grow even bigger. He is a grower not a shower, and damn it gets big. I get on the bed slowly, making him watch me. I move straight to his dick, barely grazing it with my fingers, down to his balls, lightly touching them. I continue to tease with soft touches, making him hiss and suck in a breath. I move myself between his legs, keeping my eyes on his as I lower my mouth to his tip, sticking my tongue out to lick off the precum already beginning to bead up. He throws his head back as I take him down my throat, moaning as I come back up to the tip. I bob on him for a bit, deep throating him until he is moaning. When he starts thrusting his hips, I pull my mouth off with a pop and move to straddle him. I move my pussy up and down his shaft, soaking his dick before I position him at my entrance and slowly take him in. I throw my head back and moan as my body stretches to accommodate his size.

"Oh God, angel, you feel so good." He moans as I start to move. I place my hands on his perfectly tatted chest to hold myself up, moving my hips until I hit that perfect spot. I start moving faster but miss his hands on my body. I try to get lost in the moment, but I realize that I won't get off until he is touching me. How the tables have turned. I reach up and untie his hands. "Take me, Sin, take it all," I say as my orgasm builds.

He wastes no time flipping us over, crushing his mouth to mine as he jackhammers into me. He is holding me close, getting deeper with every thrust. I come hard as his name leaves my lips in a harsh rasp. He pulls out and flips me over before I have completely come down from my high. I feel his hand start to rub my pussy, moving my cum up to my ass.

He slams his cock into me as he inserts a finger in my ass, taking my orgasm to new heights. "Oh fuck, yes, take my ass, Sin. Please." I beg for him to just do it. I want it, my body wants it. He inserts another finger in my ass, stretching me.

"Oh God, oh God." My voice is a whisper. "Slap my ass and go back to the place only you have been. Please." He does as I ask as he pulls out and just puts the tip in my ass.

"Yes. Yes," I yell out as I back up into his dick. He slaps my ass, hard. I can't help the moan that escapes even though it hurts for a few seconds, but the shocks of pleasure override the pain. He moves in and out slowly, making me push back. I move my hips as he starts to move faster, almost twerking into his dick. I start to rub my clit as he picks up the pace. My entire body almost convulses as I come again and again. Sin doesn't relent. He is practically growling when he comes, slapping my ass again, sending another shockwave of pleasure through me before I come down from the last one. We both collapse on the bed, breathing heavily as he pulls me onto his chest.

"You okay, angel? Was I too rough?" he asks, kissing my temple.

"You can fuck my ass anytime you want. I had no idea how much I would like it until the other night. Now I want it all the time," I reply breathlessly.

He kisses my head, then lifts me and stands us up, carrying me bridal style. I lay my head on his shoulder, still coming down and exhausted. "Let's take a bath, angel."

CHAPTER 20
Savvy

I have never felt as treasured as I have in the last few days. Sin has turned my entire world on its axis, and I can't imagine my life without him now. We have had our fun with Bash, sending him texts that seem like the ones the idiots would send him. We even had Cami go outside our window and take a video of us looking like we were having sex, but it was just for show. We have played the part perfectly, acting as if he still has a leg up on us.

Sin let me read all the messages on the phone they found on Mike. I can't believe some of the things they wanted to do to my friends and Sin. Mike took a liking to Cami and actually asked Bash to keep her as a pet. Like what? A fucking dog? I saw red on that one and was a little pissed I didn't get to help chop the bastard up myself.

Abby, Jill, and even Cami understands now what we are up against with Bash and want to help. Cami seemed to relax a bit more once she knew the guys took care of the idiots. We all have. We have been out on the lake every day, going to Dripping Springs and Goat Island to take the goats some apples. I was proud that none of us jumped off Dripping Springs topless. Jill was close, but when Joe said he would take his trunks off and jump in with her and fuck her in the water in front of everyone if she did, she backed down. It took her a few minutes to not take it as a challenge. I think she knew he would and kinda wanted him to claim her in that way.

Joe is good for Jill. She was always a wild one in high school and may have met her match. Joe is more of a Dom like Jill prefers. She told us about him tying her up in the hotel their first night. He is a kinky fucker, and she loves it.

Abby has her kinks too. She told us about Jasper liking to use toys and all kinds of BDSM play. She let him fuck her ass before he fucked her pussy. Apparently, she likes being tied up in all sorts of ways and prefers anal. I get it. I practically beg Sin to fuck my ass now. I don't know if Sin will ever be able to tie me up or do any of the things I'm still not sure I want. He is so afraid he will hurt me. It's sweet, but I want to give him total control. I know he would never hurt me intentionally, but I also know if he accidentally did, he would never forgive himself.

"All packed, angel?"

"Yup, and ready to go home. I can't wait to get back and get all my stuff unpacked at your place."

"Our place, angel. I want it to feel like your home too."

Sin has been on this kick of what's mine is yours and I would be lying if I said it wasn't nice, but I still want to hold onto my independence. I will not accept handouts, even from the love of my life.

"I know, I know, our place. It's just going to take some getting used to."

"You have the rest of our lives to get used to it. I have to admit, I'm ready to get home and have you to myself more."

"We will still be with our friends; they live there too." I try and remind him we have roommates.

"Angel, the compound is huge, and everyone has their own wing. Each wing has been made into a personal home. I know I didn't get to show you much before we left, but I think you will be surprised at how much less we will see everyone."

"I guess I hadn't thought about how big it is. We can still have meals together and stuff though, right?" I ask because I really have no idea how big it is. I mean, the show made it look big, but that was just a set that was built in Conyers, not the actual place.

"Of course. We can live as one big family, or we can have as much space as we want from each other. It's really up to all of us." He reassures me with a sweet kiss.

"I know we will all want our space at times, but I like the idea of us all being together. I feel like everyone will be safe if we are all together."

"Don't worry, angel, we will take care of business and all be safe soon. I promise. He will never get near you or any of our friends again."

"We have to stick to the plan, that means he will get near me one more time. Then we can all live happily ever after."

"You chose this plan, I never agreed to it." He furrows his brows at me from across the bed as he finishes folding and packing his things.

"We all voted, and you lost, babes. We are sticking with the plan. I can hold my own, I promise." I try to reassure him, but I know he isn't happy with what I have decided is the best course of action.

"Mike got another text after we pushed the limits with that video. Bash wants blood, angel, and I'll be damned if he gets any of yours."

"What does this one say? I'm coming to get you? I'm so scared." I yawn for dramatic effect.

"This is not a joke. I need you to be safe and take this seriously if we are going to beat him at his own game without anyone else getting hurt. I also texted your bio mother, she knows you are coming home. Have you decided whether you want to meet her yet?"

He catches me off guard. He hasn't brought her up in a couple of days. He told me all about her when I asked and even more about Lottie. I wish I had got to know my sister. Growing up with a dick-head brother sucked, but I think having a sister would have been nice. It just sucks that I will never actually know her. I don't want that to happen with my birth mother. I know I'll regret it if I don't look her in the eyes at least once and ask why she gave me up. I don't blame her for my upbringing or the lack there of. I just need to know how she could give her baby away. I don't know if it will make a difference, but I want to hear it from her.

217

"I want to meet her, but I'm nervous. What if she doesn't like me?" Sin busts out laughing, comes around the bed, and pulls me into a bear hug, kissing the top of my head.

"She will love you, angel. She thought that you didn't want anything to do with her when your eighteenth birthday came and went and she never heard from you or your pops. She said since you turned twenty-one this year that she thought maybe, but when she still hadn't heard anything, she tried to get ahold of your pops to see if there was a chance. When she finally got ahold of him, he said you didn't know about her, and to just let you live a normal life and leave you alone."

"I still don't understand why Pops lied to me my entire life. I get that she is in the drug business too, but Pops was obviously into some shady shit in NOLA and God only knows where else. What makes him think he is any better than her?" My mind is still reeling with the fact that Scarlett isn't my mother and that my dad lied about everything. Even my age. I didn't go back to the ranch and now I'm glad I didn't. She wanted to see me. She waited for me to come to her.

"Angel, there's more. She called me this morning when I went for my run."

"And?"

"Sylvia sent Bash the year you turned eighteen. She knew you lived in Oklahoma, close to Grand Lake, but that's all she knew. She sent him, hoping to find you and see if you knew about her and bring you back. Bash said he never found you. She had no reason to think he was lying, so she let it go, until recently. She had no idea about y'all's relationship, or what he did to your friends. She just wants to know you. I'm gonna be honest here, she is a bitch, but I think she is being sincere."

"He fucking knew Sylvia was my mother the whole time?" I'm seething at this point.

"No, she just said that you were someone she needed to find, not who you actually are. She said your name would be Savannah Barrett, around eighteen years old, that's it. She didn't want to risk it with how he felt about Lottie. I knew they had an affair at one point. I caught her in a lie about Bash, then Jasper followed them and confirmed it. I let it go because she promised it would never happen again, that she loved me. I found her diaries after she died and I read a bit, but I quit after the realization hit that I wasn't the one she was in love with. I was the better choice according to Sylvia. That's the only reason she chose me. Sylvia knew about the affair the whole time but told her the day she married she would have to cut it off and be a good wife." He wears a mask, shadowing his emotion.

"Christian, I'm sorry. This is opening so many old wounds for you."

"Shh, angel, I told you that in order for you to heal, you needed to let it out and be honest. I'm doing that with you. I haven't talked about any of this since the day we had Lottie's celebration of life, other than with you. I need to finally heal from this too. I guess I'm trying to practice what I preach." Sin hugs me a little tighter.

"Thank you for opening up. I know that wasn't easy to admit. Just know that I love you, and I will always be here if you need to heal from anything." I want him to feel it all. I know it sucks, but when I let go and let myself feel it all with Sin, it helped me heal. I want to be that for him too.

Sin holds me close for a few more minutes, pulls back, kisses my forehead, and says, "Let's go home, angel."

I get butterflies instantly thinking about our home. Not just what the home is, or where it is, because honestly, home could be anywhere as long as I'm with Sin.

We all pack into the three vehicles, deciding we are all driving back together. Jill and Abby only packed a couple suitcases and had a couple of boxes each. The guys said they could ship everything to NOLA, but like me, they don't have much. Sin and I drop the Jeep off at the closest Hertz and hop into the middle captain's seats in Bash's blacked-out Hummer with Jasper driving. Abby is riding shotgun, and Cami and Charlie sit in the back row of seats making out. They are so cute.

I decide to finish the book I had on the plane, loving the twist ending. I remember I have a few THC gummies I picked up at Minerva in Langley. I get them out of my purse. "Anyone not driving want something to help them relax?"

"Oh, yes please." Cami holds her hand out from behind me, and Charlie follows suit.

Sin just looks at me as I pop the sour watermelon gummy in my mouth and chew, making a face when it gets to the weed taste and swallowing with only a slight gag.

"Yeah, I'm good, angel. That face tells me I won't like it." Sin laughs at me, reclines his seat, and goes back to playing on his phone. Abby finally says yes too and takes one.

Within thirty minutes, we are all laughing and dancing and singing song after song. I decide to lay back after belting out "Bitch" by Meredith Brooks. Sin leans over and kisses my temple and covers me up with my new favorite knitted baby blue blanket I took from our cabin. I snuggle up to it and take a deep breath, inhaling my favorite scent, Sin.

Bash

Looks like I'll be seeing my girl soon. I will punish her for fucking my brother, and she will forget all about him once he is in the ground. The boys have been keeping a close eye on my girl. I could have done without the fuck video, but I have to admit, I have jacked off to it multiple times.

"Are you ready to go, baby?" Doc has her overnight bag in her hands, ready to go to the lake. I told her we needed to get away, just the two of us to help me heal. The rehab facility is just too depressing, and a weekend with her on a boat would make it all better. She practically jumped at the idea. She really is a nice pet to have. I may keep her around after I get my Savvy girl back. I may also send her over to the highest bidder if she does good this weekend, depends on how much time I have to train her properly.

"Yeah, let's go, baby girl. I can't wait to see you in that tiny bikini I picked out." I lay it on thick with her because she is like every other chick out there and just wants to feel loved and pampered. She has daddy issues, so she is easier than most.

We leave her penthouse apartment in the city and head for the airport. She got me out of the rehab facility last night so we could have a night together at her place before we flew into Oklahoma this morning. She even thought going back to where the trauma occurred would help. This bitch is just too easy.

She has no idea that Savvy burned down the cabin. I'll put on a good show for her when we get there. I'll have a fucking breakdown in front of her and then fuck her ass to make myself feel better. She knows it's the release I need. I'll find them while she is tied up waiting for me. It will be a fun game to play, for me. Savvy will come around once my brother is gone and she can put her focus back on me.

I get in the driver's seat and start up the red Audi R8. I undo my slacks and pull my dick out, stroking it a few times, getting it hard picturing Savvy. Doc gets in and notices, giving a huff.

"I'm not ruining my makeup; I just spent an hour trying to look pretty for you." She obviously doesn't get the assignment. I reach up and grab the back of her hair, making her cry out, and shove her face on my dick.

"I didn't ask, baby. Suck my dick before I yank you out of the car and fuck your ass again for getting sassy." She sobs but starts deep throating my cock immediately.

"Good girl," I praise her.

I keep ahold of her hair and force her head up and down faster, thinking of my Savvy girl. I will say that the good ole doc here gives way better head than Savvy, but nothing will ever top her sweet little cunt. I feel my balls tighten as I picture Savvy looking up at me with those mesmerizing eyes. I push the bitch's head down on my cock as I come down her throat, pumping my hips harder as she flails, trying to breathe. I pull her head off my dick and practically toss her back over to her seat.

"Thanks, I can relax a bit now on the drive. Just wait till you see what I have planned for you on the plane." I give her a wicked smile. My dick gets hard again as I watch tears fall out of her smeared black eyes, running down her cheeks as she tries to hold in her sobs.

"You will eventually just get to where I don't have to ask, you will just do it out of habit, and because you want to, baby girl. You are doing good as a new sub. I knew you would. I will fuck you on the plane, maybe even in the airport. You will learn that I will fuck any part of you I want, when I want, and how I want. Understand?"

"Yes, sir," she blubbers out. She fixes herself back up on the drive to the airport. Stupid girl, I'm just going to fuck it up worse once we get there. She doesn't understand yet that when she pretties herself up, all I want to do is fuck it up. She will quit trying so hard and only do what I tell her very soon.

CHAPTER 21
Sin

We have been back in NOLA for three blissful days of fun and I have been trying to spend as much time alone with Savvy as she lets me. We have been taking the girls on tour after tour of the city to let them get accustomed to the culture and food without worry, knowing exactly where Bash is and what he is doing.

Bash was last spotted in Ketchum this morning in his rental car getting gas at the Woodshed with a pretty woman in the front seat with big black sunglasses on. They left there, then headed out of town.

At least she is still alive. He hadn't said anything about her since they arrived. He followed them to the Turnpike; I'm assuming he is on his way here. Turns out her friend TJ came in handy and let us know when Bash arrived and where all he went. Luckily, I asked him to take her pops to our new cabin. I knew Bash wouldn't be able to figure out his guys were gone until he got out and would find someone to take it out on.

He wanted her pops as leverage and would have got him had we left him at home. Bash did stay at the ranch for a while. Scarlett's car was there so he could have tried to use her as leverage, but he didn't. He just keeps sending messages saying what is going to happen to Savvy and her friends once he gets a hold of them. The girls don't even seem worried. They just laugh every time he threatens them.

Now, we aren't answering his messages, but we can see who all is.

Kind of.

This dark web shit Bash is a part of goes pretty high up on the food chain. That's just the ones we can figure out. I have every contact in Mike's phone on who is and isn't involved in Bash's madness.

I would be lying if I said that the list was short. We have taken out most of the rats that we know on our end and are watching others to get more info on whoever they have pulled into it on one little phone, mostly the ones labeled as pawns weren't encrypted as heavily.

Jasper is a very skilled hacker and can get into anyone's personal shit online in a matter of minutes with just a phone number. Message logs with conversations on just how deep Bash was into the Black Market. We have found some pretty disturbing shit on half the elite male population in New Orleans and way beyond. Bash is significantly more disturbed than I could have ever imagined. We were so focused only on Bash's messages from the new number we didn't pay attention to the rest of Mike's contacts until Savvy asked.

Bash's new business ventures weren't in drugs. He has become the broker of the fucking year in training and selling women to elite men who want a pretty complacent trophy on their arms for sick parties they have to share these girls with other buyers and brokers. They keep them as pets at home and refer to them as such. One says he has a new red retriever who finally got her training in line when Bash took her for a week, basically promoting the fact that he not only can get you pets, but train ones you already have as well.

The picture with the message is a pretty, very young, redhead with sad pleading brown eyes and freckles. She has a studded pink diamond collar on with someone holding a matching leash. She is on her knees wearing a see-through baby pink gown that you could visibly see her pierced peachy-colored nipples through. Her hands rest on her thighs, showing sharp, pointy baby pink nails. Her pink pouty lips are spread apart with what Savvy called a horse bit that has been modified to fit her specifically. It has a black rubber bar that fits into her mouth and a metal chain on each side that holds it in place around her head. I can't get the image out of my head. All I can think about is helping her.

Bash started out small a few years ago, about the same time he came back from Oklahoma, and it took off from there. He has finders who pick up these girls who are new to town and they willingly leave with said finder to go have a good time. She is never seen or heard from again and no one ever remembers a new face in town when there are hundreds a day. Their families never even know whether they made it to town or not. They just vanish along the way as far as they are told.

The problem is, the finders are under the names of parishes with a bishop chess piece, which I assume they are a finder in. Their phones are completely encrypted to where it only gives the parish no matter what he does and nothing more. All the contacts are labeled as emojis of chess pieces with one other emoji. Bash has a fleur-de-lis and the king piece as his contact name. I know it's Bash by the way he acts like he is big shit on here.

We can't get the queen, or the knights either, pawns just have their names. Obviously, pawns are expendable. They are only there to take the fall and be errand boys, moving pets. However, the pawns talk more to each other and give real names, making it easier to figure out some of the contacts.

This is the first hack I have ever seen Jasper have trouble with, but he is determined to crack it. It's only a matter of time before he gets all the names. The problem is, we are running out of time. We're getting ready to have to put the girls on lockdown until we get him, and they are not going to be happy about it. We got them a brunch tour they begged for to have a girls' day with Sylvia and have a little fun before everything goes to shit. We all agreed it would be fine as long as a couple guards followed close by.

Savvy met Sylvia yesterday and they have been talking on the phone nonstop since. She loves her new mom and is almost obnoxiously adamant about spending time with her today. I looked at

Bash's itinerary and they won't land in NOLA until 6pm, which gives them plenty of time to hang out for a bit before we have dinner here.

"Hey man, did you get notice that the girls are good and made it to the tour okay?" Charlie asks as he comes out to the courtyard, sipping his coffee.

I look up at him, pulled out of my own thoughts. I was actually ecstatic to get the girls out of the house so we could get everything ready for the caterers tonight.

"Yup, they are at Maspero's having hurricanes and gumbo as we speak," I reassure him.

Jasper and Joe make their way out into the courtyard. "Operation get her to say yes is underway, gentleman," Jasper announces with his chocolate peanut butter protein shake in hand.

We have three hours and twenty minutes to go meet the party planner to pick our colors and shit we want for the table. The caterer is close to the party planner's place where we will pick out appetizers, a main course, and desserts. We didn't want to involve the girls because they have big mouths and tell each other everything. Not that we don't, but fuck, we have limits. They don't.

"Let's go get this girly shit done and get back here before the girls get back. Is Nick meeting us?" Joe grumbles.

"Yeah, he will meet us at the party planner's shop. He is the one who recommended her," I explain.

We all head out after we finish our coffee and breakfast. I didn't eat much. I'm excited and nervous at the same time.

"Have y'all noticed the girls acting weird. I mean Jill has been acting as if we don't have a care in the world and Bash coming back is almost a good thing. Like she is excited," Joe pipes in from the backseat.

"Yeah, Abby has been the same way, not taking this on realistically," Jasper replies.

"You know, Savvy has been that way since the lake. She isn't worried at all. It makes me question their sanity more than ours to be honest," I chime in, feeling like the guys might be on to something.

"Cami has been a little on edge actually. I just assumed it's wedding stuff driving her mad already," Charlie replies with a slight chuckle.

"You guys don't think they are keeping something from us, do you?" Jasper looks pale, like something just dawned on him.

"I'm sure it's just that they are in a new city and are trying to be tough with what could possibly be coming." Joe shrugs his shoulders.

"Or the girls have a plan of their own. We should bring up the plan again at dinner, just to see how the girls react and see if we can pull whatever is going on out of them," Charlie chimes in again, and it makes me stop and think for a second as we're getting out of the car at the party planner's place off Decatur.

Savvy

It has been such an amazing few days. We have had a blast showing Jill and Abby our NOLA and the guys have no clue what is about to happen. We have kept them blissfully in the dark about our plan. We figured out quickly at the lake that the guys only see us as damsels in distress and are going to try and have their own plan to keep us away from taking out Bash. We decided that we have minds of our own and are perfectly capable of taking out the fucking bastard ourselves. Our plan was set in motion before we ever got back to NOLA. I had Sin make the call to my mother to meet me. Just me.

We had a plan set with the guys, but they kept changing it to keep us safe. Meaning they pushed us out of the plan and pissed us off. They really should know us all better by now. They will learn.

"Savvy, your package will be delivered around two thirty." Sylvia smiles as she takes a sip of her hurricane, looking proud of herself. When I look at her, it's like I'm looking into a mirror that tells me what I will look like in thirty years. She is pretty and has the same long black hair and same blue eyes as me. Since I met her, I can't stop staring at her. She is my mom.

"Thank you, Mom." I call her that because it's the only thing she has asked for and even though I don't fully trust her yet, she hasn't given me a reason not to. Plus, it's nice to call someone mom and actually receive a smile from her just for saying one word.

We both cried a lot when we met yesterday, but she explained why she did what she did and didn't lie. At least I don't think so. She seemed genuine with everything she said to me. She just wants a chance to finally be my mom. She has a lot of regrets, giving me up was her biggest one. I can't judge her, she could have aborted me and I wouldn't be here, so I'm grateful for that.

When I met her yesterday, I told Sin I wanted to do it alone. Not because I actually did, but because I knew I was going to ask for a favor, and I wasn't sure how she would react. To say she jumped at the opportunity to do anything for me would be an understatement. When I told her what I wanted from her, she was all too eager to help in any way she could. She feels guilty that she sent Bash to find me.

Now, we sit at brunch with all of my friends that Bash hurt, minus one, going through the motions until we get back to our package and our old friend.

"Are we sure this is the way to go, keeping the guys out of it? I hate lying to Charlie, and I'm really bad at it. He knew something was up this morning when I wasn't in the mood to be his breakfast." Cami huffs, crossing her arms over her chest.

"We already have everything set up. We have worked really hard to make sure this goes off without a hitch. He will be out of our lives, and we can all move on. The guys will be proud once it's all said and done." Abby throws her hands up, acting as if she is shocked at Cami's statement. Everyone looks at her like she grew another head.

"Hey, no one said we weren't doing it. It's already put in motion. We have Bash. We are going to follow our plan to a T because it's the right thing to do," I reiterate.

"I'm just nervous. I've never done anything like this and what if something goes wrong?" Cami is about to lose it, I can tell. I put my hand on hers.

"There are going to be five of us and one of him. We will be fine." I try to settle her nerves.

"Girls, let me give you a bit of advice from someone who has been around the block a time or two. Take the fucker out. He has done nothing but bring chaos and pain to all of you. Use that pain to get the job done. Plus, I had my guy sedate him. He will be out for a while before y'all get to have your fun. Don't let this man or any other tell you what you are or aren't capable of." Sylvia gives us a bit of encouragement, letting us know this isn't her first rodeo. I know where I get my fire from.

I give Sylvia a hug. A big hug. "Thank you. I needed to hear that. I know this isn't your typical girl party we are having later, you guys, but fuck. Think about everything he has done to every one of us. Plus, countless other women. He deserves everything we are going to give him and more. We will finish this tonight! Then we are all free. We won't have to stay locked up to be safe. We take out the mother-fucker tonight." I hold up my glass and wait for each girl to do the same.

"It ends tonight!" We all cheer and clink our glasses.

CHAPTER 22
Sin

We finally finish setting up all this shit to be delivered and set up around 3 p.m. while the girls are getting ready. I can't stop thinking that the girls are going to try something and that scares the shit out of me. They really don't know who they are dealing with. I step out of the caterer's shop and pull my phone out again.

I keep checking my phone for updates. They are headed back to the compound now. They haven't wandered off track or anything. I may just be paranoid because I know what my brother is capable of and if something happened to Savvy or any of the girls because we were careless in protecting them, I'll never be able to forgive myself.

"Let's get back, the girls are on their way," I say as we all load up in my Jeep.

"See, they are fine, they wouldn't go behind our backs. They know we would be pissed." Jasper tries to lighten my mood.

"Yeah, I mean, we are all still new and I don't think they would want to break our trust this quickly." Joe backs him up.

My phone dings with a message, the girls were just escorted back in. "Y'all are probably right, they are back at the compound safe and sound just like they promised."

We make it back home and it's eerily quiet. We holler for the girls but get nothing in response. We split up and go through the entire compound and come up empty handed. We all meet back in the courtyard frantic. My phone dings.

233

> Jet: Bash came in on an early flight and we lost him. He never left the airport that we saw. The girl he was with is still here. We have searched the entire building, he isn't here.

"We definitely have a problem. The girls are here somewhere. They were escorted in, and the gate locked. No one could get in or out. Bash came in on an early flight and they lost him. Call everyone and find him." I run my hand through my hair, unable to catch my breath.

"How the fuck did they lose him? How long has it been since they lost him and the girls were dropped off here?" Jasper is pissed and seeing red.

I look at my watch. "Twenty minutes maybe."

"You boys need to calm down. Have a seat and let's have a little brunch of our own, shall we?" Sylvia walks into the courtyard, pushing a silver cart with matching trays with silver domes with fleurs-de-lis imprinted into the metal.

"What the fuck are you doing here? Where is Savvy and the rest of the girls?" I demand, frustrated because I know I need to eat to get my blood sugar up and because I'm now scared shitless my brother has my reason to live.

"Savvy said you would need to eat because you forget breakfast sometimes, your sugar would be low if they were running late with their errand, and you would lose your shit. Don't worry, the girls should be coming up any minute." She takes the trays one by one, like she is practically floating on air, and places them on the table, removing the lids.

I've never seen her like this. We all look at her as if she is nuts, but sit down, with her at the head of the table, and start eating. We know she is as crazy as they come. If she has the girls, we need to play it cool.

"I don't think you understand. Bash—" Sylvia cuts me off.

"Bash is being dealt with; how do you think your guys lost him?

234

Hmm?" She chastises with a smirk as she takes a sip of sweet tea from her straw.

"Sylvia, if you put Savvy in danger. I swear—" Bitch cuts me off again, laughing so hard she almost falls out of her chair.

"I would not put her or any of those girls in danger. I had that motherfucker sedated and tied up with a big pretty bow around him and delivered by a caterer to the back yard. The girls are doing what they see fit. You all should be ashamed of yourselves for trying to push them back instead of giving them the kind of closure with that asshole they need and deserve. They are perfectly capable of taking care of themselves. They outsmarted each of you and are getting the job done. I wasn't going to let her do it alone. I helped. Now she will let me be a part of her life. That's all I've wanted. That being said, I lost one daughter, that won't happen again. Next time, stand beside her instead of in front of her and let her choose her fate. That goes for all of you." Sylvia lets us have it and we probably even deserve it.

"We just wanted to protect them," Joe responds first.

"There is nothing wrong with that but choose your battles and see that they are just as capable as you are, and just love them."

We all jump from our seats when we see the girls come into the courtyard covered in blood, looking like zombies. They almost look sadistically demented. They are all wearing strange outfits. There is another girl with them that I have never seen before, at least, I don't think so.

"Angel, are you okay? What happened? Who is the new girl?" I hold my hand out to her. Her eyes light up a little when she hears my voice, then walks toward me. But she stops abruptly before I can touch her.

"Guys, this is Mia. We would like to shower first. We decided to make a home movie for you to watch.

"I notice there is a VHS player in the theatre room." Cami, the only one who isn't completely covered in blood, hands me a VHS tape. "You guys can watch and figure out how to clean up the mess. We will show you where he is when we are cleaned up. Deal?" She doesn't sound like she is in shock or anything. The blood on them is obviously not any of theirs.

I furrow my brows and let out a breath. "Deal." What else could any of us say to that.

Savvy

47 minutes earlier

When we finish brunch and are escorted back into the compound, we know we only have so much time before the guys will be back from the caterer. We have overheard so many conversations from the guys that we know they are planning something special for dinner. That's how we knew to use a caterer's truck.

As soon as the guards are completely outside the gates, we all run to the library and open the bookcase, the secret passageway leading us to what Marcel in The Originals called his Garden. I was right, it is real.

Lucky for us, Cami is a New Orleans native who loved studying the architecture and original plans to most of the buildings in NOLA. She had seen the original plans for the compound and knew there were secret passageways and underground tunnels that you can take outside of the compound but haven't been used in years because the city blocked most of it off back in the 1920's. We found it the night we got back to NOLA while the guys were sleeping. We followed the tunnels to a hatch-type door that took us a bit to open, but we finally managed it with a shit ton of WD40. It led straight out behind the compound but still inside the gates. The rest of it has been blocked off completely past that.

We make it to the back and see him tied to a dolly with a giant red bow wrapped around his neck. Mia is sitting on the ground next to him, waiting for us.

Nice touch, Mom. I giggle a little.

We hurry and get him back down in the tunnel and close the hatch. You can't even see it from the outside, it just looks like grass. We wheel his lifeless body to the area we decided had the most room for what we wanted to do.

We have candles lit all around the center of the room. We have chains bolted to the ceiling, walls, and floor to put him in any position we want. We have had to put all of this together at night while the guys have been sleeping the last couple of days, and they have been none the wiser. We are a little crankier and have bags under our eyes from planning every second we have to get this done, but they haven't caught on.

Now that we are in the safety of the cave-like area, we all hug Mia.

"No time for pleasantries. Y'all ready?" I ask, unsure myself.

"Let's fuck him up." Mia smirks, looking almost evil.

We all hurry and change into the outfits we chose to make it a spectacle. We want the last images in his head to be of us as our most sadistic selves with outfits that make us feel powerful.

Cami is ready in her red maxi dress that has a pentagram cut out of the back.

I look around and everyone is almost ready. I finish lacing up my tennis shoes and make my way over to help Cami finish setting up the chains. Bash stirs a bit but not much. We all untie him from the dolly one arm at a time and attach the handcuffs. Once we get the modified bridle I made for him in his mouth and strapped to the back of his head, we move on to his feet. When we are done, he looks like he is almost suspended in the air, feet barely touching the floor. We chose to keep him from being able to say anything to us. A muzzle for the dog he is.

Abby brings over the butt plug Mia picked out with the lube. I have to admit, she got the biggest one she could find. She stands behind him in her black leather dominatrix outfit, looking like she is ready to crack a whip.

Abby squirts a little dollop of lube on the tip while Mia holds it out. The rest of us grab his chains and maneuver his body to bend over. Whoever brought him was nice and left him naked except for the bow. Saves us time.

Mia grabs the chains we put around his waist and pulls back as she shoves the butt plug in Bash's ass. His eyes shoot open, his body flails as much as it can, while indecipherable screams leave his mouth but the modified horse bit and bridle I made muffles it all as spit flies out of his mouth and down his chin. I smile and wink at him once he calms down and focuses his vision on me. We all let go of his chains and let him hang.

Cami pushes play on her phone and "Goddess" by Xana bounces off the cave-like walls, making us all smile. She has a white sage smudge stick burning, filling the room with smoke. She told us it would help cleanse us of the evil we are about to do. She has three minutes and thirty-seven seconds to do what she wants to him.

We all decided that, because our time was limited, we would each pick a song that makes us feel in control and is also telling him off in a way. These will be the last words he ever hears. They should have meaning, not for him, but for each one of us.

Cami takes the piercing equipment behind him, he struggles and yells, but can't do anything. Cami hooks a long chain to the bridle piece and pulls to keep his head up. We want to make sure he isn't able to move much with what we have planned.

She pierces his back with the first bar all the way through, making him scream out again but he can't do anything but let the spit fall down his chin. Whatever he is trying to say just comes out garbled. She does the other side to match. Bash's screams lighten once again as she attaches the cables to each end of each piercing, then hooks them onto the chains from above.

"See, Sebastian, you are our puppet now, pet," Cami yells out as she pulls the chains, only locking them when his screams get too shrill. He hangs by the skin of his back now, only the tips of his toes touching the ground beneath him. She comes around, getting in his face. "I wonder if this is how any of your victims felt. Are you scared yet?" she asks menacingly.

The song stops after Cami punches him in the nose. She stops, turns around, and leaves the circle of salt she had to have. Hey, if it made her feel better, we all said do it. She takes Jill's place as she enters the circle, making sure to step over the line of salt, not to disturb the circle.

"Dark Side" by Bishop Briggs fills the silence, making Jill smile a wicked, red-lipped evil grin. Bash's eyes go wide again when he sees her scalpel. She decided that since she wants to finish nursing school and maybe keep going to be a doctor, that she would wear a nurse uniform, like for Halloween, and learn how to use a scalpel. Luckily, Sylvia was able to get us everything we asked for and gave it to me yesterday when we met so that we could finish setting everything up last night.

Jill goes straight up to him and kisses his cheek, leaving pretty red lip prints. She pulls back, lifts the scalpel to his cheek above the lip print, and glides the blade down slowly, almost soaking in his screams.

Blood trails down his face as his breathing gets heavier and heavier. She continues making methodical slices all over his body. His wail almost fits along with the song. I'd be lying if I said it wasn't music to my ears. Her face stays calm, almost like a porcelain doll as she skillfully ends the three minute and twenty-nine second song with the blade slicing his left eye.

Silence fills the area once again.

She flips him off and walks outside of the circle, taking my place as I enter it.

"Nightmare" by Halsey fills the space quickly as I'm dipping my wrapped hands in resin, then into a box of broken glass. "Do you remember making me watch Kickboxer over and over because you actually like Tong Po? I thought you would appreciate the sentimental aspect of it all." I smile wide as the prayer stops and I hit him in the mouth just as the first word of the song is said with the beat.

"You wanted me, bitch, I'm right here and I don't owe you shit!" I hit him again and again, remembering all the lies he told me, all the things he made me do, the videos he recorded. Every hit I make hits one of the cuts Jill made, making them tear open. I don't stop until the song is finished. I just see red and all the damage he caused. I got three minutes and fifty-two seconds back. That's more than most girls can say.

I go over to the table and pick up the necklace that I wore for so long, hoping it would find its mate again. I place the half of a broken heart up to catch the magnet and let the chain fall. "You can take this to hell with you." I let the final words out, knowing it's almost over.

I look back at him as I walk outside of the circle with my head held high, breathing heavily. It takes everything I have not to go back and fuck him up worse when he tries to smile, choking on his own blood, dripping from his mangled still-pried open mouth.

Abby grabs my arm before she enters the circle, knowing he was taunting me to end him. He doesn't realize it yet, but the worst is yet to come, so I smile wide at him, happy with how much his face looks like hamburger meat.

I take my seat as "i hope ur miserable until ur dead" by Nessa Barrett flows through the space, making us all dance and sing along in our seats, encouraging Abby to do her thing.

She looks adorable in her cut off overalls and white crop top with a baseball cap on backward with her hair in a double braid.

She grabs some bolts, a hammer drill, and a tall wood pole attached to a metal plate at the bottom with two flat shelves coming off of it, one at his face, and the other at his crotch. She bolts it to the ground and goes back to the table, getting a smaller drill, screws, and a long metal clamp.

She walks back over to him, singing the lyrics the entire time. She sets the drill and screws on the bottom shelf, right by his little dick. His eyes are wild yet heavy. She won't fuck him up too bad, she is just getting him ready for Mia.

The fact that he chooses to piss himself in this very moment is just icing on the cake.

She takes the metal clamp and puts it in his mouth, pulling out his tongue past the bit. She forces him far enough where she needs him, then, one handed, she puts the screw in the drill, luckily its magnetized, and drills the screw straight through his tongue into the board as she bobs her head and sings along. Blood spurts out, mixing in with his falling tears. Luckily, she put goggles on, or blood would have sprayed in her eyes.

He used to love to see me cry in bed. I'm sure he was the same with us all.

He realizes quickly that the more he moves, the worse it is. She moves down to his dick, grabs it with the clamps and repeats the process, placing the screw in the middle of his dick and screwing it into the board.

He screams until he passes out but comes to when she gets the smelling salts off the table and shoves it up his nose. He wakes up quickly, tearing his tongue a bit in the process. The song ends with her screaming the last lyrics in his face.

Silence fills the space again. Faint sobs are all that can be heard. She steps out of the circle as Mia finally gets her time. She picked the shortest song, but it has the meaning she wanted. She is wearing a pretty red dress that looks hookerish but accentuates all of her curves with tall black stilettos.

"Break You" by Marion Raven flows through the space, saying the words we all want to scream at him. She grabs several BDSM sex toys off of the table along with a choker chain that is usually used to train dogs.

The chain has little spikes that poke into his skin. She puts the chain on him like a leash. She takes the Kong Dong she asked for and shows it to him.

"I'm going to show you the same courtesy you showed me. She drenches it in lube, then walks behind him and rips the butt plug out, but he doesn't dare move, just squeals through the blood bubbling out of his tongue on the board.

"You need to shut the fuck up and take this dick like a good little bitch!" She screams the words out as she pushes the giant rubber dick up his ass. She has to really work to get it in there.

Bash rips his tongue and his dick at the same time, pulling them off the boards, flailing around as blood pours from his penis and his mouth.

Hmm, he looks like the fucking snake he is with a fork tongue and matching dick now. I internally laugh at my own joke.

It takes her over half the song, but she manages to get most of the Kong up his ass before he passes out again. His entire body was trembling before it went slack.

Mia stops, proud of herself. She leaves the rubber dick in his ass while she goes and gets the smelling salts and grabs her knife. Her song ends and we all move to the circle. The silence is eerie. We step into the circle, clasping hands. Cami said we needed to, so we are giving her whatever she needs to get through this.

"Bitter Sweet Symphony" by The Verve begins playing as we all make our way to the table to retrieve our chosen knives and go to Bash, all standing in front of him, ready to end it all. Mia shoves another smelling salt up his nose, making him come to, but barely.

"We wanted you to see us for this." Mia almost growls at him, looking sadistic as fuck.

"This song is over seven minutes long. I read once that the human brain doesn't shut down when you die. It will actually continue to function for seven whole minutes after you die. We thought this song was the most peace you deserved while you go," Jill explains as his eyes widen.

He hangs there, body slack, drained. He is hanging on by a thread. If we left him here he would still die from blood loss, but we all agreed.

We all take a deep breath and go for an artery like we promised. None of us will ever know which wound ultimately killed him. We pull our knives out, drop them at his feet, and walk away. Cami grabs the VHS tape and leaves the recorder there that Mia brought.

We all walk hand in hand to the door leading to the back of the house, never saying a word. We take our time, silent in our thoughts as we climb the steps into the sun and make our way to the courtyard where Sylvia promised she would keep the guys calm.

CHAPTER 23
Sin

We are all sitting in the theater room, sipping on bourbon, when the girls finally come in, looking much more like themselves.

We watched the video several times. To say it was disturbing to see the women we love so angry and murderous would be an understatment. We actually gave them props for the way they did it. Watching Savvy beat the shit out of him with glass covered hands was epic. She really is savage when she needs to be.

They never put themselves in danger and took the bastard out in the best way possible. Their way.

We did, however, make a pact to have each other's back in case one of us ever pisses them off to the point of them being murderous. Not gonna lie, we are now scared shitless of our perfect girls. We knew they were capable, but they went beyond anything I would have ever imagined.

The caterers have all come and gone, setting everything up while we watched the girls take their vengeance on my brother over and over. Then we decided we needed alcohol to handle whatever they were feeling tonight.

We made them all a few shots. It's what we do after a kill.

Nick has been asking who the new girl is and if we think she would be into him. We have all told him to take his shot but to be gentle with her because of what Bash did to her. She absolutely had the worst end of it all. He agreed.

Savvy comes out in a pretty blue sundress with white HeyDudes and her hair down in messy curls just like I love. She rushes over to me, sits in my lap, and kisses me, wrapping her arms around my neck.

She pulls back. "What do you have planned for tonight?" she asks, grinning from ear to ear.

"Angel, first, why don't you girls have a drink. I think we need to talk about what happened and get it cleaned up. The sooner it's done, the sooner we can move on to what we all have planned for tonight." I try to get us back to the topic of the hour and face what they did.

"Oh, I was thinking about that." Cami comes up for air from Charlie's mouth to chime in. "Burn it. It won't take long down there, and it will basically incinerate him and the evidence. We already threw our bags of bloody clothes back down there. We just need the video to finish the job."

"Where the fuck is this place?" Jasper finally asks, a bit harshly, what is going through all our minds, while the girls act as if nothing happened.

"Fine, let's go." Savvy stands up abruptly, huffing, and the girls follow suit, leaving us sitting dumbfounded.

They move over to the bar, all throw their shots back, and walk toward the door. Cami goes to the VHS player and takes the tape out before making her way to the door with the rest of the girls.

"Y'all coming?" Cami asks in a duh voice.

We all stand and follow them to the library. Cami opens the bookcase and leads us down to their crime. She giggles as we descend.

I have to admit, watching the video a few times helped soften the visual once we made it to their little secret circle.

"How did y'all find this, and how did I not know about it?" I ask, genuinely curious.

"I'm kind of a nerd when it comes to old architecture in NOLA. I remembered seeing some of the old plans before, showing the secret passageways. We just had to find the right room with the secret door," Cami admits proudly.

I take in the sight of my brother hanging lifeless. I know I shouldn't feel bad for him, but he was my brother. I didn't miss Savvy putting the necklace on him to give him his heart back. I saw the hurt in his eyes. I had never seen that expression on Bash before.

I get down on one knee and say a silent prayer. He may not have been a good person or a good brother, but I am, and I won't walk out of here without saying a few Hail Marys and asking her forgiveness for my angel and the rest of the souls my brother has harmed.

We have the girls direct us to the exit that goes outside and make them go sit in the courtyard and wait for us to clean this up. None of them argue.

"This is a bigger mess than dumb and dumber at the lake," Charlie grumbles.

"I say we burn it all like Cami suggested, we have plenty of gas cans in the basement." Jasper, of course, is over this shit already.

"Fine. We will just set it ablaze in this area with the candles that are still lit and go out the same way the girls did and meet them in the courtyard." I give in because I'm over this shit too.

Savvy

We all walk back to the courtyard. There are white twinkle lights set up around the entire area. We knew the guys were planning something special tonight but we didn't know what. There is one long table covered with white tablecloths and accented with a couple silky sapphire blue tablecloths placed over the white showing the corners still. There are three silver candelabras holding white stick candles, and what looks like snow globes showcasing Royal lilies inside water, magnifying them. It's a beautiful set up.

"The guys outdid themselves here, don't you think, Savvy?" Sylvia walks into the courtyard as we stand gawking at the beautiful table.

"It's beautiful. Did you know about this?" I ask.

"No, I'm not privy to Christian's plans. We have always had a bit of a strained relationship. I plan to change that. I want us all to be able to be in each other's lives. I'll work on my relationship with him. Tonight, I want you to enjoy whatever this is, and we will talk more tomorrow. I'm proud of you, Savvy. I wanted to tell you that before I left and make sure you are okay." Sylvia hugs me, kisses my cheek, and looks at me with a look only a mother could give.

"Thank you, for everything. I'll never forget what you did for all of us today. It's nice to finally have a mother who has my back."

I look around at the other girls. To look at us, you wouldn't know that we just tortured and murdered a man in cold blood. Right now, we seem normal and feel nothing but relief.

Tomorrow may be different.

"I'll always have your back, lovely. I'm your mother, that's what we do. You will see someday." She smiles brightly at me, cupping my cheek in her perfectly manicured hand.

I hug Sylvia again, the girls say thank you, and I walk her to the gate.

"Can I come over tomorrow and you tell me more about Lottie?" I ask before she leaves.

"I would love that. I'll go home and get out all of her photo albums. I have a few boxes of her things if you would like to have them. I think she would like that." I see tears well up in her eyes at the mention of Lottie. She doesn't let them fall, just kisses my cheek, gives me a big hug and leaves.

"How is everyone feeling?" I ask as I walk back to the table with the girls who are all sitting, just staring out into space. They all look at me with wide eyes.

"Do you think the guys are mad at us? Jasper seemed more pissy than usual." Abby almost sobs.

"No, they aren't elated we went behind their backs, orchestrated a murder and actually did it without them, but I don't think they are mad. Surprised maybe," I reply. I thought they were upset because of what we did, not that the guys would be mad. I actually think we are all handling this better than we should be.

"Charlie isn't mad, just surprised. They were relieved we were okay." Cami tries to help.

"What if Joe doesn't want me after this? I didn't think about consequences." Jill sobs.

"That would never happen, sweetheart," Joe replies, walking with the rest of the guys toward the table looking all dapper. They are all wearing slacks and dress shirts, looking yummy.

I smile when Sin winks at me. I knew he would be upset that I went behind his back, but I also knew he would understand. He looks nervous for some reason though.

Charlie starts pouring champagne and handing each of us a pretty glass flute.

We are all gathered in a circle around the table, none of us wanting to sit. Sin raises his glass with his other hand in mine and turns to me.

"Angel, I have loved you from the moment I saw you in the cathedral, hell, maybe even the restaurant. I never knew that I could feel a love this deep for anyone. You have turned my entire world upside down and I couldn't be happier. I love you, Savvy."

He sets his flute on the table and gets down on one knee. I gasp at the thought of what he is actually doing, raising my free hand to my mouth.

"Savannah Grace, I want to grow old with you, I want to have babies with you, I want us to live a fairy tale life that most only dream of. Will you agree to always stand beside me as I will you and be my wife?"

He opens the pretty blue box, showcasing the most beautiful ring I have ever seen. It's white gold, has a perfect oval diamond in the center with sapphires on each side that travel all the way around, covering the band. Tears spring to my eyes as I look into Sin's. I love this man with everything in me and I want to live the rest of my life showing him just how much.

"Yes!" I practically yell as I jump up and down. He slips the ring on my finger, and I practically tackle him. He barely stands us up instead of falling over. Everyone cheers and laughs. I look around at the people I care about most in this world and say a silent prayer, thanking God, if there is one, for keeping us all safe.

Once Sin lets me go, the girls all swarm and want to get a good look at my ring. They all oohh and ahhh, making me feel special. I can't help but notice Mia looking lost in her own head.

"Hey, you okay? I know we haven't had a ton of time to talk except on the phone, but I owe you an apology in person. I'm so sorry I didn't believe you." Mia puts her hand up to stop me.

"We're good, Savvy. I won't waste another second of my life on that asshole, and neither should you. We were all dickmatized by that fucker and now it's finally over. I want to move on. What I was thinking about was your friend Nick over there. Is he single?" She surprises us all and we can't help but laugh as she gets the biggest cheesy grin on her face.

"Nick!" I yell out over everyone's chattering. He comes over with a quickness.

"Mia, Nick. Nick, Mia. You're single, right, Nick?" I raise my eyebrow at him.

"Yup, single as a pringle." He jokes nervously, making Mia laugh.

Perfect.

"Why don't you two sit together at dinner, you could get to know one another better," I offer. They go straight to the table and sit down together, looking mesmerized by each other.

I fucking love love.

EPILOGUE 1
Savvy

Cami wears a beautiful white long-sleeved gown with a high collar. Her lacy veil and train flow behind her a good four feet, giving her a royal look, and Charlie wears a white tux. Standing in front of everyone in Jackson Square, they say their vows as we watch them promise to love one another as long as their souls shall be, they shall be one. Witch weddings and customs are so neat.

Once they finish with their kiss and everyone cheers, the entire party follows them out to the street for their very own wedding parade, finally stopping at Nick's bar.

We make our way inside for the reception. Mia helped Nick get the bar ready for the party.

Mia is going to school for business management and is ready to start her own wedding planning business. Cami said she would be her first client. She has done a beautiful job and we are so proud of her for opening up to Nick. He really loves her. Mia is going to be busy next year planning all of our weddings.

The rest of the guys didn't wait long after Sin proposed to me to put a ring on their girl's finger. I have decided I want a spring wedding, while the others prefer summer and fall. I'm planning a wedding at home in the courtyard.

Living arrangements have been amazing. Mia and Nick moved in a few weeks ago and we all have our own routines but always make plans to have Sunday dinner together no matter what. The guys are gone some with business and we all wind up watching movies together and just hanging out. No one gets in anyone's way. I love it.

I spend time with Sylvia on the daily. She is hilarious. Pops is supposed to be coming in March to stay a few weeks for our wedding, and you could say we are all blissfully happy, living our best lives with the people we love.

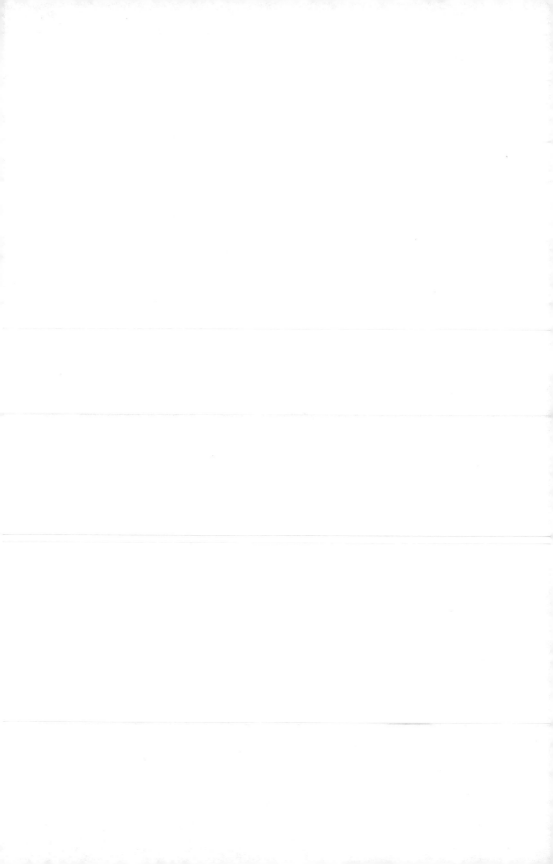

EPILOGUE 2
Savvy

1 year since Bash

"Good morning, angel." Sin comes up behind me at the counter where I'm waiting for my Pop-Tarts to pop out and wraps his arms around my baby bump, rubbing his hands up and down as he kisses my neck.

"Good morning." I smile, turning in his arms to give him a proper kiss.

"What are your plans today? Anything special?" he asks skeptically, like I don't know what today is.

"The girls and I are going to Maspero's to celebrate one year trauma free." I smirk at him.

He lets out a breath, seeming to be a little more relieved. "That's great, angel. Don't forget we have dinner with Sylvia and my dad tonight," he reminds me. I have pregnancy brain and I am extremely forgetful right now.

"I won't. I'm excited to see Mom today. I think they have some news for us if their trip went how Sylvia thought it would." I smirk at Sin and his eyes get big.

"How did you guys know?" he asks dumbfounded.

"Because y'all are easy to read. He has been nervous as fuck around her for the last couple of weeks since he planned the trip to

257

Hawaii," I explain. I give him a kiss and grab my strawberry Pop-Tarts and a glass of milk and head out to the courtyard. Sin follows and sits with me.

"Are you ready for our ultrasound tomorrow to find out the sex?" he asks all of a sudden. I don't have the heart to tell him Cami's mom already told me it was a boy and I'm only going through the motions for him.

"Yup." I try to sound enthused as I take a huge bite to keep me from speaking.

"Charlie already told me Rose told you what it is. Why not just tell me if you believe her?" He finally asks what he really wants to know.

"Because I know you don't believe in that stuff. I'll tell you if you want to know." I smile before gulping down half my milk.

"I want to know! Just tell me already so we can start shopping." He begs in the cutest way, pushing out his bottom lip.

"Start buying some blue shit, babe, it's a boy!" I shout happily, knowing he wanted to know if his little vision in the cabin was right. He can say he doesn't believe, but I believe enough for the both of us.

Sin jumps up from his chair and picks me up out of mine and spins us around, planting little kisses all over my face.

"Sin, stop, I'm gonna throw up if you keep spinning. He sets me back in the chair as we both laugh.

"Ready to go?" Mia asks as she enters the courtyard with Jill and Abby as Cami waddles behind them. She is seven months pregnant and over it already with this summer heat.

"Yeah, Mom is meeting us there," I reply.

Once we get to the restaurant, we get seated and wait for Sylvia. We go ahead and order strawberry lemonades and start looking at the menu when Mia's phone dings. She picks it up and goes pale instantly.

"What's wrong?" Jill asks first as we all just stare, not knowing what is going on.

She turns her phone around as a tear falls down her cheek.

> Unknown: Enjoy your little brunch anniversary this year, none of you will make it to the next!

Acknowledgements

I want to thank my family for being understanding of the time it took to create this story. My husband J for always pushing me to chase my dreams and for making me believe I can do anything. You are my rock, and I can't ever imagine doing life without you.

To all the people who helped me along the way, you know who you are, and I can't tell you how grateful I am that you all came into my life.

Made in the USA
Monee, IL
09 November 2023

46084205R00149